LOSING

CONTROL

by

Althea Lawton-Thompson

Losing Control © 2005 Althea Lawton-Thompson

Published in Atlanta, Georgia.

This novel is a work of fiction. Any references to real events, businesses, organizations, and locales are intended only to give the fiction a sense of reality and authenticity. Any resemblance to actual persons, living or dead, is entirely coincidental.

Printed in the United States of America

ISBN-13: 978-0-9968068-0-0

10 9 8 7 6 5 4 3 2 1

For my favorite chocolate M&Ms who allowed and encouraged me to write. To the twins, Isha and Sofia - you know who you are.

LOSING

CONTROL

Chapter One

Baltimore, Maryland
Friday, May 4, 2001

ZUMA SWUNG HER LEGS FROM THE silver sports car and leaned back to grab her purse from the passenger seat. Standing, she smoothed the short skirt of her suit and bent to reach for her suit jacket lying in the back. Slipping her lean arms into the expensively tailored jacket, she headed for the garage elevator. As the doors slid open on the ground level, she began walking purposefully toward the tall glass building of Shearing Wireless Technology.

She leaned into one of the double glass doors at the entrance and barely glanced at the balding, old security guard watching her exposed legs with admiration from behind the security desk. Once at the elevator, she impatiently pressed the upward arrow and brushed non-existent lint from her lapel as she waited. With a ding, the doors slid open and, after a soft *woosh*, the elevator began its assent to the upper levels of the Shearing building where Zuma and the other directors, vice presidents and C-level officers of the wireless giant worked. She stepped from the elevator, turned left, and strode toward heavy doors with "Marketing" engraved into the wood.

"Betty, hold all my calls for the next ten minutes and bring me a bottle of water," she said curtly to the woman sitting behind the reception desk.

Crossing the expansive floor of cubicles, Zuma entered her corner office at the end of the hall and paused to admire the view. A year ago, she'd been sitting in one of the windowless offices on the other side of the floor as one of many marketing managers. Now, she gazed absently out of one of the floor-to-ceiling windows to the traffic stopping and starting on the busy street below. She needed to focus on the company's new product launch, but it was hard to focus on anything with the possibility of a merger looming. She absently stroked a lock of honey-colored hair as she considered her future.

Shearing Wireless Technology and Ladd Tech Corporation, two of the largest producers of wireless technologies, were talking merger. It seemed to be a trend in telecommunications: Bell Atlantic and Vodaphone, MCI and Worldcomm. It was nothing new, but now it was personal. Zuma's position as marketing director of segmentation was not as secure as it once was. If the two companies merged, they'd never keep all of the marketing people from both powerhouses. It would either be her or her counterpart from Ladd, and if it were the latter, she'd be in the market for a new job. With a mortgage, a car note, and no one to split the bills, there was only one option — Zuma Harris's name would have to remain outside the door of this office.

"Here's your water," Betty said, startling Zuma with her quiet entrance. "The conference call for two o'clock has been pushed to three by product development, and you have new messages on voicemail." Betty stated everything matter-of-factly and hesitated a beat, waiting for Zuma to comment.

"Three o'clock?" Zuma asked harshly, more to herself than Betty. "No good. I have a four o'clock with the Pdata team," she said, whirling around to pick up the phone on her desk.

Cutting her eyes with dislike at Zuma's back, Betty turned and walked out of the office.

Zuma began speaking into the phone's receiver. "Jim," she said by way of a greeting.

"Development pushed the conference call back to three o'clock, and I have a four o'clock with Pdata. I'll start the call and stay on until three forty-five. After that you've got the ball. And you better not drop it."

She listened briefly while the marketing manager made a few comments, then ended the call, typing an adjustment in her PDA. Zuma knew her direct reports didn't like her, but she wasn't there to make friends. Making friends with subordinates didn't get her the director's corner office — socializing with the right executive-level big wigs did.

As she screwed the top off of the water bottle, her cell phone sang a melody in her purse. After a sip, she stood to retrieve the little bag. The phone continued to sing as she pulled it out and flipped it open.

"Zuma Harris," she answered sharply, without looking at the caller ID.

"Hey, baby," came a deep, baritone voice.

Zuma took another sip of water and rolled her eyes slowly upward as she prayed for patience. "Malcolm. What did I do to deserve this pleasure so early in the morning?"

Normally, the sexy voice of a chocolate tower of muscles would excite Zuma. Today, however, she was completely focused on remaining the only African American female executive at this company or the next one.

Malcolm's voice broke into her focused thoughts. "I thought I'd give you a ring before my client meeting."

"Hm, that's nice, but I'm about to get on a conference call, and I need a few minutes to prepare," she said, flipping through a stack of files on the corner of her desk.

"No problem. I'll see you tonight at about seven then, cool?"

Distractedly, Zumba agreed. "Um hm. Sounds good. See you then." She quickly flipped the phone shut, forgetting about Malcolm and anything else outside of the company's walls. Opening a drawer, she grabbed the resident bottle of Aleve and popped two in her mouth before taking another quick sip of water. It was going to be a long Friday.

* * *

The minutes and hours ticked by and, eventually, the meetings and conference calls were done. Zuma sat back in her office chair and looked at the same view that had started her day. With a weary sigh, she stood to pull on her suit jacket and began re-stacking her files. As she was putting the papers she would need to review over the weekend in a leather briefcase, the phone rang.

Shit, where's Betty? Why isn't she taking this call? she wondered, glancing at the clock. Zuma saw it was already six thirty, and most of the people on the floor had left to enjoy what was left of Friday. Grudgingly, she picked up the receiver.

"Zuma Harris," she said, in her usual clipped manner.

"Hi, Zuma. Glad I caught you."

Zuma immediately recognized the voice and found herself gripping the receiver harder than necessary.

"Hi, Margie. I was just about to walk out the door." Zuma felt her pulse quicken as she waited to hear what the director of human resources could want at this hour.

"We have a new marketing intern coming next week, and I thought it would be great if you'd be her mentor. I'll be out of the office at a conference next week and wanted to let you know, so you wouldn't be caught off guard on Monday."

Slowly, the breath Zuma had been subconsciously holding released, and her heartbeat returned to normal. These days, a call from human resources was a serious cause for concern.

"Sure, no problem," Zuma replied, with fake enthusiasm.

After exchanging a few more office pleasantries, Zuma hung up the phone and considered the call. *The intern must be black, Zuma thought. They wouldn't assign her to me if she wasn't.* Before the phone could ring again, Zuma grabbed her bags, hit the light switch on the wall, and walked briskly out of the door.

After an hour of fighting Friday downtown traffic, she pulled into a crowded parking lot full of happy-hour patrons. The noise level in Decibels Bar and Bistro rose as Zuma walked into the private lounge area reserved for VIP guests. She quickly dismissed the hostess when she spied Malcolm sipping a beer in a corner booth.

Malcolm saw her petite figure in the tight suit before she saw him. He shifted in the booth as he appraised her sexy stride coming toward him. Her legs were shapely, and the four-inch heels she wore made him shift again. *Damn, she's fine,* he thought. As she bent to give him a soft peck on the cheek, her golden hair brushed his face, and he glimpsed the curve of her breasts. When she unbuttoned her suit jacket and slipped her five foot four caramel frame into the booth next to him, he welcomed the opportunity to move and make room for his growing excitement.

Everything about Zuma was sexy to Malcolm. She was professional, paid and, most importantly, fine as hell. Looking at her large breasts beneath the curved neckline of her silk shell, he had a flashback to their date last Friday. Zuma had taken him to her house, and they'd spent an hour sexing on the floor of her living room. It had been their first date after meeting at a networking event two days before. After the Friday night sexcapade, he was surprised when she didn't call him the next day. Or the day after that. Most women he got harassed the shit out of him, desperately blowing up his cell. By Wednesday, though, Zuma still hadn't called, and he realized he was aching to connect with her again. Eventually, he'd gone against his own man code and dialed the cell number she'd slipped him at the networking social. When Zuma finally answered, she barely allowed him to speak. She'd cut him off mid-sentence and abruptly asked, "How about this Friday night?" He was shocked at her quick, brief response but hungrily agreed to meet her at Decibel's.

Now, here they were, and he forgot about his frustration at having to chase her as he surreptitiously glanced at her nipples pressing against the silk of her blouse.

"Hey, sexy," he said, using the tone that usually made women do anything he asked of them. And things he didn't.

His deep voice and full lips did cause a little stirring in her midsection, but she wasn't one for dumb small talk or manipulation, unless she was the one manipulating. She contemplated ordering a glass of wine but realized she had no desire to converse with Malcolm. She only wanted him for one thing.

Giving him her profile, she said, "I'm ready to go. Are you coming?" Without waiting for his reply, she brushed against his arm as she stood and straightened her clothes. She watched him groping in his jacket pocket for money to pay for the beer. Pleased, she turned and strode as purposefully out of the room as she had come in.

When they arrived at her house, Zuma went up to her bedroom to change while Malcolm removed his Armani suit jacket and slung it over the arm of the leather sofa. He sank into the deep cushions of the chair, removed his shoes, and grabbed the remote for the big screen television. Out of habit, he punched in the numbers for ESPN and watched NBA stats scroll across the screen, absently loosening the tie from around his thick neck. He smiled at a highlight of one of his alma mater's players on the screen. It hadn't been that long ago that he was a college football starting lineman, being highlighted regularly on ESPN. His body was still thick and hard from the regular workouts with some of his clients. As a sports agent, he wanted his clients to feel that he was more than their agent — he was their friend. Working out with rising NFL and NBA stars kept him in shape and in business.

Deep into ESPN, Malcolm didn't notice Zuma walk quietly into the room until her sheer, white cover-up suddenly reflected in the screen of the television. Before he could turn around, she had slipped one of her hands around his muscular neck to undo the top buttons of his oxford shirt. He felt her hot breath on the back of his bald head as she removed his tie to unbutton the remainder of his shirt. Instantly aroused, he tried to pull her around the sofa, but she was quick and pulled his shirt out of his pants with a jerk, removing her arms from his grasp with the motion. He rose as she appeared before him. Malcolm parted his lips to speak, but Zuma placed her index finger lightly on his mouth, coolly telling him to remain silent. She liked to set the scene and, when men talked, they tended to ruin the mood.

She slowly unhooked his belt and unbuttoned his slacks, keeping her eyes on the growing bulge beneath her fingers. Pulling down the zipper, she eased his pants over the firm muscles of his butt and let his dick free to stand at attention. Liquid heat began to spread between her legs as she stroked the silky fabric covering his hard shaft.

Malcolm stepped out of the pants, staring at the dark outline of her nipples and the shadow of a landing strip below the belt of the sheer cover-up. Just as he was about to reach out for her, Zuma turned to lead him up the curved staircase. Passing the living room, Malcolm glanced at the spot where she'd fucked him on the thickly carpeted floor a week before.

In the darkened bedroom, he could just make out the outline of a large bed covered with accent pillows. But Zuma passed the bed and continued walking through a small dressing room. Malcolm watched, mesmerized, as her butt cheeks alternately rolled up and down, causing the white fabric to crease and wave with her steps.

The moonlight shining through the skylight was the only illumination in the bathroom. It reflected off the mirrors covering two of the walls and gave a surreal glow to the oversized room. There was a large jacuzzi tub next to a glass-enclosed standing shower along the far wall of cool marble. Zuma walked sexily to the shower, removing her robe and letting it fall to the floor. The moonlight glistened off her back and shimmied over the curves of her bottom. Stepping into the shower, she turned on the multiple heads at varying levels, then stepped back to take Malcolm's hand.

"Take off the rest of your clothes," she whispered.

Malcolm felt his excitement increase at the directive. He watched Zuma roll the firm nipple of one breast between her fingers as she licked her lips and looked directly into his eyes. With the forefinger of her other hand, she toyed with the landing strip of hair between her thighs. Two other fingers joined it and began to stroke farther and farther into the darkness.

Malcolm's hardness poked into his stomach as he stumbled over himself trying to remove his socks. The buttons on the sleeve of his shirt wouldn't release, and he couldn't get out of his silk boxers fast enough. He recognized how uncool he was behaving, but, for some reason, he couldn't pull himself together.

Zuma continued the slow manipulation of her own body, enjoying Malcolm's frustration and increasing her own arousal. Slowly, she backed toward the shower. Malcolm tried to regain his cool, but all he wanted was to ram his pulsing dick inside of her. Subconsciously, he started to stroke the mushroomed head of his erection as he moved toward her.

Zuma opened the glass door to the shower and stepped down two steps to stand under the hot sprays coming from all directions. Water dripped from her breasts and elbows as she tipped her head back and smoothed the dampening hair from her face.

Malcolm walked up to her and let his hardness slap solidly on her flat stomach. She opened her hazel eyes and looked directly into his dark ones as she grabbed his dick, made slick by the warm water. Releasing it long enough to squeeze aromatic shower gel into her palm, she rubbed her hands together and slowly massaged his thick, veined erection. She felt her arousal growing as rivulets of water ran over and around the dark muscles of Malcolm's shoulders, arms, and chest.

Slowly, she turned around, forcing him to bend at the knees so she could place his dick between her legs and stroke him with her hands while moving her hips forward and back. They both watched his dark hardness moving in and out of her slender fingers. Malcolm held a high, full breast in each of his hands and stroked her nipples. He felt like he was going to explode, but he knew she was in control, and it wouldn't do any good to try to change the rhythm of things.

Zuma forgot who she was with, and she didn't care. All she wanted was to bring herself to orgasm. She turned around and grabbed his smooth head with both hands, pulling his face down to her breasts.

Sitting on the stone seat along the shower wall, Malcolm began flicking her nipples with the tip of his tongue while he kneaded her ass with both hands. Moving one hand farther down her backside, he placed his middle finger deep between her legs and felt the warm, slick sensation. A tremor went through his body when Zuma began moaning and grabbed his hand to guide it, rhythmically, in and out of her heat. Looking at her face in the shadows, he saw drops of water fall from the lashes of her closed eyes onto her parted lips, and he knew he couldn't wait any longer. Normally, he would slip on a condom from his pants pocket, but all rational sense had fled in the intensity of the rising steam.

He stood, picking her up with him, and thrust deeply into the hot, slippery opening. She wrapped her legs around him and held on to his thick neck while she leaned back into the sprays of water. His lips found one hard nipple and sucked as they rode each other fast and hard.

Eventually Zuma commanded, "Put me down."

He reluctantly pulled out and put her down, but when she turned around and positioned herself on the low step in front of the steamed glass door and spread her legs wide, he was ready. Coming up behind her, he stuck his throbbing erection into the tight hole of her ass. She braced herself on the door, letting him thrust forcefully. After a few minutes, he picked her up and sat back on the stone seat. Straddling his lap backwards, Zuma held onto his knees as she pumped her slim hips up and down. She looked down to watch his dark shaft moving in and out of her while he stared at the cheeks of her ass spread wide over him. She turned to look at him over her shoulder. He was biting intently on his bottom lip, and the hot passion in his eyes increased her own enjoyment.

Knowing she was close to the end, she abruptly stood, turned around, and straddled him. He stood, too, as she wrapped her legs around him. Their breathing and movements joined into one rhythm. Even their moans were harmoniously in tune. The tattoo emblazoned on his shoulder and chest glowed in the moonlight and flexed with his thrusts.

Malcolm came so violently that he slipped and fell, hard, on the stone seat, bringing a panting Zuma down with him. Breathing heavily in the steam, he felt his groin throbbing and knew he couldn't move. All he could hear was their breathing and the sound of water spilling down the drain. He closed his eyes, waiting for his heart rate to return to normal.

Beside him, he felt Zuma rise. He opened his eyes and watched her pull a pink shower puff from a marble shelf in the shower and begin to soap it. As though he weren't there, she scrubbed herself clean and rinsed off. Stepping up and out of the shower onto the bath mat, she reached for her body towel and wrapped herself, drying her arms and neck.

"Let me know when you're leaving so I can lock the door," Zuma tossed over her shoulder, as she left the sweating bathroom.

Malcolm was used to kicking a chick out of his bed or quickly washing up and leaving a conquest. But a woman kicking *him* out was foreign to him, and his ego made the emotions of surprise and anger fight for space in his brain. *Who the fuck does she think she is?*

With questions clouding his head, he stepped out of the shower and quickly dried off with the extra towel hanging on the rack. He grabbed his damp clothes off the floor and awkwardly dressed himself as he stomped through the darkened rooms. With silk boxers sticking to his thighs, he tripped over furniture he couldn't see and stifled a yelp when he stubbed his toe on the edge of something hard in the dark. His anger was simmering by the time he made his way down the stairs and found his discarded pants on the floor.

He spied Zuma through the sliding glass doors, sitting on the deck in a short terry robe, talking casually on a cordless phone. She laughed, high and tinkly, as she ran a hand through her wet hair. *Bitch*, he thought, grabbing his jacket and stomping through the foyer.

Zuma glanced backward when she heard the door slam and stopped pretending to talk on the phone. She walked into the house, locked the doors, and set the alarm before going into the study. She sighed as she sat behind a modest wooden desk and glanced at the small clock in the corner.

Only 9:30 p.m.

Her eyes wandered to the picture of her parents hugging and smiling on the corner of the neat desk. Sighing again, she closed her eyes and leaned back in the chair, wistfully thinking. Her parents always seemed so happy together. She wondered how they were adjusting to the year-round heat of Fort Lauderdale. It had only been a couple of years since they'd retired and packed up their tiny house in North Carolina.

North Carolina. What happened to the little girl she used to be, spoiled by her parents and adored by everyone in their small town? At thirty-three, she wasn't a little girl anymore, and she hadn't been one in a long time. Zuma was totally focused on her career and proud of what she'd accomplished, but it was times like this, when she was alone and had forced another man out of her space and mind, that she thought about the early years when she was a foolish girl from a country town. The years that forced her parents to scrimp and save to transfer her from embarrassment and rumors to a new life — a false life with a new identity.

Slowly opening her eyes, she tugged lightly on the desk's top drawer and pulled out a thin, worn checkbook. Writing her parents' names on the payable line, she finished filling out the check and folded it in a blank sheet of copy paper like she did every month. Forever trying to repay what she felt she never could.

Walking from the study, Zuma sealed the envelope and placed a single stamp in the upper right hand corner before dropping it on the kitchen counter by her purse. She poured herself a glass of wine and returned to the study to review her notes from work.

Chapter Two

EARLY MONDAY MORNING, Iris stepped confidently from the elevator and turned left as she'd been directed in the human resource office. Stopping at the large mahogany reception desk, she smiled at Betty seated behind it. Betty didn't return the favor.

Undaunted, Iris said, "Hello. I'm Iris Pena, the new marketing intern. I believe I should be meeting with Zuma Harris." She waited patiently as a sullen Betty picked up the receiver of a telephone under the lip of the desk and pressed two buttons.

"Ms. Harris, Iris Pena is here to see you." The receptionist listened motionlessly before looking up at Iris. Covering the mouthpiece, she asked, "Did you have an appointment with Ms. Harris today?"

"Um," Iris mumbled, shifting her weight to one side and twisting to dig into her shoulder bag for a letter. Handing Betty the letter, she said, "The woman in human resources indicated Zuma Harris would be my mentor."

Betty glanced at the letter and said into the phone, "Margie Castor in HR arranged it." After a pause to listen, she finished the call and directed Iris to have a seat in one of the chairs in the reception area.

Iris glanced around at the posters of various Shearing products with their catchy slogans and signature logo hanging on the walls. Relaxing, she pulled out a magazine from her leather bag and began thumbing through it.

Eventually, the secretary stood. "Miss," she said blandly. "Ms. Harris will see you now." Pointing down a long walkway flanked by cubicles and small windowless offices, Betty directed, "Just follow this hallway to the end. Ms. Harris's office is the last one on the right."

Before Iris could thank her, the woman had moved her attention to a stack of papers in the bin on her desk. Iris turned down the corridor, noting the buzz and movement on the busy floor. As she came to the expansive corner office, she knocked on the frame of the open door before entering.

Speaking sharply into the telephone headset she wore neatly over her shoulder-length bob, Zuma motioned for Iris to enter and sit in one of the chairs in front of her desk.

"I don't care what their reasons are for the change. I want that date solidified, and I want it confirmed today before four o'clock. Send me an email with the update asap."

Zuma pressed a button on the cord hanging from the headset, and efficiently typed a brief email on her laptop. After clicking the nearby mouse a few times, she focused on the screen, quickly speed reading the email from human resources about Iris Pena from Florida A&M University. She didn't take the time to finish the entire email with the rest of Iris's educational background. Her time was too valuable.

Zuma turned to look at the young lady sitting across from her. She had a smooth, peanut-butter brown complexion and a heart-shaped face. When she smiled, Zuma noticed her perfectly aligned teeth were the whitest she'd ever seen. They matched the bright white of her large brown eyes framed by thick lashes. The girl's high cheekbones were accented by one deep dimple, giving her an innocent, youthful look. But it was the unruly mass of natural twists and curls framing her face that made her appearance exotic and uniquely beautiful.

As Zuma visually summed her up, she coolly said, "Welcome to Shearing. I apologize for not being better prepared to receive you, but we're in the middle of a few major developments and weren't expecting an intern until the summer."

Zuma stood and walked around her desk to shake Iris's hand. When Iris stood, Zuma noted the young lady was much taller than she was, even in her conservatively low-heeled pumps. Inconspicuously, Zuma looked at the girl's body. She was not only tall, but curvy with perky, little breasts and a tiny waist. Jealously, Zuma noted the skirt of her suit pulled at the hip where it was fitted over thick thighs and a firm, high, black-girl butt. The kind of butt Zuma worked religiously, and unsuccessfully, with a personal trainer to develop.

Iris smiled as she shook Zuma's hand with a firm grip. "It's a pleasure to meet you. Actually, I would have waited until June to come." She paused, thoughtfully, before continuing. "In my research on Shearing, I noticed talks of a merger. I wanted to experience the negotiation and preparation for such a process, so I negotiated with our internship office to come early in May." This was said without pretense and very matter-of-factly.

Zuma watched as Iris sat comfortably off-center with her legs casually crossed at the knee and an elbow resting on the soft chair arm. Agitated by the calm mention of the impending merger, Zuma stiffly said, "The merger to which you refer does not exist. Even if we were in that stage of a merger, *you* wouldn't be involved in the negotiations."

Taken aback by the sudden change in Zuma's tone and demeanor, Iris grew silent. She smiled without showing her teeth and sat straighter in the chair.

"So, from what school are you visiting? Florida State?" Zuma asked with a smile to match Iris's. The email from HR told Zuma the girl was from the historically black university in Tallahassee, not Florida

State, the popular white university in the same city. But for some reason, she wanted to ruffle the calm assuredness of the girl.

"No, it was Florida A&M University, but that's a common mistake people make," Iris corrected.

Zuma Harris didn't make mistakes. Except on purpose. Just as Iris was going to add that she'd completed her undergraduate degree at the School of Business at FAMU and was currently completing her MBA at Columbia University in New York, Zuma interrupted.

"Forgive me. We have so much going on here that petty, unimportant details sometimes slip," Zuma said in a cutting tone, still smiling.

This is not starting the way I imagined it, Iris thought to herself. Out loud, she said, "No problem. I completely understand. Since I know how busy you are, you can tell me where to sit, and I'll introduce myself around the floor." Iris bent to retrieve her bag and purse from beside her chair, attempting to bring an end to the unpleasant conversation.

Zuma had the distinct feeling that Iris had just taken control of adjourning their meeting, and she didn't like it. She coolly commanded, "Sit. I'll have a member of my staff show you around and help you select a desk."

Before Iris could respond, Zuma turned her chair slightly and pressed a button on the speakerphone. Hearing a greeting, Zuma said, "Barbara, please come to my office for a moment. Thanks." Without waiting for a reply, she hung up. Turning slowly back to Iris, she said, "Barbara Peters will show you around. I have a two o'clock conference call this afternoon, but I'll attempt to meet with you after lunch around one thirty."

With that said, Zuma stood and walked around her desk to wait in the doorway, as a gesture to Iris that the meeting was over — on *her* terms. Iris stood with a smile, showing her perfect teeth, and took

Zuma's hand, thanking her for her time. Then she turned gracefully out of the door.

"You must be Barbara," Iris said pleasantly to the heavyset, pale woman approaching the office. Zuma knew without seeing Iris's face that she was smiling that bright smile.

There's something about that girl I don't like, thought Zuma as she closed the door to her office and returned to the priorities of the day.

Zuma attended meetings, participated in conference calls, and worked right through lunch without realizing it. When her stomach growled, she stopped focusing on Shearing long enough to order delivery from the Chinese restaurant down the block.

While she waited for the food to arrive, she reviewed her to-do list. She'd have to schedule another staff meeting soon. She wanted her team behind her one hundred percent on the marketing proposals for the new Pdata product launch coming next month.

Eventually, Betty brought in a tasty-smelling bag and set it carefully on the edge of the desk. Zuma pulled a box out of the bag and began eating, unconscious of what the food actually tasted like. She was completely focused on the work spread out before her as she forked noodles into her mouth.

The message light was blinking on her desk phone, and she continued munching on shrimp lo mein as she checked the voicemail. Listening, she made notations in either her PDA or on her laptop, but when she heard the voice of the marketing vice president, Bob O'Brien, she stopped abruptly. His harsh New England accent seemed loud coming through the phone, causing her to frantically press the down arrow on the volume. Having missed the beginning of his message, she pressed "1" to replay it from the beginning.

"Zuma, this is Bob. Important all-day meetings are scheduled for this Wednesday, Thursday, and Friday in the executive boardroom. Give me a call as soon as possible so we can prepare."

Prepare? Was it regarding the merger? Instantly, Zuma felt her armpits grow damp. She pushed the food off the desk into the trashcan and called Betty for a bottle of water. As she fished around in her drawer for the bottle of Aleve, she heard a knock on the doorframe and looked up to see Iris. What the hell did *she* want?

Without being invited, Iris stepped into the room with a notepad and pencil.

"Yes?" Zuma said, not attempting to hide her impatience.

Hesitantly, Iris replied, "You suggested we meet at one thirty."

Zuma quickly looked at her watch and noted it was one twenty-nine. Damn, the girl was punctual.

"Something came up and now is not a good time," Zuma said distractedly. "Look, Iris, I apologize for not having the time to really get you acclimated, but you'll have to take a rain check." As Zuma finished speaking, she picked up the phone to dial Barbara. Before she could push a button, though, Barbara was at the door.

"Wow, talk about ESP," Zuma mumbled to herself. Out loud, she said, "Barbara, I won't be free today to direct Iris. Please find something for her to do."

"That's exactly what I was coming to suggest," Barbara said.

Without waiting for further instructions, Iris moved toward the door. "Thanks, Zuma," she said, and began chatting amiably with Barbara as they walked onto the marketing floor.

Mentally dismissing the girl, Zuma nervously began dialing her boss's extension. The first real indications of the impending merger had just appeared.

Chapter Three

IT WAS STILL EARLY ON TUESDAY evening as Iris walked leisurely up South Charles Street, glancing in boutique and shop windows. She felt a vibration under her arm and unzipped her purse, digging for the cell phone. Without looking at the caller ID, she said, "Hello," pleasantly.

"Hey, girl, what's up?" she heard her best friend, Rey, bark into the earpiece. His sharp New York accent always warmed her heart and made her think of home.

"Hey, boy! Just checkin' out the scenery in this place. Where're you?" she asked, letting her own New York accent come out.

"I just got back in the country, and I'm staying in Miami for a few days. Got any free time?"

Iris paused in front of an Indian clothing store to study a blue sari as she mentally considered her schedule.

"I could come down on Friday if you're there for the weekend."

"Cool. I can meet you at the airport in Lauderdale or Miami. Just let me know your flight info."

"Okay, I'll email you my itinerary tonight. Love you."

"Love you too, girl. Take it easy up there in Baltimore. I don't wanna have to kick somebody's ass."

"Bye, fool," Iris laughed.

"Peace."

Iris clicked the phone shut and turned on the next street. She quickened her pace as she came closer to a gray high-rise apartment building.

"Hi, Fred," she called to the doorman, breezing into the lobby with a smile. "How's Cassie?" she asked, referring to the doorman's pregnant wife.

"Gettin' on my damn nerves," he laughed. "That baby better get here soon."

Iris giggled and squeezed his arm as she walked past. "Tell her I said hi."

"You got it," he replied, looking after her tall, curvy frame walking to the bank of elevators.

She was like sunshine when she came into the building. Even though she had just moved in the previous week, it seemed like everyone knew her — the security guards, the doormen, and even the old janitor that cleaned the lobby. She had everyone, men and women, wrapped around her pinky finger.

She was one of the only residents in the expensive apartments who not only spoke to them, but really saw them. She even remembered the things they told her. No question, Fred loved to see "Sunshine" coming up the street with her bright smile and easy laugh.

The elevator opened and Iris stepped inside, pressing the ancient metal button with "33" imprinted on it. She ran her fingers through her tangled hair, fluffing up the curly natural, as she critically studied her reflection in the closing elevator doors.

When the doors slid open, she stepped out and walked on the plush carpet to the end of the corridor. Stopping in front of the last door, she inserted one of the three keys on her platinum key ring with

"I.A.P." engraved on both sides. Once inside the apartment, Iris dropped her keys, purse, and leather bag on the cherry wood table in the foyer and padded on stockinged feet to the large bedroom off the hallway. She paused in front of the small stereo and CD player on the entertainment center in the corner of the spacious room and pressed the red power button. Scanning the CDs thrown carelessly on the top of the console, she picked up Afrocuba's *Eclecticism*. After placing it in the CD player, she pushed the forward arrow until it stopped on her favorite track and pressed play.

Bopping to the fast melody and singing in rapid Spanish along with the chorus, she threw her suit jacket on the cluttered bed and pulled the silk top over her head, dropping it in the dry-cleaning bag behind the closet door. After removing her skirt and stockings, she grabbed a fuchsia sports bra and a pair of black running shorts from the bureau. Dropping to her knees, she searched for her Reebok DMX running shoes under the comforter hanging off the edge of her low Scandinavian bed. She continued to hum along with the music playing loudly on the surround speakers as she walked into the kitchen and located a bottle of water on a shelf in the refrigerator.

By the time Iris donned her headphones and started a slow jog down the busy city street, she was feeling light and free. Fred, the doorman, watched her round butt jiggle slightly as she reached the corner and paused, waiting for traffic to cease before crossing. *If I wasn't a married man...* He didn't finish the thought as an old Jewish couple from 304 asked for assistance with their shopping bags.

* * *

Iris didn't realize the stir she was causing in the lobby when she returned from her run. The chiseled definition of her abdomen was glistening with sweat. Her muscular legs flexed as she walked leisurely into the lobby, humming along with the music in her headphones. She smiled and waved to the lobby workers as she jogged to the elevators.

21

Her breasts and butt bounced lightly with her steps. While she waited for the elevator to arrive, she closed her eyes and rolled her head slowly around her neck. Residents, guests and staff alternately glanced and stared at the shining, brown-skinned beauty with the mass of windblown hair.

Once in her apartment, she headed straight for the bedroom, kicking her shoes by the bed and stripping off wet clothes as she went. By the time she was in the bathroom, she was naked. She briefly admired herself in the mirror over the sink counter. Her skin was smooth and without blemish. Her breasts were small but full, with large, dark nipples. Looking at her body's profile, she smiled as she lightly rubbed her hand over her high, round butt. Her passion for running definitely had its benefits.

As soon as she bent to turn on the faucet in the shower, the phone rang. With a frustrated sigh, she turned off the water, ran to the bedroom, and grabbed the cordless phone from its base on the low nightstand. Breathlessly saying "Hello," she sprawled carelessly on the floor, waiting for the caller to speak.

"Iris? It's Papa."

"Papa!" Iris exclaimed when she heard her father's voice. "Donde esta?" she asked in quick Spanish. Her parents were always flying or driving somewhere and she usually started a conversation with "Where are you?"

Her father laughed at her question before answering in his native Spanish. "We're in the airport in Miami. Our plane's boarding in a few minutes."

"Where are you going?"

Iris heard young voices in the background crying, "Abuelo! Abuelo!" He obviously had her nephews with him.

"We promised Carlos and Sonja we'd give them a break, so we're taking the kids to Orlando."

"Papa, why didn't you just drive? It's only a three-hour trip to Orlando from Miami," said Iris, laughing as she imagined her parents trying to keep her five- and four-year-old nephews entertained for three hours on the Florida Turnpike.

"Yeah, right," he laughed. "Espera!" he said sternly in the background. Iris knew he was fussing at one of the active boys. "Here's your mother," he said in an exasperated tone and disappeared.

"Hi, honey," said Iris's mother in her usual soft voice. "Are you settling in okay?"

Switching easily to English, Iris answered, "Yeah," with a little sigh.

Hearing something in her daughter's voice, Iris's mother asked, "How's the internship so far?"

"Let's just say, it's not what I expected."

"You've only been there two days, honey. What could possibly have happened in that short time?"

Iris could imagine her mother sitting in the airport with her legs crossed, watching the people walk to their various gates. She guessed she was wearing expensive jeans and a silk twin set, because the airports were always freezing in Florida. She visualized her mother's salt-and-pepper hair, cut close and brushed smooth to her scalp like one of the singers from the '90s musical duo, Zhane.

"My mentor is a woman whose picture is next to the word 'perfection' in the dictionary. Her clothes, her hair, her office, everything. And she obviously doesn't like me," Iris said, doodling with the laces of her sneakers by the bed.

"Ah," said her mother knowingly. "Just remember, no one is perfect. Except me." She got the laugh she wanted from her daughter. "Seriously, honey, behind any image of perfection is usually some hidden insecurity."

23

Forgetting about Zuma, Iris began describing her peers at the office. "I love the marketing team, though, Mom. I get the feeling they don't like my mentor. She's the department director."

"Hm," her mother said thoughtfully. "That's unfortunate for her. The best way to succeed as a leader is to have the respect and support of your team. She may have some level of respect, but I doubt she has the support."

"You're probably right. Either way, I'm planning to learn as much as I can and get out of there in August."

"Iris…" her mother began with a sigh. Iris prepared for a lecture. "I want you to start thinking about what you're going to do, and where you're going to stay. You can't keep moving from place to place."

"Why not?" Iris whined with a frustrated pout. "I'm not married, and I don't have any kids. This is the best time for me to do this. Besides, it's an adventure."

After another sigh, her mother responded. "Okay, we'll have to talk about it later. Our flight is boarding. We'll call you from Orlando."

"I love you, Mom. Give Papa and the boys a kiss for me."

"Love you too, honey. I will."

Thinking about her parents, Iris dropped the cordless phone on the bed and returned to the bathroom. She stepped under the warm spray of the shower, and imagined her father gathering the boys, speaking half in Spanish and half in English.

Her parents had met at a retail marketing consortium in Manhattan. Her father, originally from Spain, was the founder and owner of a small multilingual consulting firm based in New York. Her mother, a marketing manager for a retailer in New York, attended a workshop he presented, and later recommended his firm to her company as a consultant for their growing Hispanic market. After working closely together for a year on a successful Spanish-language campaign, he asked the professional, articulate beauty on a date. Despite the racial climate of the late '60s, Papa claimed he found the dark-skinned African American woman exotic and wouldn't rest until she was his. Later marrying, they moved to a neighborhood in New Rochelle, just north of the city. As her father's business grew, her mother's marketing reputation and the creation of corporate diversity initiatives propelled her up the corporate ladder with various retailers. Despite their hectic schedules, they started a family, giving birth to a boy they named Carlos and, five years later, to a beautiful little girl named Iris Alexis.

Iris dried off and began slathering fragranced lotion on her toned arms. Thinking about home always made her think of Rey. With a start, she realized she hadn't booked her trip to Miami. She finished pampering and threw on a lavender cotton tank top and matching bikini briefs.

Flipping open her laptop, she double-clicked on the airplane icon. As she typed in BWI, for Baltimore Washington International, and Friday's date, she smiled at the thought of her childhood friend.

His real name was Raymond Hargrave, and his family lived in the same neighborhood as hers. They'd been in the same class in third grade and had become inseparable over the years. As a youngster, he was always telling people what to do, so Iris had named him "El Rey" for "The Boss." The name stuck and, over time, simply became Rey.

When they were sophomores at FAMU, Rey, a computer information systems major, was given a class project to create a website. Having traveled extensively with his parents for their travel agency, he decided to create a site that told the real story about vacation destinations from a traveler's standpoint. It provided information on things like which cities were good for families with kids, where to avoid in various seasons due to weather, when native holidays were being celebrated, and which cities were not safe and why. By their graduation in nineteen ninety-seven, the popularity of the site had created a stir among hotels, resorts, and restaurants in various locations. Rey began charging for online advertising and, using improving web technology, he offered virtual tours by digitally streaming video clips of cities, resort properties, popular restaurants, famous clubs, and annual celebrations onto the website. Hotels, restaurants, clubs, and tourist boards paid big bucks to be a part of the growing sensation.

Six years from its inception, the thriving company now had a full and active staff, but Rey still relished traveling, partying, and womanizing all in the name of building business and creating tax write-offs. When Iris was free, she would join him and a few of their friends for a weekend adventure, enjoying the excitement until her departing flight brought her back to reality.

While she waited for the flight options to come up on the computer screen, her thoughts turned to what she would eat for dinner. With the money she'd earned and saved working for her father, plus the monthly allowance her parents insisted on putting in her bank account, she definitely had the money to eat at the most expensive restaurants in the city every night if she wanted, but she felt like cooking tonight. After selecting her flight, inputting her credit card information, and emailing the itinerary to Rey, she went to the kitchen to begin preparing dinner.

Chapter Four

Wednesday, May 9

IRIS ENJOYED THE SPRINGTIME WALK from her apartment building to the Shearing offices on Lombard. Walking in with several others rushing to work, she paused at the security desk. "Good morning, Will. How are you today?"

The old man smiled up at her. "Hey, Iris Pena."

He said her whole name as he'd remembered it from reading her new personnel badge the day before. He didn't have many names to remember since regulars rarely stopped at the desk. "Lookin' good today," he said letting his eyes wander over her curvy hips in a conservative, navy, skirted suit.

"Well, thank you. If I didn't know better, I'd think you were flirting with me," she said in a voice of mock shock.

At first, he wasn't sure if she was joking or serious. But when he saw the smile playing around the corners of her mouth, he laughed. "Have a good day, Iris Pena."

"You too, Will," she said, strolling toward the bank of elevators.

Behind her, Zuma entered the building, hearing the end of the conversation. How the hell did they know each other? The girl had barely been here two days. Whatever. The toothless, old security guard was no one Zuma wanted to know and she surely didn't want him to know her.

Prancing snootily by his desk, she waited in the elevator hallway. Once on her floor, she pushed through the doors of the department and almost stopped mid-stride, unable to disguise the shock at seeing Iris and Barbara parked in front of Betty's desk. Strangely, the three women were socializing with one another, something Barbara and Betty had never done. Regaining her composure, Zuma walked by with a general, "Good morning, ladies."

"Morning," they chorused before continuing their conversation. Pissed at their easy dismissal of her, Zuma's hazel eyes narrowed as she walked to the end of the hallway. Dropping her computer bag and purse on the desk, she walked back to the front.

"Ladies, I assume you realize it's eight thirty-five," she said stiffly.

She was pleased to see Betty's face turn in stony embarrassment as she reached for the top envelope in the overflowing bin. Barbara's face became a shade of pink as she erected herself from the casual lean she'd had on Betty's desk. But Iris, unaware of the discord, intoned a bright and cheery, "Talk to you later, Betty. Bye, Zuma," before she turned with Barbara and casually walked to the opposite corner of the floor. Zuma heard Iris's distinct voice tossing greetings to others as they went.

Despite her command of the situation, Zuma simmered over Iris's carefree attitude. And more importantly, why was the dumb girl wasting her time talking to *Betty*? Iris should have been trying to get on *her* schedule. She stalked over to the throng of people gathering around a bank of cubicles outside the doors of Barbara and her counterpart, Jim's, offices. As she approached, the pleasant chatter ceased almost immediately.

"Iris, I need to see you in my office." Without waiting for a reply, Zuma turned and switched back to her office.

With a shrug to the people in the group, Iris moved to the imposing corner office.

Zuma was already seated behind the desk and shuffling papers when Iris entered and sat stiffly in one of the chairs. After a purposefully extended pause, Zuma stopped her shuffling and sat back in her leather chair. Looking directly into Iris's large brown eyes, she began.

"Iris, I'm concerned with the amount of time you spend socializing on the floor. You've only been here a couple of days and you haven't *attempted* to learn what we do here. Instead of socializing with the secretary, you should be trying harder to get on my schedule. I'm sure this is not what Florida A&M sent you here for." Without pausing, Zuma continued in an even, smooth tone. "I want you working with Barbara today on the final Pdata marketing package for my review next week. She'll be staying late tonight to finalize it and you can stay with her. I'll be off the floor at meetings for the rest of the week. When I return on Monday, I expect a report from you describing the product and the part we in segmentation play in its rollout." Zuma stopped, waiting for Iris's response.

Iris debated whether to mention that she had graduated from FAMU years ago and was actually working on this internship as a requirement for Columbia, but something told her that wouldn't help her cause. So she smiled instead, showing her one dimple.

Zuma felt her pulse quicken with building anger. *What is this bitch smiling about? Just wait until I send her review back to Florida A&M. She won't be smiling then.*

In a controlled voice, Iris said, "I know I've only been here two days, but I've taken that time to get to know the staff and pick their brains on the various projects on which marketing is working." Taking a nervous breath, she continued.

"I'm fully apprised of Shearing's new Personal Data product.

29

Barbara and I spent most of yesterday with Rick York in the data division of development learning the in's and out's of the product so we could capture the main points for the in-store brochures and signage." Iris paused as she watched Zuma's slanted eyes grow to slits. She continued speaking with a forced confidence she increasingly didn't feel.

"After gaining a better understanding of the product, Barbara and I revised the collateral based on our research and what we thought end users would appreciate. We planned to present it for your approval this afternoon." Waiting a beat, Iris added, "Is there something else you'd like me to do in your absence?"

Zuma knew her face was flushing. *This bitch is gonna make me lose my composure.*

"Well, it sounds like you've gotten off to a good start," Zuma said tightly. Then, abruptly changing her tone, she added, "Why don't we have lunch together today? As your mentor, it's important for me to get to know you." She forced a smile, attempting to look pleasant.

Watching the Jekyll and Hyde change in Zuma, Iris realized she didn't have a choice in the matter of lunch. "That would be great, thanks," she replied with a fake smile to match Zuma's. "Should I meet you here?"

"No, I'll come get you. That's all." The false smile was still pressed on her face.

Rising, Iris straightened her skirt and retreated to the floor.

Zuma released the long breath she'd unconsciously been holding. Irritated by the outcome of the brief meeting and Iris's curvy hips, she snatched her leather bag from the closet and threw the folders she needed for the nine o'clock meeting inside. *Yoga breathing, remember the yoga breathing,* she told herself, straightening the papers falling haphazardly in the bag.

By eleven thirty, Iris began mentally preparing to spend an

uninterrupted lunch hour with Zuma. Pulling her cell phone from the purse hidden in her small desk, she quickly walked to the break room in the far corner of the floor. Relieved at finding the room empty, she pressed the speed dial for Rey's cell number.

"Wassup?" he answered on the first ring.

Hearing loud music thumping in the background, Iris said, "I'm scared to ask, but where are you?"

Speaking loudly to be heard over the music he said, "I was just thinking about you. You'd love this joint. I'm meeting a client at a sports bar near the beach."

"Ugh. I'm jealous! I wish I was there, but I will be soon. Did you get my email yesterday?"

"Yep. The info's already in my head."

Just as Iris was about to tell him her dilemma, he interrupted her thoughts. "Hey, girl, gotta go. Client's here."

Disappointed, she said, "Okay. I'll talk to you later. Good luck with your meeting."

Hearing something in her voice, he added, "Is everything cool?"

"Yeah. I'll call you tonight, okay?"

"A'ight, peace." Iris heard the phone disconnect and, reluctantly, flipped the cell closed. With a deep sigh, she returned to her desk.

Thirty minutes later, Zuma and Iris walked out the double glass doors of the lobby. The sun shined down, making the breezy May afternoon comfortable. Both women dug in their purses for sunglasses.

"Where are you parked?" Zuma asked.

"I'm not," said Iris good-naturedly. "I walk." She tilted her head back to let the sun warm her face.

"Walk?" said Zuma with disdain, leading them toward the garage's door. She imagined Iris taking a crowded, dirty bus to work and smiled subconsciously.

As they stepped out of the elevator into the sun shining on the garage's roof, Iris knew without being told that the tiny silver sports car in the furthest corner space was Zuma's. It matched everything else about the petite, perfect, little woman. With a muffled beep, the lights flashed and the doors unlocked.

After turning on the air conditioning and adjusting the radio to 88.9, the local jazz station, Zuma pulled out and wheeled around the curves to the street below. Driving a few blocks, she stopped at the valet station of a discreet little restaurant hidden in the middle of the block. Zuma exited, snatched the valet ticket from the attendant, and walked primly up the steps without waiting for Iris. Iris quickly stepped out of the passenger side, smiling apologetically at the attendant, and followed Zuma into the dark lobby of what looked like a row house, the narrow brownstones native to Baltimore.

Zuma tapped one reptile-skinned shoe on the carpeted floor as she waited for the hostess to return to the podium in the hallway. Iris's eyes adjusted to the dim interior, and she admired the rich antiques, overstuffed lounge chairs, and tables placed throughout the room. Off to the right was a bar with more couches and chairs lining the walls. Expensive fabric hung from windowed walls.

When a thin woman with sparse blonde hair glided to the podium, she smiled graciously at Zuma. Raising an anorexically slender arm draped in sheer black fabric, she extended her hand and purred, "Ms. Harris. A pleasure to see you today."

Zuma smiled widely at the rail of a woman and limply took her hand, "Good to see you, too, Myra. Any tables in the private dining room today?"

"For you, of course." Myra seemed to float in black smoke as she led them through the dimness into a large dining room furnished with square tables covered in starched linens. The men seated throughout the room were in suits and ties. The few women present were dressed as conservatively as their male counterparts in dark, long-skirted suits. A few of the men paused in their conversations to look at Zuma as she passed silently behind Myra.

The hostess paused in front of a small table in a more private room at the back of the house. Only two other tables had occupants, and they were deeply engrossed in conversations. One of the tables was covered with spreadsheets and reports.

Myra waited for Zuma and Iris to be seated before removing the linen napkins from the table and, starting with Zuma, draping them ceremoniously over each of their laps. She then handed them large menus with small cursive writing on heavy parchment paper.

"Thank you, Myra," Zuma said, as the woman glided away.

Before Iris could open the menu, an Eastern European server arrived at their table, greeted them with a thick accent, and poured water into their glasses. After describing the specials for the day, he asked if there were any questions. Without waiting for Iris for comment, Zuma ordered one of the specials with grilled fish for both of them. Iris checked her temper and reluctantly handed the server her menu. He bowed slightly, took the menus, and backed away from the table.

Absently, Iris thought about one of her mother's many insights on corporate America. *Black American women are sometimes the hardest people to work for as a woman of color. They can be petty, jealous, and the meanest crabs in the barrel.*

Iris looked at Zuma's perfectly dyed hair, flawless makeup, and pretty linen suit. She knew the gorgeous black woman across from her was exactly the person her mother had described.

"So, let's get to know each other a little better." Zuma smiled and waited, giving Iris a silent cue to begin talking.

The last thing Iris wanted was for Zuma to know too much about her, so she made a quick decision to stroke Zuma's ego and get the focus off herself.

"I know you've worked hard to become the marketing director of segmentation. How did you get to where you are?"

Zuma's smile genuinely broadened as she delved into a lengthy description of how she started with the company as a management trainee and worked her way up from one marketing position to another. According to her account, there were only a few other females and one African American man at her level or higher. By the time Zuma finished her dissertation, the salads had been eaten and they were working on the main course.

Zuma wiped her mouth daintily with the linen napkin and paused to sip from her glass before asking, "What about you? I know you're still in school, so there's probably not much to tell. Have you interned with other companies?"

Iris contemplated telling her about her father's company. She'd spent three years working as an account manager for him before returning to college to get her MBA. She'd also completed two internships as a business student at FAMU.

But she'd only done one internship for Columbia, so Iris said, "You're right, there isn't much to tell. Shearing is my only internship with this degree." Attempting to redirect the conversation again, she followed with, "Where did you go to school?"

Zuma slowly finished chewing her food and, after taking another sip, replied, "I'm a graduate of Hampton University."

Iris noted the pride in Zuma's voice.

"Hampton is a great university. I actually spent some time there…" Iris let the sentence hang for a split second. "…on a high school trip to the HBCUs."

Something told Iris that Zuma wouldn't appreciate hearing that her mother had graduated from the elite institution in the '60s. Her family often returned for homecomings or football games when Iris would wear her FAMU paraphernalia while her brother, Carlos, sported his Howard alumni sweatshirt. It was a friendly, family rivalry, and they enjoyed teasing one another when one of the popular black universities lost a football or basketball game during the year. The Hampton-Howard football game was an annual event for the family. They'd stay at a hotel in historic Washington, D.C. and spend the weekend tossing jokes and ribbing each other during the metro rides to and from the game.

Interrupting Iris's thoughts, Zuma haughtily said, "Then you're obviously familiar with the great reputation of the school."

"Yes," said Iris mildly, "I am."

As the server removed plates from the table and offered them coffee, Zuma cleared her throat, and Iris knew their conversation was about to take a turn. Once the man left, Zuma leaned her forearms on the table and clasped her hands together, pressing her breasts up through the opening of her double-breasted jacket.

"Iris, I've noticed that you tend to spend an inordinate amount of time getting personal with the lower-level people working at Shearing."

Just then, the server returned carrying a small coffee cup on a saucer. He stared at Zuma's exposed breasts as he carefully placed the fragile china next to her. Ignoring him, she continued.

"I'm sure no one has taken you under their wing in a real corporate setting, but as your mentor, it's my job to educate and assist you in the unspoken areas of appropriate business behavior."

Iris shifted in her chair as she fought to maintain a neutral look. Forcing herself to breathe evenly, she waited for Zuma to continue.

"Getting to know the security guards and secretaries on a personal level is really not appropriate. I've noticed you socializing on more than one occasion with Betty and the man in the lobby. It's really not acceptable." She paused long enough to take a sip of the coffee.

"Your actions should make it clear what position you hold at the company, even though you're just an intern and not really a member of management." She paused again, this time searching for the right words. "I'm not saying you're better than them, but you really must limit the amount of time you spend with those people."

Iris felt her face grow hot. Instead of sharing her true thoughts, she simply said, "I'll keep that in mind."

"I suggest you do if you want to progress in Shearing or any other company." Zuma sipped her coffee and sat back to admire her nails.

She glanced at her watch, calculating how much time it would take to get back and up to the boardroom before most of the other executives. Removing her napkin from her lap and dabbing at her mouth one final time, she said, "I guess we'd better get going. Excuse me." Standing, she sauntered to a dark corner in the room where Iris assumed the ladies' room was located.

Iris exhaled deeply as the server returned. He looked disappointed as he glanced at the empty seat across from Iris. Setting down the bill in a black leather holder, he slowly cleared the remainder of the dishes from the table, obviously hoping for another peek at Zuma's cleavage. Iris opened her purse, preparing to pay for her portion of the meal, when she saw Zuma returning.

"Don't bother, I've got it," said Zuma, slipping gracefully into her chair. "I doubt you could afford this meal on a student intern's budget." She opened a reptile-skinned purse, identical to the material of her shoes, and pulled out a matching slim wallet. After placing her gold company card in the leather holder, she handed it to the man and finished sipping her cooling coffee. Iris had had enough and excused herself.

In the restroom, she checked her teeth for foreign particles of food and swiped her lips with Blistex as she let her temper cool. When she stepped from the restroom, she saw Zuma glance her way before striding importantly past the men with papers strewn across their table. They didn't even bother to look up.

Smiling at Zuma's failed attempt for attention, Iris followed her through the dark rooms into the bright sunlight and waited on the red-carpeted steps for the attendant to bring the car around. This was going to be one hell of an internship.

Chapter Five

A SLIVER OF SUNLIGHT SHINED on a corner of the boardroom as Zuma sat tensely in one of the many chairs surrounding the enormous table filling the room. It was obvious plans for the merger were going through. She glanced up from the stack of papers outlining Shearing's products, services, and the commercial and consumer markets they reached. There were pages on pages of statistics regarding penetration, retention, and churn.

In consideration of the merger, each company was creating a transition team. The teams were responsible for presenting each of the products and services their company offered for comparison of compatibility, redundancy, and profitability. The meetings today and tomorrow were preliminary fact-gathering meetings to prepare the marketing presentation for the chief marketing officer to share as part of Shearing's transition team.

Looking around the room, Zuma realized she was one of only two people of color and the only woman. It was nothing new, but she sat a little straighter, always aware of her appearance in case someone may be looking. And they always were.

It used to bother her that her white counterparts commented on her impressive presentation skills and articulation, like they expected all black people to speak Ebonics or something. But now she relished the response she received whenever she stood in front of the men in her department. She knew they weren't only impressed with her great articulation.

Most of them were probably looking at her legs and chest, both of which she showed off as much as possible. She'd learned having a sharp mind is valuable, but showing some skin could take an attractive woman places a sharp mind wouldn't. As far as Zuma was concerned, power was power, and she'd take it any way she could get it.

Realizing the topic had turned to business segmentation, she interjected with a swing of her hair and a lean to reveal a hint of her assets. As all eyes riveted on her, she felt the pleasant thrill of her control. Making random eye contact around the table, she began. "Okay guys, let's talk penetration and retention in regards to our commercial accounts. If you'll look on page thirty-seven..."

Chapter Six

Thursday, May 10

IT WAS THURSDAY, AND IRIS almost skipped to work with the realization that Zuma wouldn't be around again today. As usual, she stopped at the security desk to greet Will before heading up to her floor. She went to Betty's desk and dropped a white bag on the top.

"What's that?" asked Betty with a surprised look.

"A hot blueberry muffin, sliced through the middle, with a pat of butter melting down the center," said Iris with flourish and a little neck-rolling attitude.

Betty couldn't help but laugh. "Thank you."

"No problem. I pick one up at the corner bakery every morning, and I thought it might put a smile on your face today."

"Alright now. That's what I'm talking about," Betty said, opening the bag and sniffing the aromatic steam wafting up.

Just then, Barbara, chattering animatedly, walked around the corner with Jim and one of the marketing assistants. Seeing Iris and Betty, she stopped at the desk. "Morning guys," she said with a smile. Jim and the assistant both waved as they walked past, continuing their conversation. Random managers and assistants called over cubicle walls to one another as they worked and socialized simultaneously.

Apparently, everyone could feel the freedom and joy of Zuma's absence. Soon, there was a small gathering around Iris's desk.

"You're crazy, Bruce!" said Iris in a friendly challenge to a large man with a mop of red hair. "You can't do it, I don't care what you say!"

"What?" asked Jim, eager to get in on the conversation.

"Jim, please tell this young lady that I can down six shots in a row and still walk a straight line," boasted Bruce.

Laughing, Jim said, "I don't know, Bruce. Maybe in your mind."

"Okay. Tonight. Kelly's. I'll prove it!" Bruce declared with an accent indicating his Glen Burnie, Maryland background.

"You're on," said Iris with a dimply smile.

As the others around the desk began discussing monetary bets, Iris turned to Barbara. "Hey, Barbara. Feel like checking out that new Thai restaurant on the corner today for lunch?"

Barbara answered immediately, "Sure, why not?"

"I'll meet you at the elevators at noon," Iris said, standing. "I have some research to do in the data department today. Something Zuma set up for me." Making a face, Iris gathered her yellow notepad and a pen and headed for the elevators.

Iris exited the elevator on the eleventh floor and walked to one of the corner offices. She knocked on the door and waited for the burly man inside to beckon her in.

"Iris," he bellowed. His voice matched his demeanor. He looked like an old high school football coach. With his barrel chest and a big stomach to match, he seemed like a giant version of a weeble-wobble. He had red cheeks that made him look like Santa's brother, and he wore a perpetual smile.

"Hi, Rick. Is this a good time?" Iris inquired as she stood just inside the doorway.

"Anytime's a good time for my favorite intern. How's it going today?"

"Good. Thanks for asking," she said, settling into a chair. "So, what are you teaching me today?"

Running a pudgy hand over his thinning hair, he said, "Unfortunately, I have to meet with the team upstairs this afternoon." He looked genuinely sad. "But, I've asked Jonathan, one of the data team managers, to spend a little time with you and answer any questions you might have."

"Sounds good to me," said Iris obligingly.

As Rick hefted himself out of the leather chair, Iris stood to follow him onto the floor. They walked down a narrow hallway with Rick pausing periodically to speak to members of his staff. Occasionally, he'd introduce Iris before moving on to the next person.

This is how it was supposed to be with Zuma, Iris thought.

When they came to a small, windowless office, identical to Jim and Barbara's, Rick stopped and knocked on the open door. "Excuse me, Jonathan, are you busy right now?" Rick asked.

A tall, slim black man in an oxford shirt, conservative tie, and dark slacks looked up and smiled. "Hey, Rick. Nothing I can't stop. What's going on?" he asked, sneaking a look at Iris.

"I'd like to introduce you to our new marketing intern, Iris Pena. She's with us until August, and Zuma Harris thought she should spend some time understanding this end of product development." He paused to allow the two to shake hands.

"Hi, pleased to meet you," said Iris with a smile.

Jonathan took in her pretty face, big eyes, and even, white teeth as he accepted her outstretched hand and held it firmly for a second. "The pleasure's mine." Gesturing for her to sit one of the chairs in front of his desk, he continued, "Welcome to Shearing."

"Thanks," Iris said as she smoothed her skirt and sat.

"Well, I'll let you two get down to it," Rick said.

Addressing Jonathan, he added, "I'm heading to the transition meeting upstairs. You and Christine are in charge until I return."

"Fine," said Jonathan. "I'm sure we can manage," he added with a crooked grin that Iris found attractive.

"See you, Iris. Check back with us anytime, okay?"

"Thank you, Rick. See you later," Iris replied, waving as he exited the office. Jonathan watched her profile. *Beautiful.*

"Well," he said. "I'm not really sure where to start."

"How about if I tell you what I learned from Rick earlier this week, and you let me know if there's more to learn?"

"Okay, shoot."

Iris talked animatedly about the projects she'd discussed with Rick. Jonathan couldn't help but be mesmerized by her speech, gestures, and facial expressions. He couldn't tell how old she was, but she looked young. He noticed she wasn't wearing a ring, but as pretty as she was, he was willing to bet she had a man. By the time she completed her overview, Jonathan knew he wanted to get to know her better.

"It sounds like you know as much as I do about our latest product. I don't really have anything to add." Even though he couldn't think of anything to tell her, he was willing to do anything to keep her in that chair.

Iris admitted to herself that she found Jonathan attractive. His sandy brown hair was cut conservatively close to his scalp and brushed smooth. His full lips were perfectly formed and his light brown face was clean shaven and baby smooth. Avoiding his green eyes, she racked her brain to think of something to ask about.

They both sat in uncomfortable silence for seconds that felt like minutes. Eventually, they both laughed and Jonathan said, "I'm sorry,

I have to be honest. I don't have anything else professional to share with you. But I don't want you to leave."

Iris felt her face grow warm. She didn't know what to say. After a long moment of looking at her hands folded on the notepad in her lap, she looked up and said, "What were you working on when Rick and I came in? Is it something you could share with me?"

Smiling at her suggestion, he quickly said, "Yes, yes. Of course." He stood, gathering the papers scattered on his desk, and moved around to her side. "Let me come over there so you can see it better," he said, wanting an excuse to get nearer to her.

She scooted her chair a little to the side to accommodate his seat at the desk. Soon they were focused on the statistics and information on the papers.

When Iris looked up to ponder a fact he'd shared, she noticed the clock on the wall. "Oh no," she said abruptly.

Startled, he searched her face with concern. "What? What's wrong?"

"Oh, I'm sorry. I have to go. I have a lunch appointment." She flipped her notepad closed and grabbed her pen from the desk.

As she prepared to leave, Jonathan struggled between professionalism and the desire to see her again. He didn't know if her "lunch appointment" was a date or not, but he had to take a chance.

"Um," he started hesitantly. "Ah… would you be interested in having lunch with me one afternoon?"

Pausing a second in her rush to leave, Iris considered his question. She heard her mother's voice in her head. *"Never get involved with someone where you work."* But she was only an intern here for three months. What could happen in three months?

"Sure, I'd like that," she responded with a smile. She stood and reached out to shake his hand. "Thanks again for taking time to share this stuff with me. I find it really interesting."

"No problem," he said, taking her hand and holding it for a second longer than necessary. "About lunch — how about tomorrow?"

"That would be nice."

"Great. Um, how about I meet you in the lobby downstairs at twelve thirty?"

"Perfect," she said, still smiling. "See you tomorrow."

"Bye," he said to her retreating back.

She made it up to marketing just as Barbara was turning back to the floor.

Looking up when she heard the elevator open, Barbara smiled and said, "Hey, I thought you'd stood me up."

"Sorry, I got caught up. Give me a minute to drop this off and I'll be right back," Iris said breathlessly, walking briskly around the corner.

Five minutes later, she and Barbara were heading down crowded Lombard Street, talking and laughing in the sun.

* * *

Zuma glanced inconspicuously at her watch as her stomach began to growl. They'd been in intense discussions about Shearing's consumer-based services, and she'd just finished explaining the penetration increase in cities like Atlanta, D.C., Detroit, and Chicago directly related to her African American direct-marketing campaign. She was on a roll, but she needed to eat. Soon.

Bob also looked at his watch. Scanning the table, he said, "I've arranged for lunch to be brought in today so we can wrap this up before dark. Let's take a little break while catering sets up and meet back in ten, okay?"

As Zuma stood and bent to straighten her notes, Bob came next to her, placing a hand low on her back.

"Good job, lady. Those numbers are impressive."

Straightening, she took a step back and turned to face him, forcing his hand to fall at his side. "Thanks, Bob. There's more where that came from," she said, hoping to impress him and have his support when the time was right.

Clearing his throat, he added, "We've called Rick from the data division to join us this afternoon and expound on a few things you mentioned yesterday and today."

Zuma's smile froze in place. Struggling to maintain a steady voice and neutral face, she said, "Rick? Why? I thought I covered all of the pertinent information."

"You're right, you hit on all of the relevant points for our *current* products, but I really think the upcoming Personal Data project is going to be a big hit, and Rick is the man with the research and predictions on this thing. If we're the first ones to release it, it will be a major coup for Shearing — and any company merging with us."

Looking past her, he saw someone and excused himself without waiting for her response. What could she say anyway?

Zuma didn't want any possible competition for the limited positions that would be left in marketing. Rick was already a part of the Old Boy golf group. Silently fuming, she excused herself to no one in particular and left the room.

Chapter Seven

THE LOUD VOICES, MULTIPLE televisions, and thumping music in Kelly's made it impossible to talk without shouting. Iris was instantly in love with the after work hangout. If this was Kelly's on Thursday, she couldn't imagine the place on Fridays.

Iris had talked Barbara into joining her, Jim, Bruce and three other assistants from the marketing department. The small group grabbed a tall bar table, and the ladies sat on high stools while the men stood around them.

"Libby!" Bruce yelled to a busty blonde behind the counter. "One round of shots!" he shouted when he got her attention. She nodded in understanding and started preparing drinks.

Iris wasn't much of a drinker, but she loved hanging out. She had tried doing shots once in undergrad and ended up vomiting on Rey's feet. He'd taken her home, tucked her in bed, and never let her live it down. She smiled at the memory and asked Jim to get her a glass of wine.

Laughing and talking, the group drank, snacked on chips, and ate buffalo wings. It was the most fun Iris had experienced in the weeks since she'd moved to Baltimore. She looked at Barbara and noticed that she, too, was having a good time. Over lunch, Barbara had shared that she was depressed, because she felt unattractive and hadn't had a date in over a year. Iris felt good seeing her genuinely laughing and relaxing. Her face was actually kind of pretty when she smiled.

They had several rounds of drinks. Laughter filled the air as others from Shearing joined their small group. By nine o'clock, they occupied three tables, and no one seemed in a hurry to leave. As Bruce proved that he indeed could *not* drink six shots and walk a straight line, Iris looked at her watch and suggested they start settling the tab. It took thirty more minutes to figure out the payment of the bill with everyone either drunk or buzzing. Jim agreed to drive Bruce home, and arrangements were made for the others not sober enough to make the trip themselves. Shouting slurred goodbyes, they emptied into the street.

When Barbara realized that Iris was planning to walk, she offered to give her a ride. Iris walked across the street to the parking garage with Barbara, and they talked about the evening.

"You know," said Barbara, as they rode up the garage elevator, "that's the most fun I've had in... I don't know how long."

"Really?" asked Iris.

"Yes, really. I'm glad you came to Shearing."

Iris tilted her head to think before answering. "I'm glad I did, too."

Chapter Eight

Friday, May 11

I T WAS 5:00 A.M. WHEN IRIS BEGAN swatting at the buzzing alarm clock. She wanted to get up early and pack for her trip to Miami. To avoid the traffic and rush, she was going to take a cab straight from work to the airport. Rubbing her eyes, she rolled out of the bed.

She considered her lunch date with Jonathan as she shuffled through the conservative skirts and dark slacks in her closet, trying to pick out an outfit for the day. *Don't I have anything sexy to wear to work?*

Finally, she found an above-the-knee cream skirt and paired it with a silk top in a similar shade. She chose a fitted periwinkle jacket to complete the outfit. It wasn't as daring as she would like, but it would have to do today.

After packing, showering, and carefully dressing, she decided to spend some extra time with her makeup. She used a fluffy black brush to dust on face powder and added a hint of brick red to her high cheekbones. Choosing a wine-colored lipstick instead of her usual Blistex, she applied it evenly, then pursed her lips to judge the outcome. With a touch of mascara to lengthen her already thick lashes, she was ready to shift focus to her hair. Parting it on one side, she added tiny decorative hair clips to hold down the thick curls from the part. Giving herself a final once over in the mirror, she decided she liked what she saw and headed to the foyer.

Looking over her shoulder, she glanced around the apartment to make sure everything was in order. Finally, she picked up her wheeled travel case, shoulder bag, and purse and shuffled out the door and down the hall to the elevator. When Fred saw her struggling with the bags, he quickly whistled for a cab.

"Hey, Sunshine. Whatchou doin'? Moving again?" he asked her in a joking tone.

She smiled at him, stopping to place the bulky shoulder bag on top of the case. It slipped off the top, forcing her to try another arrangement. While she fought with the bags, Fred stepped outside and spoke with the driver of the taxi that pulled up. He returned to where she was struggling and, taking her travel case and shoulder bag, said, "This is on me. Just tell him where you wanna go."

"Oh, Fred. You didn't have to do that! I can pay him."

"Like I said, this is on me," he said with finality and held the door for her. After she was seated in the back, he placed the bags next to her and slapped the driver's hand.

Peeking his head in the open back window, he said, "Have a good trip, Sunshine. See you when you get back."

With genuine gratitude, she smiled back at him. "Thanks, Fred." They waved to each other as the driver merged into the busy morning traffic.

Once they arrived at the Shearing building, the driver got out and took Iris's bags.

"You don't have to do that," Iris said to him.

"Fred told me to take care of you," he replied, holding the door open for her.

She could tell there was no sense arguing, so she stepped out and self-consciously tugged on the short skirt as they walked to the entrance. The only reason she'd worn the uncomfortable skirt was to impress Jonathan, and she knew it. But today, Iris wanted that affect Zuma created when she entered a room in her short, tight suits — heads turning and tongues wagging.

Will was waiting with the door held open when Iris and the taxi driver arrived at the entrance. Iris had dug out a five-dollar bill from her purse and tried to hand it to the driver, but he refused the money, repeating, "Fred told me to take care of you. Have a good trip, Ms. Sunshine."

Will held out his hand for the two bags as the young driver spoke a greeting to the older man. "Sunshine. I like that name. It fits ya," he said, carrying her bags to the elevator. After pressing the button for her floor, he stood like a sentinel next to her.

"Will, really, I can carry them to my desk."

"Uh huh. I know you can," he replied, standing motionless with the bags in his oversized hand.

When they arrived on her floor, he followed her down the hall. Smiling, he greeted Betty warmly. "Hey there, Bet. How's it going today?"

"Alright, Will. What you doing up here?"

Will tilted his head toward Iris, "I helped her with her bags."

Betty smiled. "I should have known it would be for Iris. No one else could get you away from that desk."

Will looked embarrassed as he told the ladies to have a good day and went back to the elevators.

"Here, honey. Leave that heavy bag back here with me. No sense dragging it around the floor with nowhere to put it."

Betty didn't realize she'd just reminded Iris of her mother. Suddenly, Iris couldn't wait to get to Miami. Maybe her parents would be back from Orlando, and she could see them while she was there.

"Thanks, Betty," she said, wheeling the heavy bag behind the desk.

"No problem. Make sure to check your voicemail, I forwarded a couple of calls for you this morning," the older woman said, returning to her sorting and filing.

"Okay. Thanks."

After sending greetings around the room, Iris parked at her desk and cradled the phone receiver on her shoulder. Listening and pressing the necessary buttons, she put away her purse and took out notes on the Pdata project. When Jonathan's voice came through the receiver, she stopped flipping papers and relaxed back in her chair to listen to his message.

"Hi. I just wanted to say good morning and let you know how much I'm looking forward to lunch today. Have a good day. See you at 12:30."

She played the message again, just to hear his voice. Saving the message, she pressed "#" for the next one.

"Iris, it's Zuma. Just reminding you to have your report from the data division ready for me on Monday." There was an audible click at the end of the brief message.

Iris made a face at the phone and promptly deleted the message. She decided to spend the morning typing up the information she'd received from Rick and add in parts from the research Jonathan had shared with her yesterday. Hopefully, she'd be done by four thirty so she could get out of the building in time to make her flight. With a sigh, she spread out her notes and turned, resignedly, to the computer on her desk.

By noon, her hands were cramped from the continuous typing, but she was done. As she attempted to review it, the words began to blur on the page. She stood to stretch her legs and back. After a minute of contemplation, she decided to ask Betty for a favor.

Betty smiled when she saw Iris approaching. "Hey, Iris. What's going on?"

Iris sighed and looked dejected. "I prepared this report for Zuma, and I need for her to review it, but it's starting to look like gibberish."

"Just email the file to me, and I'll send the corrected report to you this afternoon."

"Are you sure, Betty? Do you have time for that?" Iris asked.

"Honey, that's my job. It's what I do. You really think the directors and VPs prepare their own reports?"

"Thank you so much. I really appreciate your help," Iris said sincerely as she reached up to rub her tired eyes. Then she remembered the mascara and stopped herself. Shit, she was supposed to be downstairs by twelve thirty, and she hadn't even freshened up yet.

Quickly, she returned to her desk, saved the report, and emailed it to Betty before grabbing her purse and speed-walking as best she could in the uncomfortable high heels and short skirt to the ladies' room.

Jonathan was waiting nervously by the windows in the lobby when he heard the elevator open. The last three times it opened it wasn't her, and he was beginning to think he'd been stood up. Not wanting to be disappointed again, he continued gazing out of the window, refusing to look back.

He heard her voice before he saw her. Turning around, he watched her lean on the security desk. Throwing back her head, she laughed at something the security guard said. He noticed the muscles in her calves as she shifted her weight from one leg to another and laughed with the old man. The skirt she wore was fitted enough to define the roundness of her butt. Looking down to confirm he didn't have a visible erection, he walked over trying to appear cool.

"Hi, Iris," he said, quietly touching her back.

"Hey, Jonathan!" she said with a smile. "I didn't know you were already down here."

"Oh, he's been down here for awhile," Will said.

Jonathan cut his eyes at the old man and attempted to pull Iris away.

"I wouldn't keep Sunshine waiting either if I had a chance," the guard said with a wink to Iris.

"Stop it, Will," she said with a flip of her hand and a smile. "I'll see you later."

"Okay, Sunshine. Take care." Jonathan glared at him, but Will didn't notice. He was watching Iris's legs under the short skirt.

To Iris, he said, "Why does he call you Sunshine?"

"Long story, but it's a nickname I seemed to have acquired."

"I can see why," he said, looking at the sun's reflection on the little silver clips holding down her curls. He wanted to reach up and touch them.

"So," said Iris brightly, "where're we going?"

"Do you like Indian? There's a great place three blocks up if you don't mind walking."

"Let's go," Iris said as an answer and fell in step next to him, ignoring the pain in her feet.

They talked comfortably during the walk, throughout the meal, and on the way back. They discovered they liked a lot of the same music, artists, and books. Iris learned that he'd graduated from the University of Maryland and was a frat man. As a sorority girl herself, she was comfortable talking frankly with him about the current plight of the black fraternities and sororities. Before she knew it, they were back on Lombard Street, and the date was over.

Neither of them was ready to part, but Iris had a report to finish and a plane to catch, and Jonathan was still filling in for Rick.

Looking at her pretty face, Jonathan asked, "Would you be interested in seeing a movie or going out to a club one night?"

"I'd like that a lot," she responded with a warm smile.

Taking a chance, he added, "Are you free this weekend?"

Her face fell as she remembered the trip. "Not this weekend, but how about next weekend?"

"Okay, but..." Taking her hand, he said in a low tone that she found sexy, "I'd be lying to you if I said I could wait until next weekend to see you."

Iris felt her face flushing and her pulse quicken. She was at a loss for words.

"Will you have lunch with me again next week?" he asked.

With a shy grin, she said, "That would be nice. Yes."

Reluctantly, she pulled her hand away. Thinking of the office gossip that could start, they said their goodbyes on the elevator. With a happy sigh, Iris floated to her desk.

Chapter Nine

IRIS'S PLANE LANDED WITH THREE sturdy bumps and a long, rumbling skid. She looked out the compact window and thought about Jonathan. She was happy to get out of town and see Rey, but she couldn't wait for next week.

Iris wheeled her bag through the terminal and walked toward baggage claim. Passing the growing mass of people around the baggage conveyor belt, she pulled her carry-on directly out the sliding doors to passenger pickup. As soon as she stepped outside, the humidity and heat surrounded her like a heavy wool coat. She could almost feel the tangles of her hair coiling tighter. Dropping her bags on the sidewalk, she removed her tight, silk jacket and tossed it over her arm.

Iris waited for two slow-moving taxis to pass before crossing the street to stand on the waiting strip under a green sign with the letter "H" on it. Miami's airport was always a zoo. Iris listened to the conversations in various languages around her as she flipped open her cell phone to call Rey.

Before she could push the familiar speed-dial numbers, she heard a honk and spied him behind the wheel of a large black truck with dark, tinted windows and shiny rims. A smile spread across his face as he jumped down from the huge SUV and walked around the front bumper to grip her in a tight hug.

"Hey, girl."

"Hey, boy," she replied, squeezing him in return. Releasing their hold, they kissed one another on the cheek. Rey took her suitcase and, flinging his thick dreadlocks out of his face, tossed it in the backseat.

"Damn, Rey," she said, reverting to her New York accent. "How'd you know I didn't have something fragile in there?"

"Because I know you," he said with a smile. His skin tone was normally a warm brown, identical to hers, but after two weeks in Brazil, one in Belize, and a few days in Miami, he was a dark chocolate. His black dreadlocks had turned various shades of brown. She could tell he'd spent a lot of time in the salt water and sun.

Checking out his muscled arms in the tank top he wore, she said, "You trying to look cute?" With a laugh, she added, "I *know* you not trying to get muscles!"

Looking her up and down, he said, "Look who's talkin' bout cute."

She blushed at his comment. She never wore short skirts. Ever. Her wardrobe consisted of jeans, running shorts, and business suits. Her totally opposite styles — conservatively professional and athletic tomboy — didn't leave much room for the cute, girlie thing.

To cover for her embarrassment, she said, "Shut up, boy and drive. What's up for tonight?"

His silver chain bracelet wiggled loosely as he pulled up the pant leg of his baggy jeans and pressed a Timberland boot on the gas. No one looking at him would think he was the founder and CEO of a lucrative and growing Internet company. The ankh tattoo on his bicep flexed as he reached up to pull the long locs from his face.

"I don't know," he said, glancing at her outfit. "You wanna change first?"

As the perspiration on her back made the soft silk stick to her, she answered. "Definitely. Damn it's hot." She reached forward to adjust the vents on the truck's dashboard. "Where are we going?"

"Shit, we ain't goin nowhere that you should be dressed like *that*," he smirked, looking at her white silk skirt and heels. He laughed and wheeled the big vehicle onto the toll road heading toward Miami Beach.

"Shut up, fool," she said, sitting back and letting the heavy dance-hall rhythms from the radio pulse through her body. While Rey weaved through traffic on the highway, she saw the brightly lit outline of the downtown skyline coming into view. She watched the dark figures of palm trees swaying in the breeze and wondered what Jonathan was doing.

Rey noticed her quiet contemplation. "Whatchou thinking about?" he asked, breaking into her thoughts.

Iris continued gazing through the window at the maze of freeways and billboards as she considered telling him about Jonathan. But she didn't want to go through the usual lecture that often included a reminder of all her past dating failures.

Turning to him, she filled him in on the latest happenings at work but conveniently omitted her lunch date. He asked her questions about the people she worked with and laughed when she described Bruce's inability to walk a straight line after downing shots at Kelly's.

As the conversation turned to Rey's recent meetings and negotiations, she glanced at the bridge passing on their right, lit from the underside by blue lights. They continued catching up as they drove by a cruise ship parked in dark water in front of the Carnival Cruise Lines dock. When the freeway ended, the truck slowed to a stop at a light, and Rey opened the windows.

The green numbers glowing in the center of the dashboard indicated it was 10:17. Despite the late hour, mothers and fathers with camcorders and digital cameras hanging around their necks ushered small children in and out of tourist traps with South Beach emblazoned on the back of short shorts and Miami embroidered on t-shirts hanging in the windows. Young college girls in tight micro minis flirted and laughed with college guys in baggy shorts and flip-flops on the corner of Fifth and Washington. At the next light, Rey turned left onto Collins, the popular South Beach club strip.

After driving several blocks, Rey turned right and brought the truck to an abrupt halt as he waited in a long line of cars to turn onto the famous Ocean Drive. Young, hip people flowed between the cars and in and out of restaurants, clubs, and trendy stores along the strip.

As they sat in the middle of the intersection waiting to turn left, a thin blonde with large fake breasts straining against the material of her tiny shirt leaned into Rey's window and said, "Hey, sexy." She swayed backward, falling onto one of her girlfriends. "I'll be looking for you tonight," she slurred, as her friends attempted to help her cross the street without tripping over her high heels.

Iris laughed, and Rey shook his head mumbling, "Trick."

Fifteen minutes later, he swerved into the curving driveway of a towering white hotel with purple and green lights illuminating the outline of the building. After a sleek, black Mercedes wheeled away, Rey pulled up to the entrance. A handsome Latin man wearing a tight red shirt with the hotel's name embroidered on the breast approached the passenger side. He was opening the door to help Iris down when he noticed Rey.

"Hey man, what's up?" he said, obviously recognizing Rey.

"Wassup, Manny? This is my homegirl, Iris," he said, coming around the truck to give the man a hard slap to the palm of his hand.

"Hello, Iris. Welcome to Miami," Manny said and shook her hand. He then reached into the backseat and pulled out her bag. Rey accepted the handle Manny offered and wheeled the case through the sliding glass doors with Iris close behind.

She took in the all-white art deco interior as she followed Rey to the elevators located between the escalators leading to and from the mezzanine. Through the glass walls of the quickly ascending elevator, she watched the beautiful people riding the escalator and milling about the lobby. It stopped abruptly with a muffled *ding*, and Rey held the door for Iris to exit before stepping out and leading the way down the hall. Iris looked up at a funky art sculpture hanging from steel wires in the center of the square formed by the hallways lining the perimeter of the hotel.

At the end of the long hallway, Rey stopped, slipped his key card into the handle of the door, and pulled it out swiftly. A green light blinked on, and he pressed the handle down, pushing open the door. He flicked on a light switch and Iris saw four stylish red chairs placed around a low square conference table. On the other side of the room was a wide plush couch with two matching armchairs anchoring it on each side. Across from the chairs, a television, stereo, and VCR sat on the three shelves of a glass entertainment center. Rey walked through the room and opened a door on the far side.

"You can have the bed in here, and I'll take the one out there," he said pointing to the pull-out couch. She followed him into the room and fell heavily on the plush down comforter of the king-sized bed.

"Man, I'm tired," she said, letting her pumps fall from her swollen feet and closing her eyes.

"You can be tired later," Rey said, looking down at her. "Get dressed so we can be out."

When Iris didn't move, he nudged her stockinged foot with his boot. "Get up, girl. Shit, we only got a day and a half to kick it. Let's do this."

Reluctantly, Iris sat up on the edge of the bed and looked at him. "Is that what you're wearing?" she asked, eyeing his white wife beater and baggy jeans held up by a black leather Kenneth Cole belt. She raised one arched eyebrow and said, "I know your ass wasn't dogging my clothes dressed like that."

They both laughed as he went to one of the large suitcases resting on a stand by the closet. "I'll change, but it won't be much different than what I got on now. It's hot as hell out there."

She unzipped her bag and rummaged around, pulling out a pair of white shorts and a top with an open back and strings crisscrossing from the shoulders to the bottom. "I'm wearing this," she said, tossing them on the bed with finality before walking into the large bathroom with her flowered toiletry bag.

After she had showered and changed, Iris decided to pull her hair back into a curly afro puff. The humidity didn't leave her much choice for her natural kinks. She applied a light coat of gold shimmer gloss to her lips and emphasized her big eyes with dark liner. When she emerged from the bedroom carrying her DKNY sneakers, Rey looked her up and down approvingly before turning off the television and rising to leave.

They decided to walk and, after putting their name on the waiting list for a crowded Spanish restaurant with loud music blaring into the street, they browsed the boutiques on the street.

Holding up a high-heeled sandal, Rey looked at Iris and said, "You'd look good in this."

Iris walked over, took the shoe from his hand and burst out laughing. "Could you see me in this?"

"Actually, yeah," he said casually.

Iris looked at the shoe again with a furrow in her brow. "This isn't even my style."

"I know. But that doesn't mean it wouldn't look good on you," he said off-handedly, and took the shoe from her returning it to the shelf. "Come on, let's get some ice cream."

"Ice cream before dinner?" Iris mumbled as she followed him out of the store, looking back at the shoe on the display stand.

After dinner, they walked in and out of various hot spots. Rey recognized someone in almost every place and spent most of the night talking loudly to be heard over the pumping music. Iris wasn't shocked. Rey always knew someone, no matter where they were. Especially the women.

Women in all shapes and sizes flocked to him. They loved the dreadlocks that hung down his back. He often had his hair professionally styled along with his trim mustache, beard, and goatee. His eyes were a clear brown that always made Iris think of iced tea, and they were framed with long curly lashes. His eyebrows were thick, and he often had one raised. He wore diamond studs in both ears, and a silver rope chain, similar to the one on his wrist, hung around his neck.

She looked at his six foot two frame and wondered when he had started developing muscles. His shoulders and arms were curved with definition she hadn't seen before. Even the muscles of his chest pushed against the fabric of his tank top. Had he always had them? And was she just noticing them now? The ankh tattoo hanging from a tattooed chain design looping his bicep undulated with every flex of his arm.

As they wove their way through the throng on the crowded sidewalk, a gorgeous woman wearing a keyhole lycra top, exposing the curves of her perfect fake breasts, stepped into their path. "Rey!" she exclaimed, opening her arms.

"Martina! What are you doing here, baby?" Rey responded with a big smile.

He wrapped his chiseled arms around her tall, curvy frame, and Iris noticed the muscles of his back flex with the movement. Martina was wearing a tight miniskirt that was hooked to her top by gold loops. Iris saw the calves of her long, slender legs wrapped in straps of leather attached to very high-heeled sandals and thought about the shoe in the boutique.

Martina flipped her long, straight, black hair over one creamy shoulder and said, in a thick accent, "I needed a break from the salon, so I decided to come party with the beautiful people." Her green eyes, surrounded by dark eye makeup, were fixed on Rey's face.

She took his hand, appearing not to notice Iris, and dropped her lids seductively. "What are you doing tonight? I'd love for you to show me around." Her lips, painted a deep, dark red, parted slightly, and she rubbed the tip of her tongue along the edge of her bleached, bonded teeth.

Holding her hand, Rey smoothly said, "I'm busy tonight, baby. But give me your cell number, and we'll definitely hook up another time."

She reached into a little purse, hanging from a long gold chain draped over her slender shoulder, and pulled out a card.

"All of my personal information is there. Call me anytime. Ciao," she drawled, leaning her hard breasts on him and kissing both his cheeks. She walked past and cut her emerald eyes at Iris, letting her know she'd seen her standing and waiting behind Rey.

Without a backward glance at the woman, Rey took Iris's hand and said, "Come on, let's check out Fat Tuesdays."

Chapter Ten

IRIS AWOKE IN CONFUSION. She couldn't remember where she was or how she'd gotten there. Her lids were heavy, and her mouth tasted like a combination of paste and cotton. Slowly prying her eyes open in the bright sunlight streaming into the room, she began to recall the night before.

They had been on the cramped dance floor of Fat Tuesdays. Some guy Rey knew kept buying them drinks. Hers was a deliciously fruity thing that hadn't tasted like alcohol at all.

As her eyes slowly adjusted to the brightness in the room, Iris sat up and smacked her lips in hopes of dispelling the awful dryness. She rolled from the mountain of sheets and groped her way to the bathroom. Ignoring the light switch, she turned the silver handle of the faucet and began rinsing her nasty mouth. After washing her face and brushing her teeth, she went in search of Rey.

Balled up in the fetal position on the sofa, he was snoring softly. Iris smiled as she noticed he hadn't even bothered to take off his boots before collapsing on the chair.

"Hey," Iris said softly, nudging him with her foot. When he didn't budge, she called a little louder. "Rey! Get up and get in the bed."

Without a word of protest, he rolled into a sitting a position and, with his eyes still closed, tripped into the bedroom and fell across the messy bed. Iris untied his boots, letting them drop onto the floor with a thud. Rey scrunched up into a ball in the center of the bed and continued snoring.

Iris shook her head and considered how many times they'd replayed this scene with their friends in London, Martha's Vineyard, Canada, and more. They partied hard and, each morning, everyone would sleep until noon while Iris woke early to go running or swimming, depending on the weather and location.

Today, she decided to do both. Pulling out a bikini top and running shorts from her travel case, she quickly dressed and grabbed the card key from the floor where Rey must have dropped it when they came in. She found her sunglasses in her purse on the bar and quietly let herself out.

The morning was glorious, and several people were already milling around the hotel lobby and private beach below. Bending to tie her running shoes, she considered which path to take. Deciding on the streets, she took off with a slow jog down the sidewalk on the beach side of Ocean Drive.

She dodged tourists, rollerbladers, and beautiful people as she increased her pace and went into a zone. Sometimes she listened to music during her runs but, mostly, she liked to hear the sounds of nature. Today, the waves of the ocean and the breeze blowing through the palms were calming as Iris thought about her internship and her lunch with Jonathan.

When she finished her run forty minutes later, she walked to slowly bring down her heart rate. As she neared the hotel, she glanced in a boutique window and noticed the shoe Rey had picked out the night before. She stopped and looked at the shoe thoughtfully.

Maybe Rey was right. She was almost twenty-seven years old and still dressing the same way she had in college. There was nothing wrong with looking sexy sometimes, even if she felt like a conservative businesswoman most of the time and an athlete the rest.

With a final, wistful glance at the shoe, she crossed the street and stopped to remove her shoes and socks before trudging through the sand. As she came to an empty spot on the beach, she dropped her shoes and stripped off her shorts to reveal a black thong that matched the trim of her brightly colored bikini top.

Walking down to the shallow surf, she waded quickly into the warm water. Swimming deeper, away from the children and tourists, Iris flipped over onto her back and floated on the buoyant salt water in the heat of the sun. As she closed her eyes, she let go of the thoughts clouding her mind and drifted with the waves, listening to her breath as it escaped with the breeze.

Fifteen minutes later, Iris swam back to the beach and began searching for her shoes and shorts on the crowded beach. She stepped over and around young, scantily clad men rubbing sunscreen on each other as she scanned the ground. Finally finding her things half-buried in sand, she was bending to pick up the shorts when she heard a low whistle. Knowing most of the adult occupants on the beach were either parents or gay, Iris ignored the whistle and shook loose sand from the damp shorts.

When she bent to pick up the shoes, she heard the whistle again. Turning, she saw Rey struggling to walk toward her in the deep sand.

"How'd you know I was here?" Iris asked as Rey came closer.

"Where else would you be?" Looking her up and down, he said, "Damn, girl. When'd you get all that junk in your trunk? I almost didn't recognize you out here."

Iris slapped his arm. "Shut up, fool."

"I'm just sayin'," Rey continued, looking over the top of his expensive sunglasses to get a better look at her rear end. "You gonna make these gay boys change their religion like that." He laughed as he bent to get her other shoe.

Changing the subject, Iris asked, "Have you eaten yet?"

"Not yet. I was waitin' for you. Come on, I'm starvin'." He handed her the shoe and waited for her to follow him to the sidewalk.

"Wait, I need to wash this salt and sand off," Iris said, moving to the beach shower heads by the sidewalk.

She handed him the shoes with her shorts and socks stuffed inside, then turned on one of the nozzles and stepped under the cool stream. He watched the water make her curls heavy as they hung around her face. When Iris tilted her head back and smoothed the black waves of hair, Rey noticed a man turn back from his woman to look at her. Rey smiled. His homegirl *was* a beautiful woman. Completely natural and beautiful.

When Iris was finished, she reached a dripping hand out for the shoes.

Rey raised a brow at her and said, "You're soaking wet. I think I can handle this while we walk."

He shook his head. Iris never took a towel anywhere. She said she liked to let the sun dry her naturally. Walking behind her, he watched water drip from her wet ringlets down her back and over the round hills of her perfect rear. She seemed totally oblivious to the men and women stealing glances at her as they passed.

Just as they were about to enter the shade of the hotel, Iris stopped and tilted her head back to let the sun shine on her face one more time before entering the frigid hotel lobby. With her eyes closed, she couldn't see the look on Rey's face. A look he promised himself he'd never let her see.

Chapter Eleven

ZUMA SIPPED THE MARTINI slowly as she gazed from under seductively lowered lids around the room. Even though the constant boom of the loud music was giving her a headache, her third drink was beginning to relax her tense nerves.

Tapping a cigarette lazily on the counter, she scanned the bar and the adjoining room of couches. Swiveling on her stool, she turned to face the bar, giving her back to the room and the phony-ass people in it.

"A light?"

The voice was deep. Very deep. But Zuma didn't turn around. She simply put the cigarette between her lips and leaned toward the flame of the lighter held in a well-manicured, dark hand.

Sitting tall but relaxed on the stool, she closed her eyes as she sucked in and mentally created the man she wanted to possess that sexy, bass voice. Removing the cigarette and holding it loosely between her fingers, she slowly exhaled, letting stress escape with the swirls of smoke curling from her nose and lips.

"May I buy you another?" the voice asked, closer this time.

"You may," Zuma answered without opening her eyes. She took

another hit on the cigarette and relaxed in the exhalation.

She sat in silence for several minutes. Zuma cracked her eyes only to find her drink and bring it to her lips. She didn't want to spoil her dream vision by looking the voice in the face. Oddly, the man didn't seem to care. Why wouldn't he just leave her alone with her cigarette and drink? As the cigarette burned low, she mashed it out in a nearby ashtray and took a final sip of her drink. In preparation to return to real life, she turned to face the voice.

With his forearms leaning on the bar top and hands clasped loosely together, he was staring intently at her. She was almost caught off guard by the intensity in his smoldering black eyes. Handsome was not the appropriate word to describe this Adonis. *Damn!*

He didn't attempt to speak, and she couldn't if she wanted to. The combination of alcohol and desire had thrown her off her game.

"Excuse me," she managed, as she slipped gracefully from the stool and made her way to the ladies' room. Squinting in the dirty mirror above the sink, she brushed her hair into shape and freshened her lipstick as two women breathlessly rushed into the cramped room.

"I told you it was him," one of the women said.

"Damn, he looks better than in the magazines!"

"I cannot *believe* Charles Wellingsley is in here. Girl, I gotta get my face on right for that brother," the first one said, leaning over the sink to better see her image in the dingy mirror.

Charles Wellingsley. The popular Black actor from England. Zuma knew the Adonis looked familiar.

Readjusting her breasts in the low-cut blouse, she turned to study her butt in the filmy full-length mirror. It was nonexistent as usual, but her legs were gorgeous, if she said so herself. And she did.

Stepping from the restroom, she looked at the bar. Charles Wellingsley was still there, in the same relaxed position. But now, a woman with lots of weave and too much makeup was sitting next to him on the stool Zuma had recently vacated. He was smiling at the phony woman, showing perfect teeth, as she talked with nonstop animation. The two women from the bathroom were on his other side, and a couple of brothers were riding his jock from the back.

Walking directly into the center of the small group, Zuma stopped between him and the phony woman, touching his back lightly.

"Follow me," she said simply, before turning around and walking, without a backward glance, to the front door.

Nothing in her history indicated that he wouldn't be behind her when she reached the club's front door. If he wasn't, it would be his loss.

Outside, the men waiting to get in ogled her and whispered comments to one another as she slowly made her way to her car parked along the curb.

She enjoyed the attention a few moments more before slipping in and pausing to glance surreptitiously around for Charles Wellingsley. He was nowhere in sight. Checking her rear-view mirror, she still didn't see him.

With a shrug, she started the engine and sat adjusting the radio. WHUR, Howard University's station, was playing '80s club music, and she pumped up a DJ remix of Cheryl Lynn's "Encore."

She took her time pressing buttons to open the sunroof and windows. Preparing to pull out, she checked her side mirror and saw a sleek, black Lexus SC430 idling with the top down behind her. She smiled to herself and pulled out in front of it. Stepping on the accelerator, she sped off in a flurry of dust and smoke with Mr. Wellingsley close behind.

Chapter Twelve

IRIS LOOKED OUT THE rectangular window of the plane carrying her back to Baltimore as it rumbled along the runway and tilted sharply up toward the sky. She replayed the weekend in her mind as the palm trees and traffic below became smaller.

Yesterday afternoon, she and Rey had driven to Miramar, a nearby Miami suburb, to visit her brother, Carlos, and his family. Carlos had moved his wife and sons there three years earlier. Iris smiled now as she remembered her nephews running through the house throwing a football and shouting. Her sister-in-law, Sonja, spent most of the afternoon breaking up fights and yelling for them to stop running in and out of the house. Her mother and father had spoiled them in Orlando, and the boys wreaked havoc both inside and out with their new toys.

As the plane leveled off, Iris placed her headphones over her ears and pressed play on the portable CD player. She barely heard the music as she recalled her conversation with Sonja.

"What's up with you and Rey?" Sonja had asked as soon as she had Iris alone in the kitchen.

Confused, Iris asked her, "What do you mean, what's up with us?"

"You know what I mean, chica," Sonja replied in her native Spanish. "You're spending the weekend with him alone in Miami at the newest and hottest hotel in South Beach. Like I said — what's up?"

Iris shook her head as she dried a pot and stooped to place it in a low cabinet. Also speaking in Spanish, she answered, "Sonja, you know we're like sister and brother. It's not even like that."

Sonja stopped rinsing the pan she was holding and propped a wet hand on her hip, letting water drip to the floor. "Number one, he's *not* your brother, and number two, he's fine as hell. Or haven't you noticed?" she added with a cocky tilt of her head.

Iris had to smile at the last comment and switched to English. "I won't lie. I did notice my boy was trying to look kinda fine. But, for real, he knew every gorgeous woman on Ocean Drive, and trust, they knew him, too. Besides, this isn't the first time we've kicked it like this."

"Yes it is. This is the first time I've seen you two alone. Where's your posse?" Sonja went back to rinsing as she waited for Iris's answer.

Unable to come up with one, Iris changed the subject. "Anyway, I've met someone recently," she said with a coy smile.

Sonja stopped rinsing again and turned back to her sister-in-law. "So when were you going to tell me, ho?"

Iris laughingly filled her in on the details regarding Jonathan. As she finished, Rey and Carlos came into the kitchen, quickly quieting them. A knowing look passed between the two women as they finished cleaning the kitchen in silence. Iris laughed when Sonja looked Rey up and down while his back was turned. Feeling the unspoken words and laughter were about them, the men quickly escaped to the pool in the backyard.

Iris's recollections were interrupted by the pilot's voice, barely audible over the plane's roar, indicating they'd reached their cruising altitude. As his voice crackled over the plane's speaker system, Iris contemplated what Sonja had said.

Rey was definitely fine and, yes, she had noticed. But they'd been friends since they were eight. There was no way Rey was even considering her that way. Especially with women like Martina hanging around and available in every city.

But then again, when had she and Rey been on vacation together alone? Never. But nothing had changed. They still did the same things, the same way, and Iris realized she wouldn't even be having this conversation with herself if Sonja hadn't brought it up.

Rey obviously wasn't interested, but a handsome brother named Jonathan was. As far as Iris was concerned, it was all good. Drifting off to sleep, she let the smooth jazz sounds of Norman Brown keep her company for the rest of the flight.

Chapter Thirteen

"HELLO, IRIS PENA SPEAKING."

"Iris, I'd like to see you in my office," Zuma said briskly.

When Iris walked into Zuma's office and sat in one of the chairs facing the desk, Zuma immediately noticed the darker hue of the younger woman's skin. *She didn't get that in Baltimore.*

"How was your weekend?" Zuma asked curiously, hoping Iris would disclose something specific.

"Good, thank you." Not knowing what to say or do, she waited nervously for Zuma to continue.

When Iris didn't expound, Zuma picked up a folder from the desk and removed a stapled report, laying it on top of the folder. Iris recognized it immediately.

"I've reviewed your report on Pdata, and it's good. Where did you get the information?"

Iris wasn't expecting a compliment from Zuma and took care with her answer. "I spent a day with Rick York and another with Jonathan

Williams in the data division. They shared a great deal with me."

"Hm, that's great," Zuma said insincerely. She paused to shuffle through some handwritten notes on her desk. "I've been thinking about how you can be an asset to our group and also get a good internship experience." Zuma paused to watch Iris's expression, but no change occurred.

"I want you to research the company with whom we're considering merging, Ladd Tech Corporation. Prepare a report for me that compares and contrasts their products and services to ours, and suggest marketing ideas that we, as one company, could employ to improve overall market penetration and retention."

Zuma passed the paper across the wide desk to Iris, then leaned back in her chair and waited for Iris to comment.

Looking skeptically at the paper, Iris responded, "Wow, that's a serious assignment."

"Yes, it is. But I'm confident after reading your report on Pdata that you can handle it and do it well."

Still cautious, Iris said, "It will require a lot of research and work. When is it due?"

"I realize it's a big undertaking. How about if you check in with me on Fridays to discuss the status of your research, and you have the final result to me by Monday, July thirtieth?" Zuma consulted her desk calendar and counted off the weeks before continuing. "Since your internship ends on August third, it will give me a chance to review it before you present it to Bob O'Brien, our vice president."

"I'll present to the vice president of marketing?" Iris asked incredulously.

"Why do you sound so surprised? I told you I'd take care of you as my intern. Let me know if you need any help — I know all of the products for both companies." Zuma sat back, resting her elbows on the chair's arms, and steepled her fingers.

"Okay. Thanks. I'll get started now," Iris said, standing and walking out the door.

Zuma stared evilly at the retreating woman's back. If college girl was as smart as her report on Pdata indicated, this research assignment might reveal something Zuma had overlooked or missed. By the time the big meeting took place at the end of August with all of the vice presidents and the CMO, she'd have the research and new ideas necessary to secure her position in the new company. She'd give Iris a good review to take back to college, and everyone would be happy.

Step one of Zuma's plan was in effect. Now it was time to start renewing some old friendships.

Chapter Fourteen

Friday, May 18

THE REST OF THE WEEK zoomed by as Iris researched the information she needed for her first Friday morning meeting with Zuma.

The first couple of days were spent reading up on the current products and services of both companies. Afterward, Iris completed detailed research on the commercial and consumer markets that comprised the majority of the sales for each. Realizing the depth of information, she decided to isolate her work to consumer markets.

Still unsure about Zuma's motives, Iris dove into the research with vigor but was cautious about what she planned to share. Each day, she added the most basic references on a poster for Zuma, but locked the detailed notes in her desk drawer.

Now it was Friday morning, and Iris sat quietly in Zuma's large office, looking past her to the skyline visible from the window. Zuma stood, leaning on the edge of the desk, looking down at Iris's poster.

Along the left side of the poster was a column of boxes with product and service names, descriptions and, in some boxes, pictures. Across the top were headings of age groups, race and nationality, geographic regions, and household income. Throughout the board, there were checks, Xs, and asterisks.

Initially, when Iris had propped the elementary-looking poster on the desk, Zuma felt her irritation building. The markings throughout the poster were handwritten in different colors. It looked like a middle school science project. But, as Zuma considered the headings across the top, she realized how many Xs and asterisks were present and knew there was more to the simple presentation than met the eye.

With her hands propped wide on the desk, Zuma asked, "So, what does all this mean?"

Iris stood and joined her. "These are various market parameters," she began, pointing to the column headings. "These," she said, randomly pointing to various Xs and asterisks, "are areas of weakness and possible opportunity."

Zuma smiled. Her pretty face lit up as she considered how she'd use this childlike presentation as a tool to prepare a *real* proposal for Bob O'Brien and the CMO. She couldn't wait to see what Iris provided for her next week. *I might even be able to introduce one or two of these items in our current meetings as something I'm working on to propose in August. Anything to keep me here a little longer.*

Leaning her hip on the desk and folding her arms under her breasts, Zuma tossed her hair over one shoulder and looked at Iris. "Good work. I knew you'd be up to the task. I can't wait to see what you have for me next week."

Zuma looked at the poster once more before dropping her arms and abruptly turning her back on Iris. Walking to her chair, she sat and swiveled to face the computer's monitor. As she began checking her email, it became obvious to Iris the meeting was over.

Iris collected the poster and retreated silently to her desk. She wasn't sure what Zuma's hidden agenda was but she knew an agenda definitely existed. Her brain began calculating a plan for successfully completing the internship with a good evaluation and, if necessary, exposing Zuma in the process. There was only one person who could help with what she had devised.

Dropping the poster along the wall of her cubicle, Iris strode purposefully to the reception desk. "Betty, what are you doing for lunch today?" she asked in a serious tone.

Surprised, Betty looked cautiously at the young woman. There was an odd look on Iris's face. "I get the feeling you have plans for my lunch hour," she said, squinting curiously at Iris. Iris nodded.

* * *

Betty sat picking at the pasta salad in front of her as Iris explained her plan and Betty's role. The older woman couldn't help but smile as Iris unfolded the strategy. *I knew there was a reason I liked this girl.*

Betty had been working at Shearing for several years when Zuma was promoted to marketing director. From the first day in her new role, Zuma had treated the older black woman with condescending disdain. Barking orders and ignoring her existence. The tension on the floor among all the staff reporting to Zuma was palpable, and there had been little joy for anyone in their department during the past year.

Not only would Betty help Iris with her plan, she would enjoy every minute of it.

Chapter Fifteen

Friday, May 25

FOR IRIS, IT WAS HARD to believe May was almost gone. She spent most of her days researching, making phone calls, and meeting with various marketing managers. Especially Jonathan. He proved to be very knowledgeable about the technology and background of both Shearing's products and their competitor's.

With her extensive background in Latin and Hispanic markets, Iris quickly noted the lack of penetration in this untapped market for both Shearing and Ladd. She made a few phone calls to a company in New York to retrieve demographics and buying trend information.

Next, she researched the direct marketing tactics for Shearing and Ladd to non-white populations, gathering samples of mailings and in-store brochures. Finally, she had her brother, Carlos, mail her colorful maps and diagrams of the cities and states with the highest population of Spanish-speaking people. Using PowerPoint, she created a color grid and legend to identify the specific nationalities of each population indicated on the maps. Once the grids and legends were printed on transparencies, she could lay them over the maps to further identify possible target markets.

Throughout the week, she tested the bilingual customer service call center for each company by calling several times and asking questions in Portuguese and different dialects of Spanish. Spanish-speaking representatives were available in their regular call center, but, as she guessed, the representatives didn't speak Portuguese and failed to understand some of the Spanish terms she used.

Iris was amazed that in 2001 companies were still missing the necessity of catering to the wide variety of Spanish-speakers present throughout the United States. Puerto Ricans, Mexicans, Cubans, and Brazilians spoke differently, lived differently, and had different political and economic American experiences.

Regardless, Iris now had the task of figuring out what to share with Zuma and what to withhold. It was the Friday before the Memorial Day weekend, and she and Betty were putting the final touches on the document. With extensive attachments and several exhibits, the presentation was impressive and several pages long.

"How long do you think it will take to finish this and get copies?" Iris asked as Betty carefully reviewed a page for typographical errors.

"I don't know. For the formal binding you want in the quantity you're requesting, it could take some time. But you need to forget about this for awhile and enjoy the long weekend." Betty looked maternally at Iris.

"I guess you're right. Zuma's already gone on vacation, so there's nothing else to do now."

"Girl, get your stuff and get out of here. I'll take care of this from here," Betty said as she watched Iris's usually sunny face hang in preoccupied thought. "Iris, let me tell you something. I've watched people come in here fresh from college with a light and full of ideas. After awhile, the light fades and, while dealing with the shit of corporate America, they become bitter and angry. Don't let Shearing take over your life. It's just an internship for you. Don't make your summer miserable over someone like Zuma."

Betty watched as the muscles in Iris's jaw relaxed. A hint of the original smile played on her face.

"The information you've gathered is excellent, and the proposal is going to look fabulous. Just keep doing the best you can, and try to forget about Zuma Harris."

"You're right, Betty," Iris sighed. "I just get pissed every time I think about the fact that the most support I've had from management here has been from everyone *except* Zuma. The one person who looks like me and should be my ally is my worst enemy."

Betty didn't have a response for the hurt she saw in Iris's eyes. What could she say when she knew the girl spoke the truth?

Eventually, the cloud over Iris's face cleared, and she said, "If I haven't said it recently, thanks for helping me with all of this. I truly appreciate your help."

With a gentle smile, Betty said, "Anytime. Now get out of here and enjoy your weekend."

"You too, Betty. See you next week."

Chapter Sixteen

ZUMA LOOKED DOWN at the small, rocky islands in the water off the cape as the plane began its descent into Boston. She quickly closed the magazine she'd been reading and returned it to the leather carry-on under the seat in front of her. Once the plane landed, Zuma rose with the rest of the first-class passengers, placed her bag daintily on her shoulder, and sashayed through the arrival gate doorway.

With pleasure, she noticed people looking at her. Stopping in the ladies' room, she checked her makeup and lovingly brushed her hair. She adjusted her clinging top to make sure it scooped low enough. The shorts she wore gave her the appearance of a round butt, and her legs looked long in high-heeled sandals. *The daily walking lunges and stair stepper are totally paying off,* she thought, looking proudly at her body's profile.

Glancing at her watch, Zuma realized she was running late. She pulled her cell phone out of the carry-on and turned it on. After a few seconds, a melody played, and her name scrolled across the screen. She had two new messages. Putting on her hands-free earpiece, she tucked the phone back in its pocket and sped toward the escalators.

The first message was from Malcolm declaring his need to see her.

She felt a familiar heat between her legs and smiled, but the smile soon turned to a smirk when she heard the familiar voice of the second message.

"Can't wait to see you, babe. Two thirty on the nose. Don't keep me waiting."

Zuma pulled out the earpiece and tucked it in the bag with the phone as she waited for her suitcases to come around the slow-moving carousel in baggage claim. After another fifteen minutes, her cases finally wound around the bend, and she maneuvered them to the floor. Pulling the two large bags behind her, she approached the sliding glass doors and stepped into the breeze of the northeastern spring day.

Blinking in the sunlight, she was reaching for her sunglasses when she heard a horn blow. After tucking the handles of the sunglasses carefully under her hair and placing them on her nose, she looked up to see a white Mercedes convertible pulling up to the curb.

She waved and waited for a bus to pass before dragging her bags briskly across the street. The trunk popped open and, when the driver didn't move to help her, she went around to the back of the car and struggled to lift the heavy bags in herself. Breathing hard, she slammed the trunk shut and walked around to the passenger side. Attempting to control her heavy breathing, she bent over in the window to let the driver get a full view of her breasts.

"Glad you made it, babe," he said, completely oblivious of her struggle as he eyed her neckline. "Get in."

Zuma opened the door and slid into the cool leather seat. Placing her shoulder bag and purse in the back, she did her usual hair flip and looked lustily at him. He leaned over, grabbing one of her breasts, and kissed her hungrily with his thin lips. Sitting back in his seat, he rubbed his swelling groin before stepping on the gas and taking off for the toll road leading to Cape Cod.

Zuma watched the sun glinting off the gentle waves of water under the bridge as the Mercedes slowly followed a long trail of vacationers coming to the Cape for Memorial Day. Dismally, she thought of past holidays when she'd been with a sexy man in California, Las Vegas, or the Caribbean. Sighing inwardly, she closed her eyes and remembered happier moments.

"We're almost there, babe. Don't worry," her companion said, incorrectly assuming she was impatient with the snaking lines of traffic.

Remembering where she was and reminding herself of the goal for the weekend, she sat up perkily and smiled at him. "I know. I'm just ready to spend some quality time with you, that's all," she lied smoothly.

Inwardly, she chastised herself. The last time she found herself in this situation, she swore she would never be in a position to have to do it again. Now, here she was, about to spend the whole holiday weekend with him. Where were his wife and family?

Eventually, they pulled off the state road and drove along a busy main street. After waiting, merging, and driving around several rotaries, they came to a neighborhood of quaint cottages. The Mercedes cruised slowly up a quiet street lined with trees and yards of sand and sparse grass. Old-fashioned bicycles of varying sizes leaned against most of the houses.

Finally, he pulled the car into the long driveway of a faded blue and gray house set back from the road and cut the engine. Two bicycles were chained together under the carport, and a children's swing-set sat rusting in the front yard. This house had definitely seen better days, Zuma thought. Sighing again, she opened the door to step out into a pleasant breeze. She closed her eyes and breathed in the salt air.

Leaving the trunk open for Zuma to get her suitcases, the man got out and walked up the front steps to unlock the door. He went in, leaving her outside to drag her heavy bags into the house by herself.

She swore under her breath as sand became trapped in the wheels of the suitcases. Stopping, she dropped one bag and grabbed the other by the handle with both hands. Bending back under the weight, she dragged it up the steps, into the house, and dropped it loudly in the foyer. Perspiration beaded on her forehead as she eyed the other case lying discarded in the sandy yard.

Zuma began muttering to herself. *Lazy motherfucker. He should be carrying these bags for me, considering what he's expecting to get.*

She repeated the struggle with suitcase number two and stood still to catch her breath. Dusting off her hands on the front of her shorts, she looked around the bright room. It was cozy, neat, and clean. Her breath caught when she saw the beach and ocean, only steps away, through the windows in the kitchen. She walked through the family room, stepped down into the tiled kitchen, and stared through French doors at the waves crashing gently on the sand. It was so serenely quiet, she didn't dare breathe for fear of disturbing the perfection of the moment. Unfortunately, the tranquility was short-lived.

She heard him before she felt him come up behind her and grab her chest, pinching her nipples hard. Zuma felt his erection poking her awkwardly in the butt as he grinded spastically against her for a few moments.

"Mm, babe. I can't believe I made it this long without touching you," he mumbled into her hair. Sticking his warm, wet tongue in her ear, he continued to roughly knead her breasts. She closed her eyes, reminding herself that this charade would provide the results she needed, wanted, and demanded. If she played her cards right, she would be controlling this game.

Chapter Seventeen

IRIS ALWAYS WENT HOME to New Rochelle for the Memorial Day weekend. Rey was flying to Baltimore to accompany her on the three-hour drive, but he wouldn't arrive until Saturday morning. Friday night was all hers.

She excitedly primped in the mirror as she waited for Jonathan to pick her up for their date. They'd been out to lunch several times, and he'd taken her to dinner twice since their first date. Tonight, they were meeting a couple of his frat brothers and their girlfriends for dinner at an Ethiopian restaurant in Adams Morgan, the trendy spot to enjoy diverse ethnic restaurants and shops in the heart of Washington, D.C.

Dinner was delicious, and the conversation was good. Afterward, the three couples walked casually up the street laughing and talking as they window-shopped. Not wanting the evening to end early, one of the ladies suggested they go dancing at Zanzibar, a popular nightclub in southeast D.C. Everyone agreed and, after discussing whose car could fit them all, they climbed into one SUV and headed toward the waterfront.

When they drove past the club looking for a parking space, Iris noticed the line of people waiting to get in the venue. She was prepared for a long wait and was actually looking forward to the opportunity to hold hands and lean on Jonathan in line. As they walked past the entrance to get in the slow-moving queue, Jonathan recognized one of the security guards. After a quick hand shake and man hug, their group was ushered ahead of the waiting patrons to the payment window. Iris didn't think the night could get any better.

They entered the crowded lobby and walked up the curving staircase to one of the dance floors. The beat of the music thudded against the walls making the room vibrate. In the darkness, strobe lights flashed on the people on the packed dance floor, causing them to look as though they were robotically moving as one.

Suddenly, the rhythm and melody of Frankie Beverly and Maze's "Before I Let Go" came on, and the room went wild. As Frankie crooned, "Aaaaahhhhhh," the DJ turned down the music, and everyone held the note together as one, singing the next words that every person in the room knew by heart. Jonathan grabbed Iris's hand and led her into a space he created among the dancers.

They danced through several songs before Iris had to call it quits and find an open space to cool off. Jonathan went to get her a drink while she mingled with his friends. By two o'clock, Iris was yawning, creating a chain reaction among the other ladies. Minutes later, they were streaming out of the club with the rest of the partygoers.

Walking a casual distance from his friends, Jonathan reached for Iris's hand and held it gently in his. Once in the truck, Iris was tucked in the crook of his arm and curve of his body. Occasionally, she rubbed her hand casually against his chest or thigh.

Soon they were back in Adams Morgan, and the couples parted ways with hand slaps, hugs, and promises to do it again soon. Jonathan unlocked the doors of his car and held the passenger door open for Iris. *A gentleman,* Iris thought silently. *I think I'm falling for this brother.*

Jonathan drove north on the Baltimore Washington Parkway, and the forty-five minute ride back seemed quick as they engaged each other in easy banter. Eventually, Jonathan pulled off the highway and drove through the lights of downtown Baltimore before turning on Iris's street.

She reached over and touched the back of his hand lightly. "Why don't you park and come up for a little while?"

Jonathan didn't hesitate to circle the block a few times to find a parking space and quickly maneuver the BMW into a tight space along the curb. Hand-in-hand, they walked down the empty sidewalk to the revolving door of her building.

Iris's mother had insisted on getting her daily maid service because of her messiness. Now, Iris silently thanked her for the service she'd ridiculed earlier. As she and Jonathan approached her apartment at the end of the hallway, she rummaged in her purse for the keys.

Jonathan had been in the lobby of the expensive building before, but never in one of the apartments upstairs. Now, as Iris opened the door, she heard him whisper, "Damn."

He walked past her, his shoes echoing on the hardwood floor of the hallway, to the living room, admiring the view of downtown Baltimore and the lights glinting off the water of the Inner Harbor. Iris quietly dropped her purse and keys on the hallway table and tipped into her bedroom to turn on the CD player.

"This is the *shit*," Jonathan whispered to himself, gazing out of the curtain-less windows. Jazz rhythms of the Baltimore band, Fertile Ground, came through speakers he couldn't see, and he turned to look around the room. The spacious area was furnished with stylish cherry wood futon pieces. The futon cushions were encased in soft, cream-colored, zippered covers with mudcloth throw pillows in various sizes spread throughout. Tall trees and healthy plants were everywhere — on the floor, hanging from hooks on the wall, and in front of the ceiling-high windows. African, Caribbean, and Spanish artwork covered the wall separating the living room from the kitchen.

Jonathan noticed framed pictures of various sizes on the shelves of the entertainment center. Moving closer to get a better look at one with Iris and an older woman, he noticed the resemblance between them and guessed the woman to be her mother. He shifted his gaze to another photo and saw the woman standing next to a tanned white man. As he continued scanning the images, it became apparent that the man was Iris's father. Jonathan noticed the similarities between them and another, younger man who he assumed must be her brother. Like her mother, she had high cheekbones and a heart-shaped face, but the single dimple and large, dark eyes were definitely taken from the man in the pictures.

Iris suddenly appeared next to him and Jonathan asked, "Is this your family?" pointing to a shot of all four of them around a sculpture in a crowded square.

Iris smiled widely, touching each image and said, "Yes. That's my mom, Papa, and my brother, Carlos. We were visiting family in Spain." She gazed lovingly at the images as Jonathan's eyes traveled from her face down the length of her body. She was wearing a tiny, white, cotton tank top, barely disguising her nipples, and matching boy shorts that rode high on her behind.

Hearing the slight accent on her pronunciation of Papa and Carlos, Jonathan commented, "I didn't know you were Spanish."

"There's a lot about me you don't know," Iris said coyly, cutting her eyes at him and moving closer.

"For instance, you didn't know I would do this," she said, slowly gyrating against him in rhythm to the music softly permeating the room. "Or this," she added, softer this time, as she gently kissed his lips.

The clinging cotton shorts had ridden up far enough to reveal a great deal of her assets, and Jonathan forgot about the family pictures as he reached around her and gently cupped her round ass. Pulling her closer, he let his erection push between her thighs, and Iris stepped back, smiling, to take his hand. Turning, she led him through the unlit hallway to her bedroom, leaving the rhythms of Fertile Ground pulsing in the darkness.

Chapter Eighteen

ZUMA PRETENDED TO ENJOY herself as she kneeled between Bob O'Brien's knees and took his hardened cock into her mouth. He moaned, gripping her hair with both hands to guide her head back and forth. He glanced down to see her full lips locked around his blue-veined erection and, with a shudder, pulled out to watch cum spill on her breasts.

"Oh," he mumbled as he fell back on the bed, breathing heavily.

Zuma rose slowly, using the edge of the bed for support, and walked quietly to the bathroom. As the water ran in the shower, she looked at herself in the small mirror. *What am I doing?* She moved back from her image and stepped over the edge of the narrow tub into the warm stream of water from the shower head.

Zuma watched the Shearing vice president's semen run off her breasts in a stream and felt a familiar rush of power course through her body as she answered her own question.

I know exactly what I'm doing.

Chapter Nineteen

ZUMA WOKE TO FIND A HAND gripping her left breast. Bob stirred next to her and moved closer to her warmth. His naked, pale body suddenly made Zuma nauseous. Lying as still as possible, she tried to borrow a few more moments of quiet before he awoke.

She could smell his odor. He hadn't showered from the day before. His shriveled manhood lay on the two tight little balls of his testicles, and Zuma tried to forget that it had been in her mouth the night before. As though feeling her gaze, Bob inched closer and ground his genitals into her slender thigh.

"Hm, babe," he murmured in his sleep. He gripped her breast harder. Zuma assumed he was having a sexual dream, because she felt the beginning of a poke in her thigh.

She pulled out of his grasp and crawled over him and out of the bed to retrieve her robe. Stepping into high-heeled slippers, she tiptoed down the stairs into the kitchen and began heating water for tea.

As a tea bag steeped in the warm mug, she opened the French doors and stood on the terrace, gazing longingly out to the ocean. *If only I was here with one of the men I actually like to sleep with*, she thought.

Hearing noises inside the cottage, Zuma instantly tensed. She listened to Bob shuffle around in the kitchen before stepping outside.

"Morning, babe. No coffee?"

Without turning around, Zuma responded shortly, "Nope."

She heard him scratch himself and shuffle back into the house. A few minutes later, he appeared next to her, naked and holding a cup of tea. Sipping the tea, he made a nasty face before putting the mug on the glass patio table and glancing at the water.

"Feel like a swim?"

She wanted to tell him she was black and didn't swim in cold Massachusetts water, but instead she smiled up at him and said, "Sure, why not. I'll go get my suit."

"Suit? For what?" he retorted, turning to look at her. He licked his lips as he looked her up and down in the sheer white robe and matching heels. Zuma saw his limpness coming to attention. "Take that off," he commanded.

This option was definitely better than swimming nude in the freezing ocean. So, she smiled and began toying with the belt of the robe. Letting it dangle loosely, she pulled the front apart just enough to show the smooth caramel skin she'd had waxed completely bare. "Is this what you want?" she asked him.

"Hm," he murmured, watching her finger herself with one hand and play with her exposed breast with the other. She did a little striptease for him, squatting to the ground and moving her knees slowly together and apart as she continued to stroke herself. Turning around and bending over, she moved the robe so he could get a clear view of her swollen lips from behind. Hearing his groans, she whirled around and lifted her breasts to lick her own nipples while propping one high-heeled foot on the patio chair and winding her hips in a circular motion.

"Come 'ere," Bob said throatily as he masturbated roughly.

Walking seductively to him, Zuma offered him her breast. He lapped at it, trailing saliva around her nipple. With a sudden violent shake, he spewed cum on the front of her robe and down her leg onto one of the slippers.

Oh no he didn't, Zuma thought to herself. *He will be getting the dry-cleaning bill for this shit. And right now, he's about to lick this...*

Chapter Twenty

I T WAS STILL DARK when Jonathan reluctantly climbed out of the rumpled bed and found his clothes. Iris lay under the sheet watching him dress. Her wild hair framed her face on the pillow, and Jonathan stopped dressing to crawl back on the bed and caress her face with his hands.

"You. Are. Gorgeous." He stopped to kiss her after each word. Winding his fingers in her curls, he pulled her close.

Iris gently pushed him back with a smile. "If you keep doing that, you'll never get out of here."

"I don't have to leave," he said, pretending to unbutton his shirt.

Laughing, Iris responded, "You know I have to pack to go home. And I can't do that with you here."

"Damn right," he said, scooting off the bed. "If I stayed here, I'd keep you right where you are, looking just like that." He forced himself to turn away from her to search for items of his clothing that were trailed throughout the apartment.

Once he had dressed, Iris pulled on an oversized T-shirt and walked him to the door. Looking at her in the wrinkled shirt, Jonathan wanted to undress her and turn back the hands of the clock. Pulling her close, he reached under the shirt and massaged the soft mounds of her ass.

He leaned back on the door and propped her against his growing excitement. They kissed as he slowly grinded between her legs. When he lifted one of her legs and began running his hands along her inner thigh, she pushed back.

"Jonathan, you better go," she said with a giggle.

"Unh, baby, please..." he groaned, pulling her to him again.

Reluctantly, she moved away, pulling her shirt down to cover her behind.

"Go! I'll call you when I get home."

"Okay. But, don't have too much fun and forget to come back," he said with a lazy smile.

Kissing her once more, he finally opened the door and slipped out. Iris leaned against the door and hugged herself after he had gone. His scent was still on her face and body, and she breathed in deeply to smell him. Realizing the time, she forced herself to move to the bedroom to get cleaned up.

* * *

An hour later, she was stuffing clothes into a duffle bag when the buzzer sounded. Running from her bedroom, she slid across the hardwood floor and pressed the intercom button.

"Yes?"

A voice came through the wall speaker. "There's a Mr. Rey to see you, Ms. Pena."

"You can send him up. Thanks," she said.

Iris rushed back to her room to make sure she had everything. Rey hated to wait. He usually had a schedule and was always ready to go. While grabbing her toothbrush and toothpaste from the vanity counter, she noticed her face in the mirror. "Lookin' good, girl," she said out loud to her reflection. Smiling in the mirror, she dropped the last two items into her toiletry bag just as Rey knocked on the door.

After hugging her close, he looked around and said, "Yo, your parents hooked you up on this one, kid." Walking further into the apartment, he nodded approvingly at the view.

"Yeah. Mom found it," Iris said distractedly, mentally reviewing her packing list.

After completing his own tour, Rey came back to her in the vestibule. "Okay, so you ready or what?" he asked, looking down at her two small duffle bags. "That's all you takin'?" He raised one eyebrow and held out his arms in the direction of the two bags.

"What? You think I need more?" Iris asked seriously. "We're going home, right? What do I need a lot of clothes for?"

"Hey, it's your business," Rey said, picking up the handles of the bags. Looking at her, he paused and frowned. "You look different," he said, squinting his eyes at her.

Self-consciously, Iris touched her face and hair. "I haven't done anything different."

Still contemplating her through slitted eyes, Rey said, "I don't know what it is, something just seems different. But you look good." Dismissing the thought, he headed toward the door. "Come on. We better get on the road if we're gonna get home before dark with the holiday traffic."

Iris slept as Rey drove north on the New Jersey Turnpike. Traffic was heavy, and it took them almost five hours to get to New York. She roused herself as the truck slowed at the tollbooth for the George Washington Bridge.

"It's about time, sleepy head," Rey said, turning to glance at her. "Damn. Wipe some of that drool off your face."

Iris reached up to touch the wet trail on her chin. Only slightly embarrassed, she took a tissue from her purse and wiped the spot dry. Arching her back to stretch, she looked around to discern their location. The lines were snaking slowly through the tollbooth as Rey maneuvered the truck into the far left lane for pass holders.

"What did you get into last night that has you so tired?" Rey asked suspiciously as they passed the stand-still traffic and merged onto the bridge.

Iris tried to hold back a smile and shook her head. "Nothing, just hanging out with some friends."

Rey knew she was being secretive, but instead of grilling her, he focused on the traffic and continued heading north to New Rochelle.

Iris sang along with an old club anthem on WBLS as Rey slowed at exit 16 and took the ramp onto North Avenue. It was almost five o'clock when they pulled up in the driveway of her childhood home. There were already several cars parked in the back of the large house.

"Aw shit. Here come Thing One and Thing Two," Rey mumbled, referring to her nephews running loudly toward them from the back of the house.

Stopping in his tracks, the older boy shouted, "Tia Iris esta aqui!" alerting the occupants of the house that Iris was there. Iris stooped to grab the smaller child in her arms and playfully chewed at his neck. He giggled and squirmed away to bat at Rey's legs like a boxer.

"Boy, you don't want none of this!" Rey said, scooping the child in the air and flipping him upside down over his shoulder.

Iris bent to receive the other child, opening her arms and smiling. "Hey, honey!" she exclaimed as the older boy ran into her embrace almost knocking her backward on the pavement. He held her tightly around the neck as she kissed the top of his curly head.

Finally making it in the house, Iris and Rey distributed hugs, kisses, and handshakes as they went from Iris's mother and father, to her brother and sister-in-law, and greeted cousins, uncles, and aunts who'd stopped by for the holiday.

"I know you better make a pit stop in that restroom!" Iris's mother chastised Rey as she caught him opening a pot on the stove and sniffing the contents.

"No problem, Mom, 'cause I plan to get in that pot!" he responded, trooping out of the kitchen.

Iris's mother shook her head and smiled, bringing Iris to the table and pulling out a chair for her to join the other women. They fell into the comfortable conversation and gay laughter of any close family. Periodically, a child ran through the kitchen and out the back door. One mother or another would randomly admonish them for running, yelling, or throwing a ball in the house, and English and Spanish were casually interchanged in their conversations.

Listening to her aunt dramatically tell a story, Iris looked at the women gathered around the table. Her mother and aunt were both chocolate-hued with chiseled features and salt-and- pepper hair. Next, her gaze stopped on Sonja, her brother's wife. The Dominican woman looked African American, but her strong Spanish accent told the truth. Two of Iris's first cousins were there as well. The daughters of her father's brother looked Caucasian. Her family was as unique and colorful as could be. And as tight as a knot.

With much fuss, Rey returned to the kitchen with Carlos and one of Iris's male cousins close behind. Holding up their hands to show they'd been washed, they went straight to the pots simmering on the stove.

"Unh unh, wait a minute," Iris's aunt said. "I'm not gonna have ya'll breathing over the food. Back up and let me dish this stuff up. Come on ladies, let's feed the troops."

As Iris stood to help, she smiled with the knowledge that she was home.

Chapter Twenty-One

BOB PUMPED UP AND DOWN between Zuma's legs, making the springs in the bed creak and Zuma's breasts wobble on the sides of her chest. With her legs wrapped around his midsection, she routinely moaned, pretending to show her enthusiasm. Waiting for him to finish, her mind wandered to the dark corners of her memory.

A moan became stuck in her throat as a long-forgotten memory flashed behind her lids. Her eyes flew open to search the face of the man on top of her. She muffled a nervous giggle when she saw Bob's red, sweating face hovering above her and closed her eyes again.

A moment later, Zuma heard, "Do you like this Zumatha?"

Again, her eyes stretched wide. She swore she'd heard the voice of her college accounting teacher addressing her by a name she hadn't been called in over fifteen years. But it was Bob grunting his pleasure over her — not Professor Simons.

Zuma manipulated her body to continue pleasing the vice president, but her thoughts were over a decade away. Reluctantly, her mind went to a tiny dirty motel room on the outskirts of her small hometown in North Carolina.

* * *

Christopher Simons, the handsome accounting teacher at the local community college, was fondling Zuma's breasts while she sat on his lap with her back resting on his chest. Sitting on the edge of a sagging gray mattress, he kissed her neck and touched her hair, whispering promises to her in the low, sexy voice that thrilled the girls in his class.

"Zumatha, you're so beautiful. When you finish school, I want you to be with me all the time," he said, tucking his strong hand into the front of her pink Hanes underwear. He stroked her with a touch so gentle it caused tremors to flood her nubile body.

Zuma leaned back on the older man's bare chest. "Really?" she whispered naively, as she closed her eyes and spread her legs further apart to accept the pleasure he offered.

Gently, he lifted her to her feet and removed his pants. Zuma's eyes became round as she stared at the tent his hardness made in the white cotton BVD briefs.

"Look at what you do to me, Zumatha. I couldn't stay away from you if I wanted to."

Hooking his thumbs in the elastic waist of her underwear, he pulled them down to her ankles and kneeled on the worn carpet floor, waiting for her to step out. He slowly and gently ran his fingers up her legs and cupped her petite buttocks in his large hands, bringing her body close enough to his face to take one hard nipple between his teeth. Closing his lips around the tip of her breast, he teased the nipple with his tongue while his hands explored the tender flesh of her inner thigh and higher. Feeling the warm wetness between her thighs, he stood and removed his own underwear before guiding her slowly to the bed.

* * *

The memory of Professor Simons thrusting between her legs meshed with the reality of the red-faced man pumping up and down on her now. A single tear escaped her closed eyes and ran slowly toward her ear. She'd fucked for a passing grade at eighteen, and now she was fucking for job security at thirty-three.

Suddenly, Bob collapsed heavily onto her chest, and the tear rolled

102

under her ear and into the hair at the nape of her neck. Gently pushing him to the side, she remembered being in this exact position with him about a year ago. Just before she was promoted to marketing director.

Zuma wiped the tear away and forced the old memories haunting her mind to disappear as she wrapped her arms around Bob and whispered something sexy in his ear. She wasn't eighteen anymore. She was in control of *this* game of sex and power. And she was determined to win.

Chapter Twenty-Two

AFTER HEARTILY EATING every crumb on his plate, Rey cornered Iris. "You ready? Mama is probably wondering where the hell we are."

Iris waved to the women in the kitchen and joined Rey in the driveway. "Let's go," she said, jogging to the black SUV.

They climbed into the truck, and Rey backed slowly down the driveway. Less than five minutes later, they were parked in front of his family's large house.

There were so many cars, trucks, and vans in the driveway, they were forced to find a space on the street. Iris could hear Al Green's soulful voice streaming out of the open windows as they trekked up the long sidewalk to the front door.

Rey twisted the knob and walked into the entry hall. People were everywhere — dancing in the family room, talking in the hallway, standing around the entrance to the kitchen.

A group of men were gathered around a table where two of Rey's older brothers and some cousins were playing dominoes. Rey playfully slapped one of his brothers on the back of the head. Everyone turned around and added to the noise level by greeting him loudly and slapping the palm of his hand.

Seeing Iris, his brothers stood and enveloped her in tight hugs. Coming to Rey's house was like coming home all over again. She teased his younger cousins, then left the room to join the women in the kitchen.

"Iris!" exclaimed his mother when she looked up to see the tall beauty standing in the crowded doorway. Iris distributed more hugs and kisses, making her way through the room of aunts, cousins, and friends she'd known since she was a little girl. "Where's my baby boy?" Rey's mother demanded, not waiting for an answer.

"Raymond! Raymond!" she shouted over the noise of the house as she squeezed through the people.

"Mama!" Rey said when he saw the top of his petite mother's head, barely visible in the mass of people gathered in the hallway. He hugged her tightly, then picked her up and spun her around.

"Boy! Put me down before I whip you. You may be grown, but I can still whip that ass." Laughter erupted in the room as Rey, smiling, lowered his mother to the floor.

"Where's Pop?"

"You know where he is," she responded before hitting his brother on the neck for putting a beer bottle on the floor. "Boy, pick that up, and put it on a coaster before someone knocks it over and spills that stuff."

Shaking his head at how much nothing had changed, Rey wove through the crowd to exit through the back door. A group of older men randomly stood and sat, smoking cigarettes and pipes as they listened to one unravel a story.

Rey had heard the story a hundred times and knew it was based on truth, but by the time his uncle finished telling it, some things would be added to increase the humor and excitement of the tale. As his uncle came to the end of the story, the men exploded in laughter and coughing – some remembering the event and others only knowing the embellished version.

"Raymond! When'd you get in, son?" his father said, noticing him in the shadows. Rey stepped forward to hug him and then went through the group of men giving more handshakes and back slaps.

"Where's my Iris?" Pop asked.

"Inside with Mama. She'll be out here in a minute."

As if hearing her name, Iris opened the door and walked toward the group of men.

"Hi, Pop!" she exclaimed, hugging the tall, wiry man who was like a second father. She waved to the group as a whole and gave everyone a general greeting. The men continued their storytelling as Rey and Iris walked back toward the house.

"I'm getting sleepy, Rey."

"Sleepy? You slept the whole way here!" he laughed. "Naw, you ain't going home yet."

With the whiny voice she knew irritated him, Iris said, "Oh, Rey, please. I'm just so tired. Come on. It'll only take five minutes to drive me back home."

"Whine if you want, but I'm not leaving." He pulled her hand to lead her up the back steps and into the house.

It was eleven o'clock by the time Rey finished playing dominoes and Iris had played several rounds of Spades.

"Come on, girl. I better take you home before you fall asleep and I can't get you out of here."

"It won't be the first time," Iris drawled, half asleep.

"Yeah, yeah. Come on, we're out."

Back at her house, Iris walked into the kitchen and looked at the women still gathered around the table, drinking coffee and talking quietly. Some of them held sleeping children in their arms, subconsciously rocking them. She waved silently as she passed through and went up the wide staircase to her bedroom.

Stepping out of her sneakers and shorts, she collapsed onto the bed without changing her top, washing her face, or brushing her teeth. It would all have to wait until tomorrow.

Chapter Twenty-Three

Sunday, May 27

THE NEXT MORNING, IRIS helped her mother, aunt, and Sonja in the kitchen as they prepared breakfast.

"What you have planned today?" Sonja asked her, mixing eggs in a bowl.

Shrugging her shoulders, Iris replied, "Nothing. Why?"

"Wanna go shopping with me?"

"Sure. Wait, are my nephews coming, too?"

Laughing, Sonja shook her head. "This is just for the ladies, chica."

After breakfast, Iris and Sonja cleared the dishes. Quickly showering and changing, Iris met Sonja by her parent's car in the back. They drove into Manhattan and traveled south toward the trendy shopping in Greenwich Village and Soho. After parking, they walked leisurely along the street of storefronts and restaurants. Iris stopped to admire a pair of Skechers sneakers in a store window. Shaking her head, Sonja dragged her from the window to the Steve Madden store a few doors down and stopped in front of a table with trendier heels and funky sandals.

"Girl, you have great legs, and you need to start showing them off."
Beckoning to the sales clerk, she held up three pairs of shoes for Iris's
size.

Iris had an immediate flashback to the shoe store in Miami as she
sat next to Sonja and waited for the attendant to return. Thirty minutes
later, they walked out with a bag of shoe boxes.

Next, they stopped in an odd-looking clothing store Iris would
never have ventured into alone. She looked skeptically at the teensy
tiny shirts with weird designs and funny-angled miniskirts with a look
of concern. Immediately locating a chair by the fitting room, she sat,
crossing her legs, to wait for Sonja.

As soon as Sonja saw her, she swore in Spanish and made a beeline
toward her. "Oh no, honey. We're here for you! Come on you sexy,
young thing," Sonja said, pulling her towards the racks of skirts.

After trying on what seemed like hundreds of outfits, Iris dropped
three skirts, two pairs of jeans, and four tops on the sales counter with
a hesitant glance at her sister-in-law. Sonja nodded her approval, and
Iris paid for the purchases. Taking a break, the two women sat at an
outdoor café sipping cool drinks and sharing an appetizer while they
people-watched. Sonja's cell phone rang, and she picked it up, pressing
buttons in an attempt to answer it.

"Damn, I wish your company would make a simple phone for
people who just want to make a call and answer the damn thing. Shit,"
Sonja muttered, continuing to press buttons and repeatedly saying
"hello" into the mouthpiece.

Finally, still swearing to herself, she connected with the person on
the other end and mostly listened, not saying much. Iris knew Sonja
was up to something by the way she kept averting her eyes. She ended
the call and suddenly stopped talking.

After a few moments of unnatural silence, Iris finally said,
"*What?*"

"Okay, chica. I'm just going to say it. It's your hair."

Iris reached up and touched her kinks. "What about my hair?" she asked cautiously.

"It's gorgeous, thick, and curly," started Sonja, "but it's time to give it a style, mi'ja."

"What do you mean a style? It has a style." Iris knew she sounded defensive, but she liked being natural. She wanted people to accept her for what she was, not try to change her to fit some outdated standard of beauty.

"No, honey," Sonja tried again. "I mean shape. Cut it into a shape. Right now, you just have a bush of curls wildly living on your head." Iris laughed at the description. "It hides the beauty of your face. If you had a good cut, it would accentuate your features and also showcase the natural beauty of your hair."

Iris contemplated. Maybe Sonja was right. She hadn't had a cut in months. "Okay, I'll do it," Iris said with a half-hearted smile.

"Good, because your appointment's in twenty minutes," Sonja said, quickly opening her wallet to pay the bill.

"*What?*" Iris spluttered. "You already had this planned?"

"Don't worry, mi'ja. Your mother and I knew you'd agree."

"*Mom?*" Iris realized she was speaking loudly when a few patrons turned to stare. She lowered her voice and squinted at Sonja. "I'm gonna get you two for this."

"That's okay, you can thank us later," Sonja said as she snatched the bags from the floor and grabbed Iris's hand, dragging her out of the patio's gate.

Chapter Twenty-Four

Sunday, May 27

EARLY SUNDAY EVENING, Rey pulled into the driveway of Iris's house. Two of his brothers and their wives were waiting in a car idling on the street.

Iris heard his voice through her open bedroom window when he stopped to speak to her father who was standing over a smoking grill in the back yard. Tentatively, she touched her bare neck where hair used to be. Looking again at her reflection in the dresser mirror, she ran her hand over the soft waves that the stylist had created with scissors, a blow dryer, and a very big brush. She had to admit, the cut was nice, and straightening her wild curls into soft waves made her face look completely different.

"Iris!" she heard Rey bellow up the stairs. "You ready?"

She heard his heavy steps on the hardwood stairs and felt ridiculous as panic gripped her. What would he say? What would he think about her hair, new clothes and high-heeled sandals?

"Iris, you in here?" Rey called as he rapped hard on the closed door, causing her to jump.

"Yes," she answered, looking at her image once more.

"What're you waiting for? Carlos and my brothers are already in their cars. Let's go, girl." She heard his steps disappear back down the steps and fade away.

They were headed to City Island for seafood and hanging out. It was a Memorial Day tradition that the children of the two families had started years ago. Rey's brothers used to bring their girlfriends, but now, like Carlos, they were married and brought their wives.

With a final shrug, Iris grabbed her purse off the bed, ran down the stairs, and slammed out the back door. Stopping to kiss her father, she jogged down the driveway to the passenger side of Rey's truck. Rey was on his cell phone and didn't even bother looking in Iris's direction. Sighing with relief when he didn't notice her, Iris fell back into the seat and began singing along with Mary J. who was crooning on the radio.

"Aight, peace," Rey said into the phone before pressing a button. As he dropped the phone into a compartment under the dash and reached for the handle to shift into reverse, he stopped mid-reach. He stared at Iris as she sang and rocked to the beat, unaware of his stupor.

"Yo! What's *up*?" he exclaimed, bringing a fist to his smiling mouth.

Iris immediately stopped singing and felt her face growing warm. She brought a hand to her hair and said, "What? You don't like it?"

"Like it? Shit. You look... I don't know..." For once, Rey was speechless as his eyes traveled slowly down from her hair to the polished toenails peeking out of new sandals. Iris couldn't think of the last time she'd seen him at a loss for words. Worse, she couldn't tell if he was going to jone on her or compliment her.

Suddenly, horns started blaring behind them, and they both remembered that two carloads of people were waiting on them to move.

"My bad!" Rey yelled out the window.

Iris shrunk into the seat and turned away from him to stare uncomfortably out the window. Sneaking peeks at her, he wheeled the truck through traffic and talked on his cell phone.

As usual, City Island was ridiculously crowded and parking was difficult. After fifteen minutes of searching, all three cars found spaces, and the occupants met to walk together.

"Iris! Ohmagod! I almost didn't recognize you!" One of Rey's sisters-in-law came up to her and brushed a hand over the wavy locks of her new hair.

"Girl, you are wearing that skirt! You better do it," said the other sister-in-law as she looked at Iris's sculpted long legs beneath the angular denim miniskirt. "Sonja, have you seen Iris?"

"Have I seen her?" said Sonja loudly. "I'm proudly responsible for this transformation." She ran her hand through the air along Iris's side, like she was a prize on the Price Is Right.

"Go head, now. I always knew you had it in you," said the first sister-in-law.

What are they talking about? They're acting like I was jacked up before. Damn, was I that bad? Iris was definitely self-conscious now. Ignoring the women who were still discussing her new look, she sidled up to Carlos, uncomfortably tugging on the short skirt.

"They are *trippin'*," she grumbled to her older brother as he scanned the menu nailed above an order window.

Carlos smiled down at her and shook his head. He'd never understand females. They wanted to be attractive and have people compliment them, but then they got angry when it happened. Crazy. All of them.

Sonja came over and asked excitedly, "Iris, what did Rey think?"

The look on Iris's face caused Sonja's excitement to immediately evaporate. "All righty then," she said in a little voice and moved away to join Carlos.

As Iris stood silently fuming and looking at the crowds of people gathering on the pier, Rey came up behind her. In his usual brusque manner, he addressed her.

113

"Iris, whaddya want to eat?" he asked, pointing his thumb over his shoulder to the order window.

Turning a mean face to him, she responded, "Nothing, I'm not hungry."

"Damn, what's that face for?" he asked with a scowl of his own.

Iris started to tell him. She was so used to confiding in him. But this time was different. Part of her anger stemmed from his confusing response to her makeover.

"Nothing. You wouldn't understand," she mumbled, turning her back to him.

Rey hesitated a few seconds, debating whether to speak or not. His better judgment told him to give her some space. Reluctantly, he turned from her and joined his brothers at the window.

After a few minutes alone, Iris sighed heavily and turned to find her group squeezing into a recently vacated spot at one of the tables. Self-consciously, she walked over and joined them. She picked a greasy fry from Rey's tray and stuffed it in her mouth as she sat. Her little personal drama had been dismissed or, more likely, missed altogether. Laughing and talking as they reached over one another for ketchup and salt, they watched the sun set.

Around eight o'clock, Carlos and Sonja begged off, offering the excuse of giving their parents a break from the boys. Everyone knew they didn't get much time alone in Miami with their family being in New York. The two would probably go to a secluded spot and make out like teenagers before heading back to their house.

A little while later, Rey's brothers and their wives left to join the dominoes and cards going on at his parents' house.

Alone, Iris stood next to Rey as he leaned over the rail, watching people ride bikes and walk along the trail. They were each deep in their own thoughts and stood comfortably together in silence.

After a few minutes, Rey turned his head to look up at Iris's profile. She looked down at him and smiled, making her dimple crease. "What?" she asked when he didn't speak.

Rey let the silence hang, debating whether to be honest. "I'm just thinking how pretty you are," he said simply. Too shocked to respond, Iris looked curiously into his face to see if he was joking or serious. Seeing her quizzical expression, he laughed, deep and rich.

"Girl, you are priceless. Why you lookin' at me like that?" he asked, still amused.

"I was just trying to figure out if you were being serious or not," she responded.

The smile faded from Rey's face as he straightened and stood facing her. The height of her sandals brought her eyes almost level with his. Reaching up, he brushed his hand over her hair and down to the back of her neck. Iris swore she could hear her heartbeat thumping in her chest as she felt a tingle in her toes from the gentle caress.

Rey looked into her dark eyes and cupped her face in his hand before softly saying, "I'm dead serious."

Iris felt like everything was moving in slow motion – her heartbeat, the people walking around them, time itself. Meeting Rey's gaze, she felt like she was drowning in the liquid brown of his eyes. She blinked to make sure he was real in front of her.

Rey hesitated again. His mind told him to stop. To let his hand drop and make a joke. But his body was on autopilot and, before she could speak, he leaned toward her and brushed his lips lightly against hers.

The instant heat that flooded her body was overwhelming, and she put her hand on the rail to steady herself. *What in the world just happened?* She was scared to move for fear she might fall.

Wanting desperately to step away from her, Rey stepped closer, moving his hand to the soft curls at the nape of her neck, and tilted her face to meet his kiss. Her lips were as soft and sensuous as he'd always imagined. With great effort, he pulled back and looked into her face. The shock he saw there caused him to burst out laughing again. And, just like that, the tension of the moment dissipated.

"You're a real trip, Iris Pena," he said, taking her hand and turning to leave. "Come on, it's getting late." Still holding her hand, Rey led her from the pier to the crowded street where the truck was parked.

Completely in shock, Iris couldn't think or act and simply followed behind him with her hand warmly encased in his. Holding hands with him like this felt unnatural, and Iris had a sudden flashback to walking like this two days ago. Two days ago with Jonathan. Funny, she hadn't thought about Jonathan since they'd gotten home. Suddenly feeling inappropriate, she gently released Rey's hand and continued walking in step next to him.

Playing cool, Rey used the newly freed hand to pull his hair back from this face. When they got to the truck, he went to her side first and unlocked the door. Holding the door handle with one hand, he hesitated, looking at her. Mentally fighting himself, he couldn't stop the desire to touch her.

Pressing her lightly against the side of the truck with his body, he brought his muscular arms around her waist and caressed the soft, warm skin of her bare back. Iris felt breathless as his coarse hair brushed her face and shoulders. He tenderly kissed the curve of her neck. His lips were soft and moist, and she could smell the rosemary, sage, and lavender in his locs.

Unaware that he was speaking aloud, Rey whispered hoarsely by her ear, "I can't help it. I can't stop."

She sighed in a combination of confused disbelief and physical desire as he slowly moved his hands down her back to rest softly on the high roundness of her backside. She lifted one of the arms that had been hanging weakly at her side and timidly laid her hand on his bare shoulder. Slowly, she let her fingers feel and explore the muscles she'd only recently discovered with her eyes and inhaled his warm scent.

She was liquid heat melting in his embrace. Mentally and physically unable to move any part of her body, she remained fused to his as he unhurriedly moved his lips from her neck to her face.

Tenderly, he kissed her cheek where he knew the dimple would be if she were smiling. With half-closed eyes, he proceeded to place feather-light kisses on her chin, nose, and both closed eyes. Eventually, he came to her mouth, gently parting her lips with his tongue. He knew there was no turning back when she responded by taking his bottom lip lightly between her teeth, deepening the kiss. Iris had succumbed to the passion within her and wanted him as much as he wanted her.

But suddenly, the image of Martina, the woman with the thick accent in Miami, came into Iris's mind. The rational thoughts that had fled earlier instantly returned, reminding Iris that she couldn't compete with the exotic beauties in Rey's harem. *And Jonathan. What about Jonathan?*

Slowly, reluctantly, she pulled back from the kiss and his warm embrace. When he looked into her clouded eyes, she could see the questions in his clear ones. Unable to speak, Iris turned within his embrace and tugged on the door handle. He stepped back, allowing her to climb up and, longingly, watched her thick brown legs move into the truck. He firmly closed the door. Taking time to cool off, he walked slowly around the truck, readjusting his boxers and the front of his jeans.

I shouldn't have done that, he thought to himself. *Why'd I do that shit?*

Unable to face her, he put the key in the ignition and revved the truck to life. He drove them quietly to her house as he bit his lip and tasted her memory.

Chapter Twenty-Five

Monday, May 28

REACHING INTO HER PURSE, Zuma pulled out three loose one-dollar bills and handed them to the porter at the curbside check-in. Taking the boarding pass and sticking it in the side pocket of her carry-on, she turned and walked leisurely back to the white Mercedes idling at the curb. Bob stepped out and wrapped his arms around her, looking down at her face.

"When can we do this again?" he asked huskily, staring into her hazel eyes.

"As long as you make sure I'm around for awhile, I'm sure we can work something out," Zuma said coyly, raising one eyebrow to make sure he got her meaning.

"If it means having you, I'll do whatever you need." He bent and thrust his tongue in her mouth. After a few seconds, she gently pushed him back by the shoulders.

"I better go. I don't want to miss my flight," she said softly, reaching up to wipe lipstick from around his mouth.

"See you later, Ms. Harris," he said, moving to the driver's side of the car. Zuma smiled and winked one eye in response as she sashayed up the curb and through the sliding glass doors. Daintily wiping the edges of her mouth with her fingers, she moved to the nearest restroom. After reapplying her lipstick and assuring a look of perfection, she made her way to the security check line.

Laying her head back on the plush first-class seat, she closed her eyes. Visions from the weekend flashed through her mind. She tried to force them away and concentrate on the week ahead, but something had changed. Professor Christopher Simons.

The long-forgotten memory of the handsome, young accounting teacher had changed something in her. Unable to push the thoughts of the past away, she painfully recalled her parents' anguish and embarrassment when they finally found out about the affair.

Zuma squirmed in her seat, trying to find a comfortable position as the recollection continued to flood her brain. There was no position in the first-class seat that would let her hide from the shame.

"Are you okay?"

Zuma jerked as her eyes flipped open. She'd forgotten where she was. Looking around, she saw clouds and blue sky through the windows. How long had she been asleep?

"Do you need anything? Are you okay?" Zuma turned, shaking, to the voice next to her. Had she made noises or been crying? Worse, had she been talking in her sleep?

"Um, yes. I, um, I guess I just fell asleep and had a bad dream. My apologies if I disturbed you," she stammered, attempting to gather her wits. Automatically reaching up to fix her hair, she readjusted herself to sit upright in the wide seat.

"Would you like something to drink?" the man next to her asked with concern as he pushed the yellow button for the attendant.

"Thank you, yes."

Zuma scrambled to find her compact in her purse and check her face. It wasn't as bad as she imagined. With a thankful sigh, she sank back and attempted to relax. When the attendant arrived with her drink, the gentleman next to her took it and placed a napkin on her tray before setting the drink down.

"Thank you," she said sincerely with a smile.

For the first time, she took notice of the older black man sitting next to her. He wasn't very handsome, just an average, normal-looking older man. His face was clean-shaven and, when he smiled, she noticed a little gap between his small teeth. His hair was cut evenly into a low afro, and little patches of gray were obvious at both temples.

"Not a problem," he replied kindly. They exchanged a few more pleasantries as she sipped her drink.

Glancing surreptitiously at his hands, she saw his nails were clean and cut low. He wore a simple gold band on his ring finger. Though he didn't look anything like her father, his gentle ways reminded her of him. How long had it been since she'd seen her father?

His presence somehow comforted her, and she found herself smiling and even laughing throughout their conversation.

As the plane landed and taxied to the gate, he turned to her with a business card in his extended hand.

"It was a pleasure meeting you. If you ever need anyone to talk to, give me a ring."

Zuma looked at the card. Elijah Pharrell, LCSW. The tag line at the bottom read, "Bringing Families Together One Case At A Time." It wasn't clear to Zuma what Mr. Pharrell did, but she passed him one of her cards anyway. She usually reserved her business cards for professional connections or sexy men, but something about Elijah Pharrell was different. Something.

Chapter Twenty-Six

TRYING TO STUFF THE NEW clothes into her small bags, Iris realized everything wasn't going to fit. Giving up, she fell back on the pillows stacked along the headboard and tried to figure out what had happened last night.

Confusion and embarrassment had prohibited her from looking at Rey on the ride home, and when he'd stopped in her driveway, she'd quickly slipped out of the truck with a simple, "See you tomorrow."

Why had he kissed her? Why the hell did she kiss him back? That was the bigger issue. The same two questions had tumbled over themselves for the last three hours, interrupting her ability to think.

That morning, she'd gone through the motions of showering, dressing, eating` and, now, attempting to pack. She hadn't paid attention to anything she'd done. Thankfully, she was taking the train back to Baltimore since Rey was staying home and working out of his New York office for a couple of weeks.

Rolling off the bed, Iris crawled around on the floor of her closet until she found a dust-covered duffle bag from high school. Shaking off dust balls, she stuffed the clothes and shoes that wouldn't fit in the other two bags into the duffle and, making two trips, dragged them downstairs to the back porch.

With nothing else to do, she stood looking at the telephone hanging on the wall. She knew she'd eventually have to call him. Taking a deep breath, she picked up the receiver and dialed the number by memory. The phone rang about five times before someone finally picked up at his house.

"Hey Iris. He's already left for your house, honey," Rey's mother said.

Taking the steps two at a time, she ran upstairs to Carlos and Sonja's room, knocking on the closed door.

"Come in," came a muffled voice. Iris entered to find clothes and shoes of all sizes strewn in piles around the room. "What's up, chica?" Sonja asked cheerily. She was placing a pile of small shirts and shorts into a blue plastic suitcase with a little man in a hard hat and the words "Bob The Builder" sewn on the top flap.

"Not much. I'm getting ready to pull out and wanted to come up and thank you."

"For what?" Sonja asked, continuing to move through the maze of clothing.

Iris looked down at her polished toenails and began tracing an invisible design on the hardwood floor. "You were right. About everything. I really, really love my new hairstyle and the clothes. I would never have had the courage to even try on what you picked out for me. I feel good, and I think I look good. So, thank you."

"Anything for my favorite sister-in-law," Sonja said, coming over to hug Iris.

"I'm your *only* sister-in-law, fool," Iris said, slapping her on the arm as they pulled apart.

Sonja giggled and said, "Have a safe trip home, and I'll call you when we get to Miami."

"Okay. I hope the boys will cooperate on the flight."

Sonja laughed and said, "Honey, we're taking the latest flight offered to make sure those boys sleep all the way home."

"*Iris*," they heard her father bellow up the stairs. "Rey's here!"

"I better go. Tell my brother I'll talk to him tonight."

"Okay, girl. Love you," Sonja said, hugging her once more.

"Love you, too."

Iris ran down the steps and collided with Rey coming out of the kitchen. He caught her as she stumbled backward.

"Oh, sorry," Iris mumbled.

"Damn, what race you tryin' to win?" Rey asked, half smiling at her.

"I know how much you hate to wait, so I was trying to hurry."

"Since when?" he asked, both brows raised in surprise.

"Whatever. I'm ready," Iris said, diverting her eyes and brushing past him to keep from drowning in his stare.

"Mom! Papa! I'm leaving!" Iris shouted, pulling her purse from the back of a kitchen chair.

"Okay, honey. Have a safe trip, and call me as soon as you get there," her mother said, coming into the room and hugging her close.

"Yes, Mom."

Her father came in and, with similar sentiments and another tight hug, stood with his wife waving from the kitchen doorway.

Rey backed the truck slowly down the driveway and drove silently to the Amtrak station a few miles away. Iris sat uncomfortably looking out the side window. As Rey pulled into a parking space and turned off the engine, they both started to talk at once. Laughing, they stopped, then started speaking simultaneously again.

"You go first," Iris said, grinning at him.

Rey took a breath before starting again. "Listen. I was out of line last night. I didn't intend to let things happen the way they did, and I apologize."

Iris sat quietly trying to gather her thoughts before speaking. "I didn't do a lot to stop you, so I guess I was out of line too. But I have to ask you a question, or I'll go crazy trying to figure it out." She paused before simply asking, "Why?"

Rey stared into her eyes. He knew he could never tell her that he'd been in love with her since elementary school. That he went to FAMU because he couldn't stand being away from her. That it killed a part of him every time she dated someone new. Or could he?

"Iris, I..." He couldn't say it. He couldn't jeopardize the relationship they'd cultivated for almost twenty years. When they disagreed or fought as friends, they always made up. Would it be the same as lovers? Finally, he blurted it out. "I love you, Iris."

"I love you, too, Rey, but that doesn't explain why."

"No, you don't get it," he said, closing his eyes in exasperation. "I'm *in love* with you."

Iris sat silently for a split second, then burst into laughter. She laughed so hard, the muscles in her stomach started to cramp, and tears leaked from the corners of her eyes.

Rey's face registered shock, then anger. "I didn't say it as a joke," he said stonily.

Fighting to regain her composure, Iris held her stomach and shook her head, wiping tears from her cheeks. "I'm sorry. I'm really sorry. You don't understand."

"Then why don't you make me understand," he said, still speaking with a quiet stiffness.

Iris met his hard gaze. "You travel around the world, partying with the most exotic women I've ever seen. Every gorgeous woman we see knows you, and I mean *knows* you. You've never even *looked* at me. And now, after I cut my hair and wear a short skirt, you tell me you're in love with me."

Iris paused and held out her hands as if to say, *Don't you get it?* When

124

he didn't respond, she said, "That's crazy!" as though it were obvious. "Instead of you being mad at me, I should be angry at *you*."

Incredulous, he stared at her. "*At me?* Why?"

Iris placed one hand on his before answering. "For playing me. I know you love me. I love you too. But you're not in love with me."

Snatching his hand from under hers, he said, "Don't tell me what I am or aren't, Iris. You don't know everything you think you do."

He turned from her, opened the door and stepped down, slamming the door hard behind him. Iris was left looking at his empty seat. With a heavy sigh, she opened the door and got out. Rey was already walking away with her bags trailing behind him and the duffle thrown over his shoulder.

By the time she reached him standing by the track, he had stacked her bags against one another on the ground and was turning to leave.

Passing her, he said, "You don't know *shit* about me, Iris. Have a safe trip." He turned to walk away, but was stopped by a strong hand gripping his bicep.

"Hold up!" Iris knew she'd raised her voice and was drawing attention, but this negro had pissed her off.

"You have some nerve, Rey," she retorted angrily, frowning up into his face. "How dare you try to read me. I've known you for eighteen years and you have never, *never* even looked twice at me. Out of the fucking blue, you kiss me and expect me to understand when you tell me you're in love with me. Should I know through osmosis how you feel about me? And what am I supposed to think when women like *Martina* seem to know you intimately? You're right, I obviously *don't* know you. But know this, I don't feel you like that, Rey."

"Oh yeah? It seemed like you were *feeling* me last night." He stood facing her anger with his own. Neither of them spoke nor moved.

Incensed by his comment and the truth behind it, Iris couldn't respond. She'd played herself last night, and he'd called her on it.

Turning around, she picked up her shoulder bag and propped her weight on one leg to wait for the train. She couldn't, wouldn't, let him see the embarrassment on her face.

Rey stood rooted behind her, wishing he could swallow the words he'd just spoken. Iris had never turned her back on him like this. Her anger was better than the finality of this silence. Throwing up his hands, he walked back to the truck and climbed in. Half expecting her to turn around, he sat in the truck staring at her back.

As the train pulled onto the track, the wind blew her hair carelessly on its breeze. Iris stooped to grip the handles of the bags while Rey held his breath, waiting, willing her to turn around.

Look at me. Look at me. Turn around and look at me.

Without a backward glance, Iris loaded her bags into the crowded compartment at the front of the car and moved back to an empty window seat. Hunched over the steering wheel, Rey watched her profile as the train pulled off with a horn blow. He continued staring at the empty track long after the train was gone from view.

Chapter Twenty-Seven

A CONGLOMERATION OF EMOTIONS rolled over one another in Iris's mind, lulling her into a fitful sleep Monday night. When she awoke on Tuesday morning and dragged herself into the bathroom, the heavy bags and dark rings under her eyes were not surprising.

Leaning on the edge of the vanity, she hung her head between hunched shoulders. Again, a brief flush of embarrassment was quickly replaced with anger, which was immediately squashed by heavy sadness. Like the day before, question after question scrolled through her brain.

Was Rey telling the truth, or was he just impressed with the outward change she'd made? How did she really feel about him? Would she have considered him *that way* if he hadn't stepped to her first? How did he really feel about her? Well, he was right about one thing — she definitely didn't know what she thought she knew.

Turning on cold water, Iris washed away the tangled emotions with the water slipping down the drain. Inhaling deeply, she began the rote motions of preparing for work.

Dressed and ready to go, she looked in the hall mirror and noticed some of the puffiness around her eyes had diminished, but the dark smudges were standing their ground. Dropping her purse, shoulder bag, and keys on the hall table, she rushed back to the bathroom and shuffled through her small collection of cosmetics. Finding a faded bottle of concealer — probably as old as she was — she squeezed a tiny amount onto her finger and attempted to blend it under her eye. The end result wasn't much better, but she didn't have time to try anything else.

Grabbing her bags and keys, she rushed out the door.

Chapter Twenty-Eight

ZUMA BREEZED INTO the marketing department and, smiling, said, "Good morning, Betty," leaving the secretary with her mouth slightly agape. Betty couldn't remember if Zuma had ever greeted her before.

In her office, Zuma got settled, turned on her computer, and began checking voicemails. She replayed a few messages, putting the necessary information in her PDA, while she waited for her computer to boot up. By the time she'd finished checking and responding to emails, returning the most pertinent phone calls, and signing a few documents, it was already ten thirty. She was checking the next item on her to-do list when the phone rang.

"Zuma Harris."

"Hi, babe."

Zuma answered cautiously in case someone walked by her open office door. "Good morning, Bob. How was your weekend?"

He chuckled, "Playing it safe, huh? Smart. When can I see you?"

"Well," she said, consulting her PDA, "we have a meeting with Rick to finalize the Pdata rollout at two o'clock. Should we try to meet prior to that?"

"I'll have Nancy book the twelfth floor conference room. Twelve thirty." The phone went dead in Zuma's ear.

She sat pensively staring out the window. Such a beautiful view. People would stab someone to say this office was theirs.

"Excuse me, Zuma."

Zuma whirled away from the view to see Iris standing in the doorway. She looked fabulous. Her hair was sharp, and her silk suit was obviously expensive. The cut lay perfectly on her curvy hips and small waist. Tiny conservative diamonds studded her ears while a simple gold chain looped her long, thin neck.

Zuma checked a sudden flash of jealous anger and pasted on a false smile. "Iris. Good morning. Come in, and have a seat."

As Iris moved closer, Zuma's sharp eye took note of the obvious and poor attempt to cover the shadows beneath the younger woman's eyes. *Lack of sleep? Too much partying? She better not come in here whining about a hangover and want permission to go home early.*

Iris cut into Zuma's silent ruminations. "Since I missed you last week, I wanted to bring you the updated report on my assignment," Iris said, opening a thin folder lying on her lap.

Zuma had totally forgotten about the damn thing as she'd moved forward with the second part of her plan. Things with Bob were progressing so well, she might not even need whatever little shit Iris came up with. But one could never be too cautious.

"Great. Let's see what you have," Zuma said, reaching for the sheets Iris handed across the desk.

Sitting quietly, Iris monitored Zuma's face as she read the information. After a minute, Zuma looked up with an unreadable expression. Iris subconsciously held her breath in anticipation of her response.

"As I expected, this is pretty good stuff. We hadn't really focused on the Mexican American market as a target group. Our most recent segmentation focus has been the African American market and, as you know, my targeted consumer marketing campaign for that group has increased our penetration by double digits. Let's see if you can come up with some statistical demographic information for Mexican Americans, and maybe I'll consider it."

Reaching across the desk, she laid the papers in front of Iris. "Good work so far."

Iris smiled, picking up the papers, and walked back to her desk. Once she was away from the open door, she tossed the papers in the nearest trashcan.

The phone on her desk was ringing as she approached, and she lunged for it, answering breathlessly. "Good morning, Iris Pena speaking."

"Hey Iris, what's up?" came a stiff voice.

"Jonathan! Hi," said Iris with a smile.

"Hi," he replied, still speaking tightly. "I thought I'd call to see if you were still alive."

Shit! How could I forget to call him? Cringing, Iris closed her eyes and took a breath before responding.

"I am *so* sorry I didn't call, Jonathan. Time just seems to get away from me when I'm at home."

"Hey, it's okay. I'm not your man, so you don't owe me anything."

"Will you give me a chance to apologize? In person? Tonight?"

Jonathan hesitated, but eventually he said, "Yeah, okay," still pouting.

"What are you doing for lunch?" Iris asked, knowing she really had to work her magic to smooth things over.

He wanted to tell her he was busy and didn't have time for her like she obviously didn't for him. But he hadn't stopped thinking about her since Saturday morning. "I don't know. Why?"

Iris could feel the ice melting. "If you can fit it in your schedule, maybe we could have lunch together."

Not wanting to give in too easily, he replied, "I'll call you back and let you know." But he knew he'd be watching the clock until lunchtime.

"Okay. I'll talk to you later, then," Iris said, knowing she'd made a dent in his anger.

After they disconnected, Iris reached up and massaged her neck and shoulders. They were tight with tension, and her tossing and turning last night hadn't helped. She'd planned to call Jonathan over the weekend, but someone or something had distracted her every time.

Looking at her Franklin planner, she realized she needed to complete the presentation materials to send to the copier. She jumped up and headed for Betty's desk.

The two women sifted through the completed pages, commenting and looking up occasionally to make sure no one would sneak up on them. "Can you arrange to get the reports in front of Bob O'Brien and the CMO?" Iris whispered as Betty arranged the papers into a neat stack.

"Honey, I can make anything happen that I want badly enough. Believe that. You just worry about the information, and let me handle the people."

"I don't know how I can thank you for your help with everything, Betty."

"You don't have to thank me. Just seeing the look on *her* face when the whole thing comes down will be thanks enough."

Chapter Twenty-Nine

LYING IN THE KING-SIZED BED in a corner of his loft apartment in Lower Manhattan, Rey stared down at people walking briskly in the falling rain. They were hunched inside dark-colored jackets as their umbrellas strained against the wind, barely able to keep the falling water off their faces. The funky, gray weather matched his mood and seemed completely appropriate today.

Unable to concentrate, he'd cancelled a morning staff meeting and rescheduled his remaining conference calls for the day. He contemplated going to his parent's house, but his mother would know immediately that something was wrong and harass him to death. Or feed him. Either way, he didn't feel like talking, and he'd lost his appetite.

Standing up and walking to the window in his socks and boxers, he leaned on the sill, staring unseeingly at the cars driving past. How the hell had they gone from kissing and caressing to anger and not speaking? Damn, he wanted to call her. He wanted to hear the voice that was as familiar to him as his own brothers'.

Even though his eyes were looking at wet figures outside, he saw her smooth face, her warm eyes, and the dimple he'd loved since he was eight. He swore he could smell her scent and feel her skin burning his palms. Licking his lips, he remembered how she tasted as the front of his boxers rose with the memory. Shit, she was driving him crazy!

His cell phone rang, breaking through the silence filling the vastness of the loft. The sound echoed off the high, vaulted ceilings as he ran and dived across the bed to grab the phone off the nightstand. It was her, he knew it.

"Rey," he answered as smoothly as possible, considering he'd just completed an Olympic event to get to the phone in 1.3 seconds.

"Hey, man. Just wanted to know if you're coming in later today." Rey's right-hand man, Rajesh, was on the other end.

Rajesh had been a CIS major at Florida State University when Rey was at FAMU, handling a full course load and working to build the website company. They'd each been working in the computer lab on FSU's campus late one night when Rajesh had helped Rey with a difficult program. When the website was still a class project, Rajesh was the only one who'd seen Rey's vision and believed in it's success and future. Aside from Iris.

"Uh, I got a couple of personal things going on right now, man."

Rajesh paused, hearing the extra hard edge to Rey's voice. "What's going on, Rey?"

Rey hesitated only a second before giving Rajesh the quick and dirty version of what had happened over the weekend with Iris. "I'm in love with her, man, but I don't think she believes me."

"Rey, I hate to say this, but I don't think you're really in love with her, either. You're comfortable with her. She's been your friend, your sister, and your confidante. She's safe, and she's pretty. You work so damn much, you don't give yourself the opportunity to meet anyone else for more than a booty call."

Through his anguish, Rey smiled at the Indian man's accented use of the slang term "booty call."

"What is love if it's not being physically attracted to your friend and confidante?" Rey asked in frustration.

"That *is* love, but it's not being *in* love," replied Rajesh.

"Raj, what the hell are you talking about? I don't think you know, man."

"I've known you two for years, and I don't see it. It would be like incest or something. Ew." Pausing, Rajesh asked, "What do you have in common, Rey?"

Rey opened his mouth to speak, but nothing came out.

"Exactly," Rajesh said. "You're from the same hometown and went to college together. That's it. What do you talk about when you're together? And, I hate to say it, but it takes two people to make a relationship work, and it doesn't sound like she's as interested in bonding as you are."

"Thanks, Raj. I feel a lot better now," Rey said sarcastically. "Look man, I'm just not up to coming in today, so you handle things."

"Unh huh. Listen, we've got another high school touring our offices this afternoon, and we need to work out the travel schedule for July and August since Audrey is going to be out with the baby. With Maurice and Malik out of the country and Rachel in California, we're running a little low on staff here, buddy. Can you help a brother out?"

Rey smiled again at the slang.

"Okay, okay. Give me an hour."

Balling up his boxers and then his socks, he took shots from across the room at the hamper in a corner. Missing both times, he shook his head as he went to the bathroom to shower. Maybe work was exactly what he needed to get his mind off of her.

Chapter Thirty

"**D**AMN, I MISSED YOU," Jonathan said, rubbing his face along Iris's neck.

"I know you don't believe me, but I've missed you, too," Iris said in a low voice, moving in rhythm with his body.

Jonathan groaned as he picked up speed, and Iris's breathing became heavy with the surge of pleasure.

"Ohh," she moaned as he thrust a final time, jerking spasmodically.

Her toes curled with pleasure as her muscles down below pulsed and contracted around him.

"Don't do that, girl!"

She laughed, breathlessly. "I can't help it."

Jonathan rolled to the side and lay quietly with his eyes closed. "What time is it?" he mumbled.

Looking at the alarm clock on the nightstand, Iris jumped up. "Shit, it's already ten to one! I thought this was supposed to be a lunchtime quickie."

"Believe me, I tried," Jonathan mumbled, standing up from the bed and following Iris into the shower.

Looking down at her bare butt, he said, "Damn, I can't wait until we make up again tonight."

Iris splashed him before quickly washing off.

* * *

Zuma jumped lightly from the edge of the conference table and pulled up her lace thong. Checking the hooks of the garter attached to her silky thigh highs, she tugged down her tight skirt and tucked in her blouse. Except for a few wrinkles, everything was perfect again.

Walking over to Bob, who had collapsed into one of the chairs with his pants and underwear bunched around his ankles, she bent low to kiss him on the lips.

"I hate to run, but I've got a lot of work to do to keep you looking good and my paycheck coming in."

Staring first at her legs, then up to her chest, and, finally, stopping at her cat-eyes, he nodded. "Yes, you do that."

Straightening, she walked with an exaggerated switch to the boardroom door. Looking back, she blew him a kiss and said, "I'll see you at two o'clock," before unlocking it, stepping out, and closing the door firmly behind her.

Chapter Thirty-One

"HI, WELCOME TO TRAVELSMART," Rey said with a smile he didn't feel.

A young woman surrounded by noisy, gum-chewing teenagers smiled back and took Rey's outstretched hand.

"It's a pleasure to finally meet you in person. I've seen your picture and read articles about you, but it's really great to actually meet you face-to-face. I'm Ebony Crenshaw, and this is my computer class," she said, waving her hand in the direction of the youth behind her.

Rey introduced Rajesh, then they attempted to get the attention of the twenty-five talkative young men and women. As agreed, Rajesh took twelve students to the second level while Rey took the rest with the teacher to tour the main level. With the students engrossed at a few of the computer stations and in the "think tank", a play room where the staff brainstormed and held meetings, Rey was finally able to speak with the teacher.

"So, how is it working with a rowdy crew like this every day?" Rey asked, handing her a soda from the vending machine.

Laughing, she said, "Believe me, it's a challenge. But it's something I've always wanted to do."

Raising a skeptical brow, Rey said, "You've always wanted to spend your days with noisy, badass teenagers?"

She sipped the soda and laughed again. "I worked for a software development company for a few years and, even though I was making good money, I felt so detached from my community, you know? I'd leave the office after working nine or ten hours and walk past these young people just hanging in the streets. I knew they were smart and bright, they just needed someone to believe in them and guide them. So here I am."

Rey nodded, thinking, while she finished her soda. After a moment he said, "We recently received a grant to work with inner city kids, educating them on computer use and navigating the Internet. Maybe we could work together with you or your school on something."

"Hey, any help we can get to mold these minds..." she paused and glanced at the kids, "...would be more than appreciated."

"Make sure you leave your information at the front desk, and we'll try to set something up."

"I'll do that," she said, looking at her watch. "It's time for us to get back." Throwing her can across the room, she made a neat shot into the small trashcan before turning confidently to gather the students. Rey nodded in silent approval.

Chapter Thirty-Two

Thursday, May 31

BY THURSDAY EVENING, IRIS had made up with Jonathan more than once and was happy to spend a quiet evening alone. Curled up on one of the large futons in the living room, she looked up from the book she was reading when the phone rang. Bending the corner of the page, she dropped the book on the ottoman and walked across the living room to the phone in the kitchen.

"Hello?"

"Hey, girl."

Iris paused, recognizing the voice. "Rey?"

"Yeah. What's up?"

"Not too much," she responded, dragging the phone and its long extension cord across the dining room to the futon. Falling into the chair, she kicked her feet up on the wide ottoman and leaned comfortably back into the soft pillows, tucking the phone between her ear and shoulder.

There was an extended silence as neither spoke. Taking a deep breath, Rey started, his words falling out in a rush.

"Listen, I just wanted to call you and apologize for everything. I was out of line in City Island, and I was wrong to throw my feelings at you. I was trippin' at the train station, and you had every right to be angry with me. I just want us to be cool again."

The silence hung heavy, and Iris could hear the television playing in the background on his end.

"Thanks, Rey, but some of the blame is on me too. Part of the reason I was so angry is because you were right. I *didn't* stop you in City Island, and I was scared of what was happening. I'm still confused, to tell you the truth, but I apologize for hurting your feelings. I want us to be friends again, too."

Rey silently mouthed "thank you" as he looked heavenward. Out loud, he said, "It's all good, then."

Just as Iris was about to respond, she heard a break on the line indicating Rey was getting a call.

"Hold on, Iris."

He clicked over, leaving her to think in peace for a few seconds, but, before she could gather her thoughts, he was back.

"Hey, I gotta take this. I'll give you a shout tomorrow, okay?"

"Alright."

Rising to hang up the phone, Iris was less than satisfied. She didn't know what she expected, but somehow that brief conversation just wasn't enough. To make herself feel better, she dialed Jonathan's number.

"Hey, baby," he crooned as soon as he heard her voice.

She felt better already.

Chapter Thirty-Three

Friday, June 1

L ATE FRIDAY MORNING, IRIS placed the copies she'd just stapled into a folder. Standing and straightening her skirt, she walked to Zuma's office.

As usual, Zuma was speaking sharply into her headset and making written notations on a stack of papers piled neatly in front of her. She waved Iris into one of the chairs in front of her desk and continued the conversation.

"Yes, Rick. We've been over and over this thing for the past month. The vendor is going to lose it if we can't get these tests to work out, and I wouldn't be surprised if they started looking for another company to supply the service."

She was quiet to listen for a few moments, but it wasn't long before she started again with renewed anger.

"I've worked my butt off selling these people on this product. You assured me it would work, and you gave me a release date that's over a month old. It's bordering on ridiculous now, and it's my reputation that will be on the line if we don't get our shit together and provide this service in the next two weeks."

Zuma was standing now, pacing in front of the vast window with one hand on her skinny hip, stabbing the air with the other.

"I don't want to have to go to Bob with this, but I will if you can't get your team to work this out, and soon. I won't continue to take the heat on this alone."

Pressing a button on the cord hanging from the headset, she removed it and threw it on the desk. Ignoring Iris, she picked up the phone's receiver and quickly dialed a number. Waiting, she clicked her manicured nails on the glass.

"Yeah, hi, it's Zuma. Do you have any free time this afternoon?"

She listened while looking intently at the little PDA propped up on the desk. "Yeah, we need to talk about the U.P.Ex deal and its delay."

There was another lengthy pause as the other person spoke.

"Thanks, Bob. I'll see you this afternoon."

As Zuma hung up, Iris shifted uncomfortably in the chair. If Zuma had the power to get on Bob's calendar that easily, she obviously had more clout than Iris thought. Suddenly, she was uneasy about her plan. What if Bob didn't appreciate her going over Zuma's head with the proposal? What if he refused to read her report unless it came from Zuma as her mentor? She'd have to sit down with Betty later and discuss another alternative. Right now, she had to deal with the status of her research.

Zuma cut into her thoughts. "Okay, Iris. Let's make it quick. I have important things to deal with today," Zuma said gruffly, turning her attention to the younger woman.

Iris handed Zuma the papers. "These are the statistics you requested for the Mexican American demographic."

She waited while Zuma skimmed the pages quickly with a furrow in her brow.

"Okay, good," she said, passing the papers back to Iris. "Keep up the good work."

Without another word, she turned back to the stack on her desk and resumed flipping through them, pausing to write notes in the margin.

As Iris rose and walked slowly back to her desk, she thought about her plan. Maybe her research and findings weren't as important as she thought they were. Obviously, Shearing had major deals going on with huge Fortune 500 companies, and her little ideas about penetrating missed consumer markets would probably be laughed off.

Sitting at her desk, she instinctively reached for her cell phone to call Rey, but she stopped with the phone in her hand. Dropping it back in her purse, she picked up the phone on her desk and dialed Betty's extension. She'd started this thing, and she was going to finish it. What did she have to lose, except a positive internship evaluation?

Chapter Thirty-Four

I T WAS FRIDAY NIGHT, and Iris and Jonathan had enjoyed a movie and dinner. Afterward, they retired to Iris's apartment. She sat snuggled in his lap, watching, as patiently as she could, as Jonathan pressed the arrow on the TV remote, flipping from channel to channel in bored frustration.

"Shit, all these channels on cable, and there's still nothing good to watch," he grumbled.

Bored and frustrated herself, Iris whispered, "I could find something for us to do," as she nibbled on the lobe of his ear.

Jonathan tried a few more channels then dropped the remote on the ottoman in surrender. He rubbed one hand along her thigh, observing the contrast of her skin color to the white bikini panties she wore. He slid his other hand under her t-shirt and toyed with her nipple until it came to attention. Pressing his nose to the top of her head, he closed his eyes and inhaled her scent. He felt his arousal growing when she shifted on his lap and began gently stroking him through the fabric of his underwear.

Iris lifted her face, and Jonathan dropped his lips to meet hers, moving his hand up her thigh to caress the warm, soft space a little higher. After several minutes of heated foreplay, their clothing littered the floor. Jonathan slipped on a condom and gently commanded, "Turn around."

Iris raised an eyebrow at the directive, and climbed onto all fours, looking back at the shape of Jonathan behind her. Placing his hands on her hips, he moved closer and began slowly riding her from the back, causing her hair to brush lightly back and forth against the side of her face. He dug the fingers of one hand in her hair, playing with her coils and curls, as he held her steady with the other hand and increased the intensity of his thrusts. He felt himself growing harder inside her as she looked back at him with parted lips from which groans escaped with each bump and grind.

Iris was lost in the passion of the sex. When Jonathan pulled her upright against him, she could feel his hot breath on her neck. She cried out when he bit into her flesh and began sucking, pulling her skin between his teeth as he continued to play in her hair. He plunged, faster and harder, between her legs, forcing her to fall back onto her hands for support. Releasing her hair, he gripped her hips again, his fingers digging into her waist, as they both called out with his final thrust.

Iris's hair clung to her damp face as she collapsed on the futon. Jonathan fell against her back, breathing heavily and tickling her neck with each exhale. Finally, he stood and walked to the bathroom, tugging at the condom as he went. Iris waited a minute before following him.

When they returned to the living room, Jonathan laid out on the futon and fell asleep with his head in Iris's lap. Stroking his hair in the moonlight shining through the window, Iris observed the sprinkling of tiny freckles on his creamy skin and the contrasting dark lashes resting on his cheeks. Her finger trailed the line of his mustache around the curve of his pink lips before dipping into the cleft of his chin. Mesmerized, she barely heard the narrator on the television, which was still on the last channel Jonathan had flipped to.

"The Olsen Twins coined the term "tweens" referring to the untapped youth market between the ages of eight and twelve. With their growing line of home videos and DVDs and a new clothing line, Mary Kate and Ashley are building an empire, and they aren't even sixteen yet."

Iris finished watching the *E! True Hollywood Story* on Mary Kate and Ashley Olsen and almost pushed Jonathan off her lap as an idea came to her. Sliding from beneath his head, she raced to her room and dropped her naked butt into the desk chair facing the computer. Typing "tweens" in the Google search box, she waited tentatively as the hourglass flashed on the screen. Not knowing what to expect, she squinted at the monitor as the results appeared.

This is it. This is exactly what I needed.

Chapter Thirty-Five

ZUMA WATCHED MALCOLM'S car back out of the driveway before turning from the window and walking to the kitchen to pour more wine into her glass. Placing the glass carefully on the desk in her study, she pulled out the worn checkbook, wrote the usual information on check number 0521, and ripped it from the bind, folding it in blank paper and sealing it in an envelope. Writing her parent's Florida address on the envelope, she dropped her pen and sat back, quietly sipping the woodsy dark liquid.

Since the trip to Cape Cod, she couldn't get Professor Simons out of her mind. Damn, he'd been handsome. And so fucking suave. He had used her, when she thought she had been using him. Zuma closed her eyes, remembering him.

I wonder where that asshole is now. Motherfucker. The prick knew. He knew, and he left me anyway. I would have done anything for him.

And then she remembered what she hadn't thought about in almost fourteen years.

* * *

"Oh, Mama, it hurts! It hurts so badly!" Zuma cried in agony.

"Zumatha, I know baby. But it won't be much longer, now," her mother said,

attempting to soothe her shaking daughter.

"I can't take it anymore, Mama. I'm gonna die, aren't I? I'm gonna die..." *she wailed in agony.*

"Baby, I wish I could take the pain and tears away, but this is what happens when you become a woman. Mama's here. It's gonna be okay, baby. Come on Zumatha, you can do it."

"No, Mama, I can't. It hurts too bad. I can't push anymore."

"Mrs. Harrison," the obstetrician said suddenly, "something's going wrong here. We're going to have to ask you to step outside." He said it matter-of-factly, rising from the low stool at the foot of Zuma's bed.

As nurses rushed in, brushing past her, Zuma's mother protested. "No! I will not leave my baby!"

A strong set of hands gripped her shoulders and pulled her firmly from the room as they moved the crying girl onto a gurney and whisked her, screaming, down the hall.

"Not my baby! Not my baby!" Zuma's mother cried after them.

* * *

Zuma's head slipped from the chair suddenly waking her. Tears were still wet on her cheeks. *Why, Professor Simons, why?*

Lifting her hands to wipe the wet streaks from her face, she saw the card. Elijah Pharrell. 410-555-2211.

Zuma held the card tightly, staring at the name and number printed on it. She looked at the clock on the corner of the desk. It was eleven thirty-two. She picked up the cordless phone, began dialing the numbers, and then waited, tentatively.

"Hello, you've reached the voicemail for Elijah Pharrell. Please leave a message after the tone, and someone will contact you as soon as possible."

Zuma hung up before the beep. What was she thinking?

Tossing the card back on the desk, Zuma stood and made her way up the stairs to the master suite. The bed was damp from lovemaking, and she was becoming nauseous from the smell of sex hanging in the air. Backing into the hallway, she went to the guest room across the hall and curled up in a tight ball on the bed. She was asleep as soon as she closed her eyes, shutting out the mess of her memories and her life.

Chapter Thirty-Six

Saturday, June 2

"JONATHAN, HOW MUCH research and data have you and the Data team gathered on the youth market?" Iris asked as she spooned eggs onto a plate in front of him.

Emptying the juice from his glass, Jonathan looked at Iris. "What are you cooking up now?"

Sitting next to him at the circular table, she picked up a piece of turkey bacon from her plate and pursed her lips. "Jonathan, just answer the question."

Chewing, he looked up at the ceiling thoughtfully. "Well, we haven't really gathered information on that particular market in our department. The people on *your* floor would have those statistics. Why?"

Iris contemplated whether to confide her plan in him. Making a quick decision, she told him about the marketing assignment she'd been given and what she suspected was happening with Zuma.

"Always keep some things to yourself. That way, you can't get hurt when someone you trust betrays you." Iris heard her mother's voice in her head and stopped short of describing her alliance with Betty and their strategy to set Zuma up.

"Anyway, I just want to ensure that I get a positive internship review, and I want to have as much ammunition to prove I deserve one if Zuma tries to trip." It wasn't a lie.

Wiping his mouth with a cloth napkin, he rested on his forearms, fixing a green gaze on her.

"What do you have in mind regarding the youth market?"

"Okay, here it is. There is something called a "tween" market for youth that's older than a young kid, but still too young to be considered a young adult or teenager. Those twins from the show *Full House* — you know, Mary Kate and Ashley — have built an entire media and clothing empire simply by targeting this market. These kids are active and smart, so why not have a calling plan for them and their parents that's restrictive but also gives them the ability to call their parents from the mall or dance practice or a birthday party?" Excited, Iris spoke quickly without pause. "There could even be less restrictive plans that allowed them to call each other. Do you see where I'm going with this?"

Even though she was speaking fast, Jonathan followed what she was saying and, playing with the corner of his mustache, thought about the real possibility of her idea.

"You might have something. Do you want me to set something up with Rick to get into the numbers and reality of this thing?"

Iris jumped up from the table, knocking her silverware to the floor with a clatter. Throwing her arms around his neck, she pushed him to the floor.

Jonathan's laugh was muffled under her weight. "Wow. If I knew I could get this type of response, I would have set up a meeting with Rick a month ago."

Chapter Thirty-Seven

Sunday, June 3

WAKING FROM A FITFUL SLEEP, Rey listened to the sound of cars outside the windows of his loft. Like every minute since Memorial Day, he thought about Iris and replayed the scene where they kissed. Damn, he wanted her. Rajesh didn't know what the hell he was talking about. *"What do you have in common? You're not in love with her."* What did his single, Indian ass know about being in love?

Rolling off the bed, he went to the bathroom and stood in front of the toilet, relieving himself. While he washed and dried his hands, he looked at his reflection in the mirror.

I look good, I'm paid, and I know her better than anyone in the world. Why is she pushing me away? Maybe she's right. I came on too strong too fast. I just need to give her some time to accept it.

Falling into a deep leather chair, he dialed the number he had memorized. Waiting for her to answer, he envisioned the waves and curls of her hair blowing in the wind.

A cracked and muffled, "Hello," came over the line.

"Iris?" Rey asked cautiously. He glanced at the hands pointing to eight fifteen on the wall clock. She was usually up and dressing for a run by this time.

When there was no answer, he repeated, "Iris?"

Clearing her throat, Iris said, "Rey? What are you doing up so early?"

"What're you doin' still asleep?"

"That's usually what people do early on a Sunday morning," she answered sarcastically. "What's up?"

"Nothin'. Just checkin' in."

As she was about to respond, Jonathan spooned her closer to the warm curve of his body before resuming a light snore. Not wanting to wake him, she carefully lifted his arm and slipped from the heat of the bed.

"Iris? You still there?"

Whispering now, she answered him. "Yeah, just hold on a second."

Instantly, Rey knew. Someone was there.

"Yo, don't worry about it. I'll just talk to you another time," he said gruffly.

He heard shuffling and a muffled voice in the background before she came back on the line. "Um, yeah. I'll call you later," she whispered.

"Peace," he said, pushing the off button before she could respond. He threw the phone across the couch as he stood up and walked to the window.

Seconds later, the neglected phone started ringing. Rey considered ignoring it but, if it was Iris, he wanted to hear what she had to say.

He snatched the phone and roughly answered, "Yeah?"

"Man, what are you going through?"

Rey's squared shoulders dropped as Rajesh's accent came through the line. "My bad, man. I'm just dealing with something here," Rey responded.

"Yeah, okay. When you're done thinking about Iris, give me a call back so we can discuss the proposal that teacher from the high school sent over."

Rey sucked his teeth. "You think you know so damn much. Let me get something to eat, and I'll hit you back in a few." Hanging up, Rey went to the kitchen.

Fuck it. If Iris really isn't feeling me like that, she won't have to worry about a brother chasing her ass.

Still trying to convince himself, he opened the pantry and reached for a box of cereal.

Chapter Thirty-Eight

Monday, June 4

ZUMA AND IRIS BRIEFLY acknowledged one another as they passed in the office hallway. Zuma observed Iris's slick hairstyle and upbeat glow, while Iris considered the haggard look on Zuma's face. Her eyes, usually bright and well made-up, were underscored by dark circles and creases. Even Barbara and Jim had commented on how little grief Zuma had given them in the last week. Iris also noticed that she wasn't riding her about the research assignment. It was almost as if she didn't care.

Moving to Jim's office, Iris peeked in and asked, "Jim, are you busy? Can I ask you a quick question?"

"Sure. Shoot."

"Have you guys ever done focused research on the youth market?"

Pushing a lock of blonde hair back from his face, Jim thought about the question. "Well, it depends on what you mean by youth. We have extensive reports on college-age people and, as you know, we offer a few different services, like prepaid, to that market. What's up? More research for Zuma?"

"Not exactly," Iris said, moving from the doorway to drop into one of his office chairs. "Have you ever heard the term "tween"?"

"Tween?" he repeated, articulating the word carefully.

"Unh huh."

"Nope. What's that?"

Iris briefly described the mid-youth market as Barbara walked in and leaned against the wall, listening.

"Yeah, I've heard about that. My niece watches Nickelodeon," Barbara said, coming in and sitting next to Iris. "They have television shows just for her age group. Some of them are pretty good, too."

"Exactly," said Iris, excitedly. "I think there's an opportunity to target that market with special technology and services, and parents will pay for it."

Looking at each other with that silent communication thing they did, Barbara and Jim nodded.

"Okay, guys," Iris said, sitting on the edge of her chair and gesticulating excitedly. "At first, I wanted to make this a part of my assignment for Zuma but, after thinking about it more, I realized that I'm really interested in how this could work. So, I wanted to know if you'd be willing to help me do the research and show me the steps to take to get it implemented. Without involving Zuma."

The two managers looked at each other again.

"The Pdata launch is pretty much over, so I might have a little free time on my hands to help you out," Jim said slowly, warming to the idea.

While Iris, Jim, and Barbara were brainstorming in Jim's office, Zuma sat at her desk reading an email from Bob about a telecomm leadership conference in New York.

Fucking him again is actually starting to pay off. With a smile, Zuma envisioned herself networking with other executives, enjoying the

New York nightlife, and being wined and dined by handsome men while their wives sat at home. It was just what she needed to break out of this funk she was in. And maybe she could make some contacts at other companies in case things didn't work out for her with the merger.

The phone's ring broke her reverie. "Zuma Harris," she answered, more pleasantly than normal.

"Zuma. Did you get my email about the trip?" Bob asked.

"I did," she replied with a smile, tilting back in her chair and crossing her legs.

"What do you think?"

"I think it's awesome, and I can't wait to pack."

"Great. Nancy will have your tickets delivered to Betty. We leave on Wednesday."

The smile froze on Zuma's face. *We.* Of course. A four-day paid sex retreat for Bob O'Brien.

As reality was setting in on Zuma, Iris sat in her cubicle across the floor, playing around with numbers in an Excel spreadsheet. She was completely engrossed and grunted in frustration when the phone on her desk rang. It rang three times before Iris pulled her eyes from the computer screen and looked to the phone's caller I.D. Recognizing Jonathan's extension, she finally picked up, hoping the call wouldn't go to voicemail.

After exchanging a few pleasantries, Jonathan said, "Iris, I have you scheduled to meet with Rick on Wednesday at ten o'clock. Is that good for you?"

"Jonathan, that's perfect! That will give me enough time to finish compiling the initial information I need to share with him."

"Good," Jonathan said, satisfied. Then his tone changed. "So what do I get for my good deed?"

"I can't say those things on an office telephone," Iris said tentatively, lowering her voice.

"Mm. That alone sounds promising."

"If you meet me in the twelfth-floor boardroom, I could tell you more," Iris whispered slyly.

"What do you know about the twelfth-floor boardroom?" Jonathan exclaimed in mock surprise.

Everyone knew that's where the top executives held their "private meetings" for two, but Jonathan didn't think Iris had been privy to the company secret.

Laughing, Iris said, "Good gossip travels fast around this place. Go to your meeting. I'll see you tonight."

As soon as she replaced the receiver, the phone rang again.

"Hey, Iris," Betty said quickly. "We need to talk."

The tone in Betty's voice was all Iris needed to hear to drop what she was doing and hustle to the front. When she arrived, Betty filled her in on the latest secretary gossip, then spread three bound copies of Iris's presentation on her desk.

"Zuma and Mr. O'Brien are leaving together Wednesday. Nancy, his secretary, called me as soon as Mr. O'Brien ordered the tickets."

Tilting her head down and raising her eyes to meet Iris's, she continued. "Nancy also said that she's scheduled private meetings in the twelfth-floor boardroom for them several times in the last month."

She waited to gauge Iris's understanding of what was becoming obvious. Seeing the wide-eyed look of surprise on the younger woman's face, Betty said, "I think you should be prepared for Mr. O'Brien to tell Zuma about anything he receives from her intern."

With a heavy sigh, Iris slumped over the desk, looking at the bound documents spread in front of her. "What do I do, then? I don't want her to think I just went over her head."

After a moment's thought, Betty said, "Give it to him anyway."

"What? You just said he'll tell Zuma as soon as he gets it," Iris said in a confused voice.

"That's right, he will. But Zuma will get one, too. It will just be a little late arriving on her desk," Betty said with a wink and a sly smile.

Chapter Thirty-Nine

Wednesday, June 6

REY IGNORED THE VIBRATION of the cell phone on his hip as he and Rajesh shook hands with Ebony Crenshaw and the principal from her high school. They had finally completed negotiations for a new educational partnership between Rey's company and the school.

As they walked from Rey's office into the lobby, his phone went off again. Rey pressed a button on the side to stop the vibration.

Rajesh turned to Rey as Ebony and the principal exited.

He rubbed his hands together and said, "The negotiations may be done, but now the real work begins. How are we going to staff the tutoring and monitor the on-site labs when our people are already stretched thin with travel and work?"

Rey opened his mouth to answer when the phone went off a third time. Mumbling to himself in irritation, he pulled the phone from the clip and stared at the caller ID. Rajesh watched his face change from irritation to concern.

He whipped the phone open and immediately asked, "What's wrong?" He listened and after a moment, his hand went limp, letting the cell phone fall to the floor with a crack.

Chapter Forty

IRIS AND JIM WERE all smiles as they returned from the meeting with Rick and Jonathan.

"Well?" asked Barbara impatiently, waiting for one of them to say something.

"He thinks it's a viable project. He's checking with finance on some preliminary numbers," Iris answered, flopping into her cubicle's single chair.

"Good work, woman!" Barbara exclaimed, holding up her hand for a high five.

Slapping Barbara's palm, Iris said, "Thanks, but this is a team effort. The process is just starting."

"I hear you. But in the meantime, let's take a long lunch to celebrate a successful first step."

Talking excitedly with her colleagues, Iris didn't hear the jingle of her cell phone deep in the bottom of her purse. The phone sang twice more before silencing.

Hours later, she sat studying the calendar resting on the corner of her small desk. She wondered how many weeks she would be able to work on the new project she'd introduced before her internship ended. Deciding to share the good news with her mother, she dug around in her purse for her cell phone.

Beep. *"3 missed messages,"* the tiny screen read. A warning sign went off in Iris's head. She quickly scrolled through the missed caller numbers. Two from Rey and one from her parent's house. *Uh oh.*

Not trusting herself to listen to the messages, she immediately called her parent's house. Her palms grew moist as she waited for an answer. After several rings, her mother's canned voice instructed her to leave her name, number, and a brief message after the tone. Shit.

Heating up with nervousness, she speed dialed Rey. He answered on the second ring.

"Iris... He's gone." Rey's voice was husky with sorrow.

Never in eighteen years had Iris heard Rey sound like this. Immediately, tears sprang to her own eyes, and she knew without him saying that Pop was dead.

Chapter Forty-Two

Sunday, June 10

ZUMA HAD BEEN CALCULATING her next move throughout every night she spent fucking and sucking Bob during the New York conference.

When their sexual relationship had begun almost two years ago, it was his title, power, and money that had drawn her to him. And it made her feel just as powerful to have such easy control over him. A sultry look or a sexy bend were the only tools she'd needed to make him jump. But something had changed. She couldn't quite put her finger on it, but she could feel it, and she didn't like it. Whatever it was, it was about to change. Zuma wasn't used to feeling played.

They sat, silently engrossed in their own thoughts, in the back of the black town car that was carrying them from BWI airport back to their respective homes. Bob scanned through his PDA, completely unaware of Zuma and her crossed, bare legs that were exposed to the thigh. Zuma surreptitiously watched him ignoring her, and a wicked smile played at the corners of her mouth as she strategized her next move.

When the car stopped in front of her house, she stiffly picked up her purse and computer bag. Without waiting for the driver, she opened the door herself and stepped quickly from the car, deftly dodging Bob's half-hearted reach for her ass.

As the driver pulled her bag from the trunk, she walked briskly up the curving sidewalk to the front door, fishing for her keys. She heard Bob panting behind her.

"Zuma, wait," he called after her.

Ignoring him, she unlocked the door and pointed to a corner in the foyer, indicating where the driver should deposit the suitcase. She stood behind the door waiting to close it behind the driver in Bob's face. If he thought he could treat her like a common whore, he had another thought coming.

"Zuma, what the hell is wrong with you?" he whispered angrily, putting up a hand to stop the closing door as the driver returned to the car to wait for him.

"What are you talking about?" Zuma asked, feigning confusion.

"Aren't you going to say goodbye?" he asked, pushing against the closing door.

"Goodbye, Bob. See you tomorrow," she said sweetly, smiling genuinely at him.

As he strained his neck to kiss her through the narrow crack, she put her hand on his shoulder, stopping him.

Opening her eyes wide, playing the young ingénue, she said apologetically, "I think we should take a little break. I'm getting too caught up in all of… this," she said, waving her hand helplessly through the air.

Zuma let him push into the foyer and looked him in the eye. "I need to give myself some space, Bob." She maintained the eye contact and innocent look as she sighed theatrically, emphasizing the pain she was pretending to feel.

"What do you mean?" Bob asked quizzically, knitting his brows together in the center of his forehead.

Looking down, Zuma brought her hand to her breast and whispered, "I didn't intend to feel this way when this whole thing started."

"Feel what way? What thing?"

"Us. I think I'm falling in love with you." After a moment of dramatic silence, she looked up into his gray eyes. "I can't let myself get hurt by a married man, Bob."

"Wait a minute," Bob began, but she put a finger to his open mouth.

"Don't. It'll be even harder for me if you try to make it better. Just let me take a little time, okay?" She fluttered her lashes and parted her lips in a way that made men lie to their wives.

Bob stuttered, "T-take a little time? What does that mean?"

When she didn't answer, he tried pleading with her. "What do you want from me, Zuma? I don't want you to be hurt, but I can't stop seeing you. Don't do this to us." He begged, lost in her eyes.

"Let me sleep on it," she said with a sigh. "I'll see you tomorrow at work, and maybe we can discuss it over lunch."

Satisfied that she wasn't completely ending things, he relaxed and stepped back through the door, turning to wave over his shoulder. Zuma waved back with a sad look, but her mouth curved into a smile as soon as she shut the door.

Chapter Forty-Two

S ITTING NEXT TO CARLOS in Rey's parents' house, Iris looked sadly at the various family photos on the walls, shelves, and fireplace mantel. Pictures of Rey's father as a young groom, a smiling new father, and others from various stages of the man he was, were interspersed with those of his wife, sons, and grandchildren. A silent tear welled in Iris's eye, and she prayed it would evaporate before someone looked her way.

"Man, remember when Pop caught us with that car in New Jersey?"

The room erupted in laughter as one of Rey's brothers reminisced with a story about Pop. Another brother chimed in, "Yo, I don't even know how he *found* us!"

Since Iris's late Friday arrival, Rey's house had been full of family, friends, and those bringing condolences. There hadn't been a moment of mourning. Only laughter and remembrances of the man that had loved a woman for more than forty years, had raised a house full of boys to men, and had been a role model for all who had the fortune to walk through their front door.

Carlos stood to add something to the conversation. He, along with most of the guys in the room, had been a part of some scheme Pop's sons had going on back in the day. As he spoke, Iris vividly recalled the night he was dragged home by an angry Pop at two-thirty one Sunday morning, years ago. She turned to look into the crowded hallway, imagining Pop walking through the high archway into the room at any moment.

"I feel the same way," came a soft voice next to her. She jumped as Rey spoke her thoughts out loud. "I keep thinking he's going to walk in and add something to the story."

Iris studied his face — the clear brown eyes and thick, hooded brows. His heavy locs, usually hanging around his face and down his back, were pulled into a tight ponytail at the base of his head. He'd had a maintenance done for the memorial service, and each loc gleamed in its newly twisted part. Despite the hint of a smile that played around the edges of his mouth, Iris felt the sadness emanating from him and saw it etched in his eyes.

"How's your mother doing?" Iris asked softly.

Rey chuckled and jerked his thumb in the direction of the kitchen. "Still being Mama. She hasn't stopped greeting, cleaning, and moving since I got here." He paused with a troubled look. "I'm a little worried that she's not sleeping. We've had people through here twenty-four seven since last Thursday, and she won't let anyone else take over her role as hostess."

It was Iris's turn to smile. "I couldn't imagine anyone else doing it like her anyway."

"Yeah, you're right. It's probably keeping her mind off the reality that he's gone." Rey's voice cracked imperceptibly on the last words, but Iris heard and understood.

As Rey turned back to the men in the room, Iris rose and walked through the crowd of people in the hallway, all laughing at old memories, and stood in the same place in the kitchen doorway that she'd stood in two weeks before. She watched Rey's mother bustle through the kitchen, placing dishes in the sink and talking animatedly with the women in the room. As though the hands of time had turned backwards, she looked up and, with the same expression and tone from two weeks ago, said, "Iris," before coming over and hugging her.

Iris hugged her back tightly. Releasing the shorter woman, Iris looked into her plump face and asked, "How you doing, Mrs. H.?"

Rey's mother placed a fist on her ample hip and looked Iris straight in the eyes. "You know, I was with Walter for forty-three years, married for forty-one. We had some real, real good times together. More than most people have their entire lives. I'm okay, because I lived love and have the proof of it all throughout this house." She waved her hand through the air, and Iris knew she meant her sons, their wives, and her grandchildren.

"Yeah, baby, I'm okay. Sometimes I'll want someone to talk to in the way only Walter and I did. But I can still do that. Anytime."

Reaching up, she touched Iris's face. "Thanks for being here, baby. You are like the daughter he never had." She let her hand drop as someone called her name. Squeezing Iris's hand, she turned and walked away.

No longer able to control the moisture building in her eyes, Iris walked out the back door and down the sidewalk toward her parent's house.

Chapter Forty-Three

Monday, June 11

O N MONDAY MORNING, IRIS was back in the office trying to focus on work. Jonathan had picked her up from the airport the night before and, at her urging, had filled her in on the tween phone project. She needed something to lift her spirits from the sadness at home in New York.

Rick had actually received a nod from finance to continue research and development of a product geared toward the preteen market. Now, they had to come up with a feasible blueprint, and it was up to Iris and Jim to validate the potential for sales.

Her mind was full of ideas when she came through the door and walked toward Betty's desk.

"Iris. Welcome back, honey. We were terribly sad to hear about your loss."

"Thanks, Betty. It was hard, but the family is close-knit and doing really well, so it's not as sad as it could be."

"That's a real blessing. A loss like that is easier when the family is tight."

Nodding, Iris blinked to fight back the threatening tears and quickly changed the subject. "What's going on here? Anything good?"

"Not really. Your girl just returned from the conference this morning, so things are pretty quiet while she plays catch up. But on another note, I sent your proposals out last Thursday."

Iris's expression changed, and she leaned on the desk as she lowered her voice. "I almost forgot about them. Do you think they've reviewed them yet?"

"Well, Mr. O'Brien and Ms. Harris have been away on a *business* trip as you know," Betty said with a smirk, "but I made sure the other two recipients received theirs Thursday."

"Other *two*? What do you mean? There were only three binders," Iris said in confusion.

Diverting her eyes, Betty answered, "Like I said, leave the administration to me, and you handle the information." Lifting her eyes in a brief sideways glance at Iris, she added, "Trust me."

Iris shook her head and headed for her cubicle. Cards in pretty pastel envelopes were stacked neatly on the edge of her desk. Sitting, she picked up the first card and fresh tears sprang in her eyes as she read the personal message from Barbara. Picking up the rest of the envelopes, she walked to the break room to read them privately.

As Iris disappeared through the break room doorway, Zuma strode confidently across the floor to her office, not stopping to speak or acknowledge anyone along the way. She was wading through the river of emails on her computer when Betty stepped in with an armful of mail and packages.

Zuma glanced sparingly at her before returning her attention to the screen. Betty placed the mail in the stainless steel bin on the corner of the desk, then stood motionless, staring at Zuma's back. Zuma had just finished typing an email and clicked "send" when she noticed Betty still standing at the corner of the desk.

"Yes?" Zuma said with impatience.

Betty didn't move or answer. She stood still and looked at Zuma with a strange smile pasted to her face.

Zuma fought to control her irritation as she blinked at the secretary. As badly as she wanted to curse at the woman standing in front of her, something stopped her from speaking at all. The two women continued to stare at one another before Zuma broke the eye contact. Disconcerted, she turned back to her computer.

That bitch is crazy, and I'm going to have to talk to human resources about replacing her dumb ass, Zuma thought, ignoring the older woman and refocusing on her email.

Betty's smile widened as she stepped quietly from the office.

Chapter Forty-Four

"ZUMA, I HAVE TO TALK TO you. I'm going crazy."

Zuma grinned to herself and turned up the volume on the telephone headset. Pulling an emory board from the top drawer, she began evening out her nails as she listened to Bob beg.

It had been three days since they'd returned from the leadership conference, and she'd managed to avoid being alone with him.

"Bob, I've already told you. I think this is the best thing for *me*. I just feel like I'm getting in too deep, and I know I'll get hurt sooner or later," Zuma lied with false sincerity.

"How could you get hurt, Zuma? You have more of me than my own wife! What more could you want?"

Zuma smiled, knowing she had him right where she needed him.

"I'm feeling very insecure about this merger, Bob. I don't know. I just feel like I really need to focus totally on my job to ensure that I *have* a job in the next few months."

Those were the most truthful statements she'd made in days, and she had no problem delivering her lines.

Bob was ready with an answer. "I have a meeting with Steve and Margie next week. I promise, you have nothing to worry about, babe."

A meeting? This was the first time she'd heard about Bob meeting with the chief marketing officer and human resource director. What the fuck was going on?

Quickly changing gears, she said, "Well, maybe you're right."

"Of course I'm right."

She could hear the hope in his voice. She didn't know when this meeting was taking place, but she knew she'd better get on his best side before then.

"I was planning to leave a little early today. I haven't been feeling well lately. Maybe you can get away, too, and meet me at McCormick's for an early dinner?"

Zuma knew Bob would not only meet her at the popular steak house, he would probably reserve a room in the hotel above the restaurant with a view of Baltimore's Inner Harbor.

"I'll have Nancy make a reservation for four-thirty," he quickly replied.

When Bob finished his conversation with Zuma and hung up, his secretary paged in. "Bob, Steve Searson is on line two for you."

Not wanting to make the CMO wait, Bob quickly connected and hesitated a second before saying, "Steve. What's going on, guy?"

"Hey, Bob. This Spanish-language proposal I got looks pretty good. Who is Iris Pena?"

Chapter Forty-Five

WATCHING THE POURING RAIN through the lobby's glass doors, Iris turned to Will at the security desk.

Before she could speak, he said, "I've already called a cab for you, Sunshine."

With a tired grin, she said, "Thanks."

"Where's your boyfriend tonight? Let me know if he's not treating you right, you hear?"

Giggling, Iris replied, "He's been working late the last few days."

Grabbing a golf umbrella from behind the desk, he stepped outside the door and held it open for her as he shielded her from the driving pellets. They shuffled quickly to the waiting cab, and Will opened the back door for her. Once she was settled, he waved and sloshed back to the brightly lit building, glowing in the darkness of the cloudy evening.

Dripping and soggy, Iris pushed through the revolving door of her apartment building, trudged to the elevator, and pressed the up button.

In her apartment, she closed the front door and dropped her bags in the hallway before peeling off her wet clothes, letting each item drop wherever she was at the moment it left her body. Wrapping herself tightly in a heavy cotton robe, she fell across the bed and pulled the phone from the nightstand.

She'd called Rey every night since she'd left New York. He'd cancelled most of his trips for the rest of the month to be free to check in on his mother. In addition, he and Rajesh had been working hard interviewing and hiring new talent to help them with the growth of the company. She dialed his home number and lay back on the pillows waiting for him to answer.

"Hello?" Rey said with a laugh.

"Hey there," Iris said, instantly smiling at the lightness in his voice.

"Hey, girl. What's up?"

"Not too much. Just checking in to make sure you're all right."

There was a pause and a muffled sound, like Rey had put his hand over the mouthpiece, as he spoke to someone in the background. Though muffled, Iris could hear laughter. Female laughter.

"Rey?"

"Sorry. Someone from work stopped by."

"Maybe I should call you back."

"Yeah, that would be good. Let me hit you back a little later. I'm getting ready for something here."

Hanging up, Iris was confused by a sudden pang of jealousy. She rolled over and picked up the remote for the television. Flipping absently through the channels, she wondered who the woman "from work" was.

Knowing she should be happy her boy was laughing considering the pain he'd endured, she was unable to erase the feeling of envy. She picked up the phone and dialed Jonathan's number.

Chapter Forty-Six

ZUMA WAS FUMING. HER FOOD lay cold and congealing on the plate she'd pushed to the side. She was losing the battle to control her emotions in front of Bob. Having finished off a salad, a steak, a baked potato and, now, devouring a disgustingly sweet dessert, he barely noticed Zuma's anguish.

Zuma turned each page gingerly, as though it might cut her fingers if she was too rough. The damn girl had given her a few sheets of paper on Mexican Americans when she had *this*. The thick binder included detailed information on at least six different Latin and Hispanic markets in the United States.

She didn't just put this shit together in the last two weeks. She had to get help from someone. That bitch.

Interrupting Zuma's deep concentration on the demographics and matching geographic map for Cuban Americans, Bob, mouth full, said, "Pretty damn amazing, huh?"

"Mm," Zuma replied deep in thought. *How the hell did she get this information? It took me a whole fucking quarter to prepare a similar proposal for African Americans. And I'm black!*

"Steve thinks it's worth looking into," Bob said, shoveling the last bite of dessert in his mouth.

Zuma froze, hoping she'd heard him wrong. "Pardon me?"

"I said, Steve thinks it looks good."

Zuma didn't comment. *How did Steven Searson, the chief marketing officer, see a copy of the damn thing? And before I did?*

"Did you help her with this?" Bob asked.

Zuma looked at him with her brows furrowed. "Of course, Bob. You don't think a college intern walked in here and just pulled this together in a month, do you?"

Bob's eyes narrowed slightly as he stopped eating and looked at the top of Zuma's bent head. She continued intently perusing the pages of the document with deep concentration.

"Of course," he said. "You just seemed so surprised when I showed the proposal to you."

Zuma realized how transparent her anger, confusion, and surprise must be. She suddenly sat up straight, giving her prettiest smile, and said, "You're right. You know me so well and see right through me every time."

She sat back and propped her elbow on the arm of her chair to give him the full explanation.

"I gave Iris an assignment when she started. I've been helping her by showing her how to do research, gather statistics, and prepare a proposal. Since you and I were traveling so much, I left her with all the information we'd gathered to do the final write up. I probably look surprised, because I didn't think she'd pull it all together so quickly. This is my first time seeing the finished product, and it is... just... so amazing." Zuma stuttered on the words of praise that she honestly felt but didn't want to admit.

Looking back at the page she'd stopped on, she murmured distractedly, "That's exactly why I gave her the assignment."

Satisfied with her answer, Bob paid the check and hastened them to the hotel room above.

As Zuma lay under Bob thinking about Iris, Iris lay under Jonathan thinking about Rey.

Chapter Forty-Seven

Friday, June 15

ZUMA'S ATTITUDE HADN'T improved by Friday morning when she walked past Betty's desk and looked in the direction of Iris's cubicle.

Betty picked up the binder resting on her desk and inserted it in an interoffice envelope. Carrying it with two other memos resting on top, she walked purposefully in the path Zuma had taken.

Betty replaced the smirk on her face with an ignorant secretary look as she walked into the large office made dark by the clouds still hanging in the sky outside. She dropped the large envelope and two memos in the bin and turned, without hesitation, to walk out.

"Wait."

Betty stopped at the door and turned back. "Yes?"

"What's this?" Zuma asked, holding up the heavy interoffice envelope, letting the two memos slip off onto the desk.

"I don't know. Iris left it for you yesterday. You left early, and she couldn't get it to you."

"Did you help her with this?" Zuma asked abruptly, squinting at the matronly woman standing before her.

"Help her with what, Ms. Harris?" Betty affected a sincerely confused look.

"Never mind," Zuma answered. "You can go." She shooed at Betty and quickly pulled the binder from the envelope.

She'd read each page so intently last night that she had the content of the proposal memorized. The irritation she'd felt then returned full force now as she looked again at the brightly colored maps with perfect color-coded legends in the margin.

Standing angrily, Zuma pushed her chair back forcefully, slamming it into the molding around the window. She stood, seething, in the doorway of her office and looked across the room to Iris's hair hanging smoothly over one eye, the other side tucked tightly behind the opposite ear, as she listened intently to someone on the phone. Her face was unreadable from the distance.

You don't know who you're playing with.

Zuma stalked across the room, unseeing of anything except the prey that lay in her path. Iris saw her out of the corner of her eye, but pretended she didn't notice the angry woman coming toward her, like a vulture to roadkill.

Looking over the low cubicle wall, Zuma spoke. "Iris, I need to see you in my office. Now." Her voice was cold steel, and her eyes matched the tone.

Iris held up one finger, continuing to listen to the speaker on the other end of the phone, and quickly jotted something down on a yellow pad on the desk.

Zuma sucked in her breath. *Did she just tell me to wait?*

Iris spoke into the receiver. "Okay, thanks so much Rick. I'll see you this afternoon. Yes. Okay. Goodbye."

Rick?

Iris hung up the phone and wrote Rick's name on a line in her

Franklin planner. Looking up, she smiled brightly, making her dimple and white teeth shine. "I'm sorry, Zuma. What did you say?"

Zuma clenched and unclenched her fists. *Remember yoga breathing, remember yoga breathing.*

"I would like to see you in my office. Now."

Zuma felt a corner of her upper lip twitching as she struggled for self control. Her face felt warm, and she knew it was probably turning a shade of pink. Unable to stand looking at Iris any longer, she whirled and walked stiffly back to her office.

Iris wanted to call Betty, but she was scared Zuma would have a breakdown if she did. Smoothing her skirt, she picked up her suit jacket and put it on, buttoning it as she made her way to Zuma's office.

The fucking yoga breathing isn't working, Zuma thought, watching Iris make her way to the office.

"Come in and sit," Zuma said tightly when Iris arrived in the doorway.

Once Iris was settled, Zuma picked up a black binder and slid it across the desk.

"Oh, you got it! What did you think?" Iris asked with feigned excitement.

She can't be serious, Zuma thought.

"I think it's good and very thorough. However, I feel it's a little too thorough."

"Too thorough? What do you mean?" Iris appeared confused.

"Where did you get the demographics and statistics?"

"I researched it."

"Where?" Zuma asked, attempting to control her mounting anger.

"Online," Iris said as coolly as possible.

"Online," Zuma repeated, unbelievingly.

"Yes, online," Iris replied, nodding her head slowly.

"And what company came up on your search online that had this type of information?"

"International Communications," Iris said as nonchalantly as possible.

Zuma made a mental note of the company name and sat back in her chair. Attempting to make Iris uneasy, she stared fixedly at the girl. But Iris only smiled back, sweetly, and crossed her legs in the casual way that pissed Zuma off.

"Why did you give the proposal to Bob O'Brien?" Zuma asked.

Iris knew the question was coming, but she still shifted uncomfortably in the chair.

"Well, I figured you were out so much and really busy, so it wouldn't hurt to submit it to both of you, in case one of you was too busy to review it."

Bullshit, Zuma thought, taking note of the sudden uneasiness her question had created. "Who else did you feel should receive it... since I was so busy?"

Iris cleared her throat and uncrossed her legs. "Mr. Searson."

Zuma's face grew warm with anger. Zuma knew she could get Bob to believe anything she said, but Steven Searson? This was going to take some creativity and scheming.

With a tight line to her mouth that couldn't quite be called a smile, Zuma said, "Good work, Iris. That's all."

As Iris stood to leave, Zuma stopped her suddenly.

"Oh, I almost forgot. What are you working on with Rick?"

"He's just bringing me up to date on the follow-up required for the rollout of Pdata," Iris lied smoothly.

Satisfied, Zuma nodded and watched as Iris walked away.

Zuma steepled her fingers and tapped them together as she

thought. *International Communications. Time to do a little research of my own.*

Iris walked past Betty's desk and gave her a nervous wide-eyed glance. "I'll call you from downstairs," she said, rushing to the elevators.

Betty nodded without a word.

Iris sighed with relief when the elevator doors slid open on the eleventh floor. She walked briskly to Jonathan's office. Peeking in the door, she saw that he was on the phone with his back to the doorway. Tiptoeing into the office, she sat quietly in one of the chairs and wiggled her legs impatiently. She couldn't wait to tell him everything and call upstairs to fill Betty in.

"Honey, I can't do that right now," Jonathan whispered into the phone.

Honey?

With his back still to Iris, Jonathan continued talking in a low voice. "Look, I'm at work, and I can't talk right now. I promise I'll see you tonight, and we can discuss it then, okay baby?"

Baby?

Iris stood up with a sharp intake of breath. Jonathan whirled around in shock. Covering the mouth of the phone, he whispered, "What are you doing here, Iris?"

Iris felt her mouth moving, but no sound came out. Looking into his eyes, she tried to back out of the room, bumping into the wall.

"I have to go. I'll call you back," Jonathan said into the phone before hanging it up and rushing around the desk to follow Iris down the hall to the elevators.

"Iris, wait!"

"No, it's okay. I know you're busy. I shouldn't have come down unannounced," Iris stammered, looking everywhere except at Jonathan. She felt a dull pain in her chest and absently reached up to touch her left breast.

184

Honey. Baby. I promise I'll see you tonight. Iris kept hearing the whispered words on mental playback.

Clasping her elbow, Jonathan attempted to pull her back. "Iris, there's something I need to tell you."

Whipping around to face him, she whispered, "No, there isn't."

"But this is important, and I want to share it with you."

Jonathan was holding her arm close to his chest and gazing at her with that mesmerizing green stare when the elevator door opened and Zuma stepped out. The three of them froze, but Zuma was the first to recover.

"Jonathan, Iris," she said by way of a brief greeting as she brushed past them.

Iris's mind raced. Suddenly remembering the lie she'd told Zuma about her meeting with Rick, she broke free of Jonathan's grasp and ran to the glass door, peeking through. As she suspected, Zuma was headed for Rick's office. *Shit.*

Turning, she rushed past Jonathan into the waiting elevator.

Chapter Forty-Eight

Saturday, June 16

REY WATCHED EBONY CRENSHAW from across the computer lab. Young kids were scattered throughout the room, chattering and clicking on keyboards. They were playing math games, working on lab assignments, or just checking out various youth-related websites.

The lab's grand opening was a week ago, but Rey had missed it with the passing of his father. So, he and Rajesh had hosted a social at Rey's apartment on Thursday evening for the new lab's staff and teachers from the school. Throughout the building, center staff and volunteer teachers were busily moving from room to room, working diligently to keep the TravelWise Youth Technology Center running smoothly and the students involved.

When Rey talked with Ebony about the idea to put his money into an existing technology program, he had no idea it would blossom into something he cared about as much as, maybe even more than, his online travel company. With this, he was able to do more than make money for his own pleasure. Now, he was helping a neglected population of kids realize the dream he'd had as a young adult.

Ebony leaned over a boy, explaining a math problem on the screen of his computer. Rey admired the patience in her voice and mannerisms. Not only was she smart, but she also cared about these kids and the future of their generation. Breaking into his thoughts, the girl next to him tapped his arm, pointed to the screen, and asked him a question. With one last glance at Ebony, he turned to the girl and her computer.

Two hours later, the children filtered out the front door, either heading for the bus stop or the subway. Rey slowly rolled his head and massaged his neck as Ebony walked up next to him.

"I still don't know how you do it every day," he said, still rubbing his shoulders.

She nodded with a grin and said, "You get used to it. And sometimes, a light goes on in their eyes, and you see the potential. Knowing I played a part in that makes me look forward to getting up and coming to see them. And they appreciate that."

As though to prove her point, a boy ran up and hugged her tightly around the waist. "Thanks, Ms. Crenshaw. See you next weekend."

"Alright, Akil. Tell your grandmother I said hello," she said, hugging him back before he ran off to catch up with the others.

Stealing a look at her profile, Rey cleared his throat. "Ebony, if you don't have plans for this afternoon, how'd you like to have lunch with me?"

With a smile and a tilt of her head, she said, "Mr. Hargrave, I'd be honored."

Even though the day was overcast, Rey felt like the sun had just peeked through the clouds.

Chapter Forty-Nine

"WHY DIDN'T YOU TELL me about this 'teen phone' thing?" Zuma tossed at Bob.

Rolling his eyes upward, Bob sighed before falling back on the mountain of pillows at the head of Zuma's bed. His erection was aching to be touched, and not by his own hands.

"Zuma, I already told you. I found out about it the same time you did. And it's called *Tween* Phone, not teen phone."

"Tween, teen. What-the-fuck-ever," Zuma ranted, pacing around the bed in white silky v-string underwear and a sheer bra of the same color that barely held onto her ample breasts as they bobbed and wobbled with her angry marching.

Bob's mouth watered as he watched her dark nipples rubbing against the material, standing angrily at attention. Under the satin sheets, he began stroking the head of his erection.

"Zuma, please," he begged. "If you'd just come over here, I could explain everything."

Bending over her vanity, Zuma rifled through the drawers in search of something. Bob continued fondling himself as he watched the white material of the v-string disappear between her butt cheeks while she bent and moved, hunting in the drawers. Finding what she wanted, Zuma stood, the stiletto slippers making her butt appear firm and round. Eventually, a trail of smoke rose from her form, and Bob realized she was smoking a cigarette. She didn't smoke often, and it was usually a sign of boredom or displeasure when she did. He guessed displeasure was the reason this time.

Sliding from the sheets, he moved behind her and rubbed his dick on the white silk triangle at the top of her ass. "Feeling better?" he asked, sensually massaging the firm nipples pressing through the sheer material of her bra.

She exhaled in answer and let him desire her. Slipping his hand down the front of the tiny panties, he felt the dampness between her legs, and his erection throbbed with wanting. Unhooking the back of the bra, he let her breasts bounce free. Slowly, he turned her around and pulled her panties down. He was so tall and she so short, that he had to kneel on the thick carpet to pull the white strings from her hips to her feet, allowing her to step daintily out of them.

Smelling her scent, he stayed on his knees and pressed his nose to the darkness between her legs. She trembled slightly as his tongue probed her swollen lips. She took another hit of the cigarette and exhaled deeply, letting his tongue explore deeper.

Without warning, the image of Professor Simons on his knees, pulling down her panties in a nasty motel room, appeared vividly behind her closed eyes, and she instantly stiffened.

Feeling the change in her body, Bob stopped, looking up.

"Zuma?"

Determined not to let the college professor destroy her twice, Zuma fought against his memory as she pulled Bob to his feet and dragged him to the bed.

"I'm sorry, sweetie. I'm just so tense and tired. Please don't stop."

Snuggling deep into the pillows, Zuma spread her legs wide and pulled his head down to complete what he'd started. Sexually excited and scared she'd turn him away again, he dove into the lovemaking with renewed fervor.

An hour later, his scheduled golf game was over, and he had to return home for a dinner party his wife was planning. Reluctantly, he stared down at Zuma's sprawled figure. As much as he wanted to reach out and touch her warm skin, he needed to get home. Slipping from the sheets, he dressed and, still staring at her perfect form, crept from the room.

Chapter Fifty

IRIS LAY ON HER LIVING ROOM floor, staring out the windows to the starless dark sky. The phone jingled next to her. Glancing at the caller I.D. and seeing Jonathan's home number, she returned her watery gaze to the sky outside.

The source of her pain had been calling throughout the night. Why did men have to be so deceitful and sneaky? Wasn't she pretty enough, sexy enough, smart enough, exciting enough? They were never happy with the one perfect woman they had. Where were the men like Papa and Pop, who loved, cherished, and worshipped their women?

Almost instantly, the phone rang again. Iris snatched it from the floor, jabbing the talk button, and yelled, "What do you *want?*" into the mouthpiece.

"Iris!" her mother's voice replied in a shocked tone. "What's going on with you?"

"Oh, Mom. Sorry," Iris said closing her eyes. This was a conversation she really didn't want to have right now.

"Baby, what's wrong?" Iris heard the concern in her mother's voice and sighed, debating how to handle this.

Softly, she answered. "Mom, I love you, and I appreciate your concern, but, for real, I just need to be alone and quiet for a little while.

Okay?"

There was silence on the line while her mother contemplated the request. "Okay, honey. Call me when you're ready. I love you."

"Love you too, Mom. Thanks."

Clicking off the phone, her mind wandered to Rey. She got up, pulled a stick from the incense holder on the bookshelf, and lit it. She watched the tip of the stick glow golden as a thin stream of smoke snaked into the air. Blowing out the flame on the incense, Iris inhaled the aroma that reminded her of Rey's hair. She placed the smoking stick in a hole on the holder and fell onto the futon with the phone in her hand.

Should I or shouldn't I? After several seconds of internal debate, Iris dialed Rey's cell number and prayed he was alone.

"Hey girl, whassup?" he answered on the second ring. Iris exhaled the breath she'd been holding.

"Nothing. Just calling to check in. How are things going?"

"Actually, not too bad. Mama's on a trip with her sisters, and Raj and I just opened a youth technology center," Rey said proudly. Iris could hear the smile in his voice.

He opened a technology center and didn't tell me? Feeling left out and hurt, she ignored the part about the technology center and commented, instead, on his mother.

"That's great about your mother. I'm really glad she's not mourning, in the traditional sense."

Rey laughed out loud. "I couldn't imagine her doing that, anyway. She's too busy to mourn like other people."

He wanted to tell her about the computer lab, but since she didn't say anything about it, he simply asked, "What's goin' on in your world?"

Iris stifled the sigh she felt and said, "Not too much."

"Unh huh. That was the weakest 'Not too much' I've heard in a

192

long time. Come on girl, I know something's goin' on. Speak."

Iris knew she couldn't tell Rey about problems with a man he didn't even know existed. And if she did, he'd do what he always did. Say "I told you so" and dog the brother out for the rest of eternity. Plus, things were different between them now.

"I just have some stuff going on at work."

"Sounds like it. What's happenin'?"

Iris filled him in on the latest drama with Zuma and the Hispanic campaign.

"Damn," he said when she'd finished.

"Yeah, and that's not all." She went on to tell him about the Tween Phone and the lie she told Zuma to protect her idea.

Rey was confused. "Why are you going through so much shit to hide stuff from someone who's going to have to handle the project when you leave in a month? It sounds like you're causing yourself more grief than necessary."

"I hear you, but you don't understand the full situation. If I don't prove to someone outside of Zuma that I'm the creator of these ideas and programs, then she can give me any evaluation she wants, and I won't have any recourse."

"Yeah, but you don't know what ties and relationships she has with the other executives and managers you're communicating and working with."

With a grunt, Iris said, "I know one. She's sleeping with the V.P. of marketing."

"Aw shit!" Rey exclaimed.

"Okay, now you understand."

They were both silent in their own thoughts before Rey spoke again.

"Um, I want to ask you something, but I don't want you to take it the wrong way."

Iris braced for whatever was coming next. "Speak," she said, mimicking him.

He walked to the kitchen and rummaged in the refrigerator, looking for something to drink, as he said, "I've been immersed in work the last couple of months, and with..." He hesitated, searching for the right words, "...Pop and stuff here. I think I need to take a break. A real break, not a working vacation. The fourth is coming up in a couple of weeks, and I thought maybe you'd want to come with me on a trip."

Before Iris could respond, he rushed to add, "Don't get the wrong idea, now! I'm not tryin' to step to you or anything. I just think we both need a break, and we usually spend the fourth together anyway, so..." He let the rest of his sentence trail off.

It had been three weeks since the Memorial Day incident, and neither of them had mentioned anything about it since the conversation when they had agreed to be friends. He was right. They did both need a break, and she didn't have any plans now that Jonathan was sneaking around.

When she didn't answer, he said, "I'd understand if you said no. But as your friend, I'm offering."

"Yes."

Expecting her rejection, he choked on the juice he'd been drinking. "What?" he spluttered.

"I said yes."

Chapter Fifty-One

Saturday, June 18

IRIS WAS TENSE AS SHE walked into the building on Monday morning. She'd spent the rest of the weekend mooning around her apartment, refusing to shower or brush her teeth, and watching Lifetime. The trip with Rey was exactly what she needed. To get away from the drama of Baltimore… and Jonathan.

As she stood waiting for the elevator door to open, Zuma stepped next to her.

"Good morning, Iris," she said in an oddly polite manner.

Iris was immediately on guard as she responded in kind. The elevator doors opened, and the morning crowd of people stepped in. Pressed close in the crowded elevator, Iris could feel Zuma's eyes on her. The elevator stopped on random floors, and people dispersed until Iris and Zuma were the only two in the airless box.

Without turning, Zuma said, "So how are things with Jonathan?"

"Excuse me?" Iris said, with a hint of attitude.

"Jonathan," Zuma repeated, turning a sweetly smiling face to Iris's stony one. "You *are* seeing him aren't you?"

The doors slid apart on their floor, and Zuma stepped out in front of Iris as she waited for an answer, daring the younger woman to lie.

Iris debated her answer. If Zuma already knew they were dating, there was no point in lying, and she couldn't tell the whole truth and admit they were having problems.

"Things are well." She attempted to speed up her pace and get to the safe haven of her cubicle.

"Good morning, Betty," Zuma said sweetly, as they passed the reception desk together.

Iris glanced at Betty and saw the questions in her arched brows. She raised the corner of her upper lip in a sneer to the back of Zuma's head, causing Betty to smile.

"Well, I'll see you later," Zuma said as she broke off and continued up the hallway to her corner office while Iris walked the short distance to her cubicle.

Barbara peeked over the low wall. "Hey woman, is everything okay? You look like hell."

"Gee, thanks."

"Well, you do. Wanna talk about it?"

"No."

Putting her hands up, Barbara said, "Okay, but if you do, you know I'm always willing to listen."

Looking up at Barbara's round face, Iris attempted a smile. "Thanks, Barbara. Really. I just have a couple of things to work through."

Barbara nodded her understanding. "Been there, done that. Remember, I'm here."

As her friend walked away, Iris turned on her computer and began checking voice mails. More messages from Jonathan. She deleted each one without listening to the recordings. A message from Rick outlining the next steps for Tween Phone brought her a sliver of joy, until she remembered that she was working with him *and* Jonathan on the project.

She studied the calendar in her Franklin planner. The fourth fell on a Wednesday this year. The office was offering Monday and Tuesday as optional personal days or floating holidays since so many people were taking them off. If she could just make it through two more weeks to next Friday when her Air Jamaica flight took off from BWI, she'd be all right. Five days in Montego Bay would definitely cheer her up.

The phone rang on her desk, bringing her back to reality. "Hello, Iris Pena speaking."

"Iris," came Zuma's syrupy response. "Since you're the creator of the Hispanic consumer marketing proposal, Bob and I thought you'd like to participate in the upcoming meetings we've scheduled with Steven Searson."

Something underhanded was definitely going on. Iris smelled the setup, but she had no options.

"Uh, okay. I'd be happy to participate," she said as calmly as possible.

"Great. I'll email you the meeting dates, times, and locations," Zuma said in her fake sweet voice.

"Thank you."

Zuma hung up the phone and pressed buttons on her PDA until she found the New York number she'd saved for International Communications. Dialing the number, she drummed her French manicure on the edge of the desk while she waited for an answer.

"Good morning, this is Zuma Harris from Shearing Wireless Technologies calling for Mr. John Hernandez." Zuma waited patiently to be connected.

If she was going to prove the Hispanic marketing idea was originated by her, she had to embrace it and make it hers. Forging a relationship with International Communications was the first step.

"Good morning, Ms. Harris. How are you this morning?"

Zuma felt a familiar tingle as she listened to the faint accent in a deep, rich voice. If he looked anything like his voice sounded, this relationship could be a win-win for real.

"I'm great, thank you, Mr. Hernandez. And you?"

"Good, good. How can I help you today?"

"As we discussed last week, I've spoken with the chief marketing officer and vice president of marketing here at Shearing, and we'd love to bring you in to discuss your company's services. Would you be available at all this week or next?"

After they confirmed the date and made a little small talk, Zuma attempted what little Spanish she remembered from high school, hoping to impress him with her effort.

"Gracias, Senor Hernandez. Tiene un dia bien," she said, in poorly articulated Spanish.

He chuckled appreciatively at her attempt. "Good job, Ms. Harris. See you next week."

Chapter Fifty-Two

IRIS WAS HEADING FOR THE elevators when Betty stopped her.

"Iris, sign this for me, please," she said, placing a covered letter on the edge of the desk.

Iris glanced quickly at the covered sheet with her name typed at the bottom and frowned.

"Betty, I'm not going to sign something I can't even see. What is this?" she asked skeptically, trying to lift the folder covering the body of the letter.

Betty slapped her hand. Seeing the mistrust in the younger girl's body language, Betty took her hand. "Trust me. The less you know, the better off you'll be."

Iris's shoulders slumped as she looked sadly at the secretary. "I've screwed everything up, Betty."

"Iris, you were put in a no-win situation. Have you noticed there are no people of color in this department except me?" Iris shook her head mournfully. "There's a reason for that. You couldn't have succeeded if you'd done nothing right or if you'd done everything right. You're too pretty, sweet, and smart. You're a threat. You only have a month left here. Try to enjoy the last few weeks, and don't let that heifer get to you. This letter is simply a safety net — only there if something goes wrong."

Pulling her hand gently from Betty's, Iris scribbled her signature on the paper and moped to the elevators.

When the doors opened on the eleventh floor, Iris straightened her shoulders, determined not to let Jonathan see her down, and walked proudly to Rick's office without looking in the direction of her former boyfriend's office door. Coming through the entrance, she smiled genuinely at Rick who welcomed her in.

"Hi there, little lady with the great ideas. Let's get to work," he said in his booming voice.

Iris sat and opened her notebook, but she couldn't help wondering where Jonathan was. "Is Jonathan joining us today?" she asked as casually as possible.

"Nope, he's in Ohio with a team wrapping up some loose ends on the U.P.Ex deal. Unfortunately, you're stuck with just me," he teased.

Relieved, Iris allowed herself to smile. At least she could focus on the project for a couple of days without letting emotions get in the way.

* * *

Zuma dialed Bob's office. After exchanging a few marketing updates, she smoothly led into her real reason for calling.

"I've scheduled an executive from International Communications to provide a presentation on the Hispanic campaign I initiated. He'll be in next week."

Bob's positive response buoyed her confidence. But, just to keep all options in play, she wrapped their call up with a hint of what she knew Bob liked best.

"So, I'll see you tomorrow in the twelfth-floor boardroom after your meeting with HR and Steven?" she asked coyly.

"You got it," Bob replied eagerly.

Zuma hung up with a smug smile and spun around to appreciate her office view. *This situation is getting better and better every day*, she thought.

But her reverie was short-lived. The U.P.Ex deal was rapidly going downhill and, before the day was out, Zuma had received the summons to fly to the client's headquarter office in Ohio. The afternoon was spent meeting with managers to prepare informational decks and, by Tuesday morning, Zuma was on a plane. Bob's Tuesday meeting with Steven Searson and Margie Castor was a long-forgotten memory.

Chapter Fifty-Three

THAT WEEK, IRIS TOTALLY IMMERSED herself in the Tween Phone project, splitting her time between working alone to compile the statistical results of various tests and sitting with Jim to prepare projections for submission to the review committee for final approval.

Jonathan's week-long absence, though a relief at first, was now a reason for Iris to brood. It was unfinished business, and she wanted answers.

Tapping her pencil on the desk, Iris chewed on her lower lip and glanced at the phone. *I should call him. Why am I avoiding him? He owes me some answers.* Iris dropped the pencil and picked up the receiver. Dialing his cell number, she continued nervously chewing her lip until it hurt. She unconsciously ran her tongue over the sore area as she wondered what to say to him. But she didn't have long to worry. The call rolled right into voicemail.

A canned voice came over the line. *"You've reached the voicemail box for…"* Jonathan Williams. *Please leave a message at the tone, or you may press '5' to page this person."* Iris held the phone, not knowing what to say. Whatever she wanted to say wouldn't be appropriate for voicemail.

She pressed '5' and waited for the prompt to enter her office number. Hanging up the phone, she sighed and stood to stretch.

With Zuma gone and most of the managers off the floor for various reasons, Iris really had nothing to do and no one to talk to. She busied herself with shuffling and re-shuffling the papers on her desk. Then, she checked email and fiddled around on the computer until there was literally nothing left to do. Eventually, she left the cubicle, making stops at the break room and the reception desk to chat with Betty.

By the time she returned to pack up for the day, the message light was blinking on the desk phone. She listened to the message from Jonathan three times before finally pressing '3' to delete it. He said he would be tied up with work and dinner meetings until late, but he was scheduled to fly in tomorrow morning and wanted to know if they could meet for a late breakfast and talk face-to-face.

Gnawing absently on the eraser of her pencil, she considered her plans for the weekend. Sonja was taking the kids to New York to stay with her mother for the weekend, and she was meeting Iris at a spa in a New Jersey beach community for a weekend of pampering. As much as she wanted to hang out with her sister-in-law, Iris couldn't help wanting to hear what Jonathan had to say. She reluctantly dialed Jonathan's number and, when the tone beeped, she left a message.

"Jonathan, I really want to see you tomorrow, but I've already made plans to be out of town. I'll be back Sunday night. Maybe we could meet for dinner?" She didn't know what else to say, so she hung up. For the first time in a long time, Iris could find nothing to divert her thoughts from Jonathan and the other woman.

Chapter Fifty-Four

Saturday, June 23

"YEAH, YOU'RE TRIPPIN' a little bit," Sonja mumbled from beneath the warm towel wrapped tightly around her face.

"You think so?" Iris asked as the aesthetician slathered a cool cream over her face.

"You have Rey telling you he's in love with you, and you're running after a negro who's whispering sweet nothings to another woman," Sonja muttered.

"What? I can barely understand you with the mummy face."

"Forget it, I'll tell you later," Sonja grumbled, sucking her teeth.

She was happy to have a break from her rambunctious boys, and Iris's little mini-drama wasn't going to stop her from enjoying the pampering weekend. *Single women are always making dumb-ass decisions,* she thought as she drifted off.

Iris, still caught up in the emotion of her situation, sighed with frustration. She wanted to talk about it and find out what Sonja thought she should do. She glanced over at her sister-in-law and was crestfallen to see the slow rise and fall of the other woman's chest.

Sonja had fallen asleep.

Allowing the aesthetician to place cool slices of cucumbers over her eyes, Iris reclined on the cushiony table and tried to relax. Sonja was always able to chill out and let go. Usually, Iris was, too, but since working at Shearing, she'd been wound tight and found it hard to be herself. Issues with Zuma, Rey, and Jonathan were turning her into a person she didn't particularly like.

A warm hand touched Iris's arm as a soft voice near her ear directed, "Focus on your breathing. Inhale as slowly as you can, and exhale through your nose. Imagine yourself in your favorite place. See the colors… hear the sounds… feel the environment. Simply let go and… breathe."

The voice was so soft that Iris wasn't actually registering that it existed. She simply followed the commands and, without realizing it, fell into a relaxed sleep, free of dreams.

Chapter Fifty-Five

Sunday, June 24

THE SPA WHERE IRIS AND SONJA stayed didn't allow cell phones on the premises or telephones in the rooms. This was fine with Sonja, who didn't want to hear from her kids until she picked them up from her mother's that afternoon and boarded their plane to Miami. But Iris was dying to find out if Jonathan had returned her call and where they would be meeting for dinner.

After settling the bill at the front desk, they browsed the spa store while waiting for drivers to bring their cars around front. Iris purchased a tub of face cream while Sonja booked another weekend in the fall.

Hugging on the sidewalk in front of their cars, Sonja's face changed as she held Iris at arm's length and stared seriously into her face.

"Iris, I'm concerned about you. Ever since you started this internship, you've changed. You're acting like the girls we used to dog out back in the day. Don't turn into a drama queen. No one likes that shit. You're young, single, attractive, and rich. Oh yeah, and just as a reminder — a sexy mothafucka named Rey's in love with you." She smiled before adding, "Make guys like Jonathan your fuck buddy, and stop taking everything so damn serious."

Iris stood staring at her sister-in-law. Instead of commenting on Sonja's advice, she hugged her again and said, "Thanks for the weekend. Be careful on the road, and call me when you guys get to Miami, okay?"

Sonja kissed her on both cheeks and waved as she climbed into the driver's side of her rental car. Beeping the horn, she pulled off with her windows down and hair flying.

I used to be free and happy like that, Iris thought, sitting behind the wheel of her truck as she watched Sonja's car disappear. Iris rarely drove the Mercedes SUV she'd purchased earlier that year. She usually kept it in a reserved space in her apartment building's garage, but she was looking forward to the freedom of driving herself the three hours back home in luxury. Popping in an old Fugees CD, she let Lauryn Hill's deep, sultry voice fill up the truck and pulled out onto the street.

Once on the freeway, she flipped open her phone and glanced quickly from the traffic to the phone's screen. Three voice messages.

The first was from Rey saying he hadn't heard from her in a few days. "Hit me back when you get a minute." Iris smiled and made a mental note to call him as soon as she finished checking the messages. She pushed buttons and waited to hear Jonathan's voice.

Instead, she heard the voice of one of her sorority sisters. "I'll be in D.C. for the fourth, girl. Call a soror and let me know if we can hook up!"

Iris made a mental note to call her sorority sister back and let her know they'd miss each other this year. She smiled, imagining her holiday trip with Rey. Thinking of Rey almost made Iris forget whose voice she was waiting to hear. When she finally heard it, she wasn't prepared for the message.

"Hi Iris, it's Jonathan. Unfortunately, I have to go out of town for a personal reason and won't be back until Wednesday. I really want to sit down and talk to you face-to-face. Can you pencil me in for lunch on Wednesday? I hope you had a good weekend. I miss you more than you know. Bye."

Out of town on personal business? What does that mean? The curiosity of what Jonathan had to say had been killing her for the last several days. Now, she had to wait even longer. She was tempted to just call him and make him tell her over the phone, but she didn't want to appear desperate.

She weaved through a tangle of slow-moving cars and, when she was back in an open space, set the cruise control and dialed Rey's cell phone.

"Eh, girl. Whassup?" he answered.

Iris couldn't deny the warmth that spread over her when she heard his raspy voice. She smiled unconsciously and talked to him for the remainder of her ride home.

Chapter Fifty-Six

Monday, June 25

THE DIRECTORS AND MANAGERS finally returned after more than a week in Ohio. When Iris stepped into Rick's office to drop off her latest test results, he filled her in on the details of the challenging, but successful, trouble-shooting deal with U.P.Ex.

"Yeah, we'd hit a little rough patch there for a minute, but that's business. Sometimes it's up, and sometimes it's down," he said jovially, reaching for the papers Iris handed him.

They spent some time reviewing and revising the information before Iris returned to her floor and headed confidently for Zuma's office. Sonja was right. She'd gotten real uptight since coming to Shearing, and it was time to stop playing all the silly games.

She waited in the doorway for Zuma to wave her in. "Hello, Iris. How are things going?"

Not put off by Zuma's unnaturally pleasant demeanor, Iris responded, "Good, thanks. I just wanted to confirm that the dates and times for this week's meetings are still on."

Using a stylus, Zuma touched the screen of her PDA a couple of times and nodded. "Yes, we are. There are no changes. Last week had to be adjusted because of the U.P.Ex deal, but that's squared away now," she said briskly.

Zuma looked up, and Iris had the feeling she was being scrutinized. Smiling she said, "Okay, thanks. See you later." But before Iris could walk out the door, Zuma stopped her.

"Iris, I'd like to catch up on your progress with everything. Let's have lunch together tomorrow, and you can bring me up to speed on your projects." Zuma said it in a way that didn't leave room for argument or options. But Iris was getting back to her old self and wasn't really concerned about spending lunch with her mentor, anyway.

With a genuine smile, Iris said, "Sounds good. What time should I plan for?"

Iris's carefree attitude didn't escape Zuma's notice. She imperceptibly scanned Iris from head to toe, noting her glowing skin, extra shiny hair, and impeccably-made designer suit. A twinge of something she couldn't determine pulled at her, but she smoothly replied, "Since we have an afternoon meeting with Bob and Mr. Searson, let's meet early, say eleven forty-five in the lobby?"

Iris confidently responded, "Sounds good. See you then," and walked out the door without a backward glance.

Chapter Fifty-Seven

Tuesday, June 26

A BREEZY AFTERNOON WIND whipped around Zuma and Iris as they walked down Pratt Street across from the Baltimore Convention Center. It had a welcomed effect on the oppressive heat of the day.

A ray of sunlight shone on the golden tresses of Zuma's bone-straight bob as she flipped her hair over one shoulder to let the breeze reach her sweating neck. Iris looked unaffected by the heat as she ran her fingers through her hair. She'd washed it and let it air dry this morning to give it the curly look she'd missed for a month. The back and sides were freshly sheared close, and the style was reminiscent of an old Halle Berry look from the '90s. Zuma looked enviously at the naturally loose curls winding around Iris's long fingers.

"Feel like seafood today?" she asked, stopping in front of Legal Seafood.

"Sounds good to me," Iris replied.

Remembering their last lunch episode, Iris was quick to peruse the menu and order her own meal when the server approached. As crisp salads were placed in front of them, Zuma started the conversation.

"I've talked to Rick about the new tween project you introduced a couple of weeks ago while I was gone." Zuma put a small green leaf in her mouth and chewed slowly, allowing the silence to stretch. The statement didn't require a response, but to ensure Iris's uneasiness, Zuma waited.

Iris didn't take the bait. Instead, she pulled a bite-sized chunk from her bread roll and buttered it before placing it daintily in her mouth. Also chewing slowly, she looked directly into Zuma's cat eyes with a nod of recognition.

"He speaks very highly of you. How do you like working with him?" she asked, placing another forkful of salad into her mouth.

Iris swallowed and tapped the napkin at the corners of her mouth before saying, "Rick is a real treat to be around. He's been completely open with his knowledge and supportive of every idea I've presented to him."

Zuma recognized the dig and smiled appreciatively. Maybe Iris wasn't as innocent as she looked.

"So, tell me more about the tween market. Rick says you're the expert." Zuma rested her fork on the edge of the plate, wiped her mouth, and waited.

Iris decided to divulge a little of the information she'd found easily on a Google search. By the time she'd finished the brief explanation, the server had removed their salad plates and brought another basket of warm bread. Zuma took a roll from the basket and ripped it in half as she listened to Iris speak in slow, even tones. It was obvious the girl was being cautious in her choice of words.

"Interesting," Zuma said simply, biting an edge off the bread.

They sat silently while the server placed their entrees on the table. Making small talk and wanting to put a dent in Zuma's high-and-mighty demeanor, Iris waited for the server to walk away before asking, "How was the leadership conference in New York a couple of weeks ago?"

Zuma stopped mid-chew. *Why is she asking about that?*

Recovering quickly, she replied, "Excellent. I love going to those things, and the company usually chooses me to attend."

Iris looked down at her plate to focus on cutting the tail off a shrimp as she said, "I thought companies sent managers needing to improve their skills to conferences like that." She looked up and smiled sweetly at Zuma as she put the shrimp in her mouth.

Touché, bitch, Zuma thought appreciatively. She enjoyed a challenge.

Her eyes narrowed fractionally as she responded, "Different companies have different philosophies about management and leadership. When you actually *enter* the workforce, you'll learn the difference between the two and understand that only top executives participate in leadership events."

Iris smiled inwardly at the tightness in Zuma's voice. They ate in silence for a few minutes. Noting the time, Zuma said, "We'd better wrap this up. I have a few important things to handle at the office before our meeting."

Iris agreed and dropped her napkin in her plate, excusing herself to the restroom. She was tousling her hair in the mirror just as Zuma walked in and stood next to her above the neighboring sink, pulling lipstick from her purse. Iris smiled at her, pulled a paper towel from the dispenser, and used it to open the door, leaving Zuma alone to sneer at the reflection of Iris's round backside as she retreated.

At the restaurant's entrance, Iris held the door for Zuma, and they stepped into the humidity of the sunny afternoon. During the first few minutes of the walk, Zuma asked a few questions about the Hispanic marketing proposal. Iris answered generically, while easily maintaining step with Zuma's short, quick stride.

Turning onto Lombard Street, Iris saw the Shearing building looming a couple of blocks away. She yearned to click her heels three times, like Dorothy in *Oz*, so she could be magically transported to her desk and away from Zuma.

Interrupting her thoughts, Zuma said, "I'm surprised you came to work today."

"Why?" Iris asked, nonchalantly.

"I thought you'd have gone with Jonathan for Ginger's birthday trip," Zuma said, sneaking a glance at Iris.

"Excuse me?" Iris blurted, before she could stop herself. She stumbled on the sidewalk.

"Ginger's birthday. I thought you'd have gone with Jonathan," Zuma repeated innocently, slowing her steps to wait for Iris.

When Iris didn't answer, Zuma turned to look at her. "You do know Ginger, don't you?"

Iris struggled to swallow her pride and anger as she answered, "No. Who's Ginger?"

"Jonathan's daughter," Zuma said off-handedly, making Iris feel stupid. "You made me think that you and Jonathan were dating, so I assumed you knew Ginger. I wouldn't have brought her up if I'd known you didn't know who she was."

Zuma was enjoying this more than she imagined she would, and she kept her pace slow to prolong the good feeling as long as possible.

Iris's curiosity was killing her, and anger was slowly heating her up. Zuma sensed a chink in the armor and decided to do a little more damage.

Shrugging and feigning innocence, Zuma added, "Maybe he went with his wife instead."

Iris stopped abruptly, causing people walking behind her to quickly shift to avoid bumping into her. Her eyes narrowed to slits as she whispered, "Wife? You're lying."

"You're right, sorry about that," Zuma said, walking back to Iris.

214

"I meant *ex*-wife. When he and *I* started dating, Paula was out of the picture."

Iris looked like someone had slapped her. But Zuma wasn't through. As though suddenly remembering something humorous, she added, "Hey, I bet he still likes to do it doggy-style. Does he?" she asked with a conspiratorial giggle.

Iris's mind raced. *She's lying. Someone please tell me she's lying.*

She stood there, her mouth slightly ajar, looking at Zuma's smiling face, watching her lips moving. She couldn't hear any words, only the sound of the wind whipping around her head and blood rushing in her ears.

Clutching her purse, she turned and began walking as quickly as the skirt wrapped around her legs would allow. Bumping into people in suits, children holding their parent's hand, and homeless people begging for change, Iris moved blindly through the crowd, blinking to push the tears away like windshield wipers as they fell in a stream down her cheeks.

What a fool. I was such a stupid fool. Iris repeated the words like a mantra, pushing through the glass doors and running past Will to the ladies' room in the lobby. She raced into a stall just in time to vomit her lunch into the waiting toilet.

Ex-wife. Daughter named Ginger. Doing it doggy-style with Zuma.

Iris knew it was true. All of it. A pang hit her in the pit of her stomach as the image of Jonathan flipping her on her hands and knees to ride her from the back replayed in her mind. She imagined Zuma's face in place of her own. She saw his hands gripping Zuma's huge breasts instead of her own petite ones.

She leaned weakly against the wall of the stall, fighting to breathe. It hurt to know he had a daughter he didn't tell her about, but most men had children. And an ex-wife was almost normal for a thirty-year-old single, straight man these days. But Zuma? He should have told her about his relationship with Zuma.

Emerging from the bathroom stall, she was relieved to find the restroom empty. She rinsed her face in the bathroom sink and attempted to fix her makeup with what little cosmetics she had in her purse. As she refreshed her lip gloss, the image of Zuma and Jonathan remained stamped in her mind.

Damn him!

Chapter Fifty-Eight

Wednesday, June 27

IRIS OPENED HER EYES ON Wednesday morning wishing the day didn't exist. Not only was she going to see Jonathan in her morning meeting with Rick, but she had agreed to have lunch with him, too. She stared at the alarm clock, wishing the numbers would click backward instead of forward.

Rolling away from the clock to slide out of bed, she thought about the afternoon meeting she was scheduled to attend with Zuma, Bob, and an outside marketing representative. She sighed heavily, remembering the last meeting with Zuma, Bob, and Steven Searson. Zuma had gone through Iris's proposal page-by-page, presenting it like it was her own. Each time Iris had tried to add something or interject, Bob was already seconding Zuma's point or piggybacking on one of her suggestions. Not one original idea came from Zuma's mouth — only memorized facts from the pages of the proposal. A few times, Steven Searson had turned to Iris and asked a question, but Zuma expertly made Iris's comments seem contradictory to what they were trying to achieve.

Trying to fight the dark negativity she was feeling, Iris purposely chose a brightly colored, well-fitting suit dress. It was cooler than a suit, shorter than most of her skirts, and the bright color contrasted prettily with the darkness of her skin and hair.

She spent extra time putting on summery eye shadow and carefully choosing the right shade of lipstick. Using a big hairbrush, she swept the curly hair from the front of her face and slipped on a slender headband. Placing a thin gold necklace with a diamond teardrop hanging from its center around her long neck, she primped in the mirror, feeling better with each pose she struck.

As she rode in a cab the few blocks to work, she reflected on Sonja's pep talk and reminded herself that she would be leaving this mess and these people in just a few weeks. She repeated a silent mantra in her head. *It's their loss. It's their loss.*

Entering the reception area and stopping to lean casually on the edge of Betty's desk, Iris said, "Hi, Betty. How's it going this morning?"

"I should be asking you that question," Betty replied slowly, peering openly into Iris's face. The way Iris had looked yesterday afternoon and her refusal to talk about anything outside of work projects had Betty concerned.

"It's all good," Iris said with a wink as she strolled past to her cubicle.

Betty tried, unsuccessfully, to read the expression on Iris's face as she walked away.

Zuma strained to see their exchange from her office, but she was too far away and couldn't hear what they were saying. Zuma thought the distance must be distorting what she saw, because it looked like Iris was smiling and being social. She wasn't expecting a smiling Iris after the teary one she'd gloated over yesterday. Quite honestly, seeing Iris's unhappiness after their lunch had been the highlight of Zuma's year to date. She was disappointed to see this renewed version of her intern. Deciding she needed to observe the girl closer, Zuma waited

218

until Iris made it to her cubicle and called her extension.

"Hi, Iris. It's Zuma. Could you please come to my office for a moment?"

"Sure," Iris answered more pleasantly than she felt.

Zuma pushed the door shut behind Iris as the younger woman sat.

Leaning on the front edge of the desk, Zuma started. "Iris, I want to — need to — apologize for the things I said yesterday. I had no idea you were ignorant of Jonathan's personal life, and I was attempting to be funny when I asked about his... um... sexual preferences." Zuma spoke in soft tones of false sincerity.

Iris wasn't expecting this speech and racked her brain for a response.

"Uh. Thanks, Zuma."

Suddenly, Iris's gut instinct turned on, and she made a quick decision to change things up. So, she said, "Actually, I should be the one apologizing. I will admit, you caught me off guard with the information you shared, but Jonathan and I are no longer..." She hesitated, fluttering her hands in search of the right words, "... together. We decided to end it in lieu of our professional relationship. I'm sure you know how that is."

Zuma smiled at Iris's attempt to save face. "Right. So, I guess when I saw you two before my trip to Ohio, you were *ending* it." Zuma lifted her hands to make air quotes around the words "ending it."

Iris was quick to reply. "It doesn't really matter either way, does it? I only have one more month here, and the rest of you will have each other to deal with when I'm gone. Is there anything else you'd like to discuss with me? I have a meeting with Rick in a few minutes."

Zuma bristled at Iris's quick comeback. "Well, I'm glad that you can be adult about things. I know it's often difficult for young people to function in the real world."

Zuma cleared her throat and walked around the desk to push a button on her PDA. "Quickly, let me remind you that we have another meeting this afternoon about the Hispanic marketing campaign. As you mentioned, you'll be leaving us soon, and it would be good if you could be present to share what knowledge you have before you go."

"Of course. I'll see you then," Iris said, rising, opening the door, and walking out without a backward glance.

Chapter Fifty-Nine

JONATHAN STARED AT IRIS throughout the meeting. He was shocked that she was smiling pleasantly and responding positively to his comments and suggestions. It was difficult for him to concentrate, and Rick had to bring his attention back to the subject being discussed more than once. When the meeting was over, Jonathan ran to catch up with her in the reception area.

"Iris, you look fantastic," he said, genuinely.

"Thanks." She smiled brightly at him.

"Are we still on for lunch?" he asked hesitantly.

"Sure. I have a couple of calls to make upstairs, but I'll meet you in the lobby at twelve o'clock, okay?"

Relaxing, he smiled. "Okay. See you in a few."

He wasn't prepared for this Iris. He knew she was upset when she'd left his office a couple of weeks ago, and she initially hadn't returned any of his phone calls. He wasn't even sure if she was receiving them. But she'd called him, agreed to go to lunch with him, *and* she was acting normal and professional. Maybe the lunch conversation wouldn't be so bad after all.

An hour later, he led her to the taxi stand in front of the building.

They took a cab around the harbor and rode over a cobbled street across from several narrow row homes erected on a hill.

Turning into what looked like a parking garage, the taxi drove around a circle and stopped in front of a restaurant. "The Rusty Scupper" was carved on a wooden sign in front.

"I know how much you like seafood, and the food is pretty good here," Jonathan said, holding the car door open for her to exit.

In the restaurant, they ascended the stairs and sat on a cushioned bench in the lobby to wait for a table. Iris looked around contentedly while Jonathan fidgeted uncomfortably with his hands and cell phone.

As they were being seated, Iris said, "You seem nervous, Jonathan."

"Nervous?" He chuckled uneasily. "Nah."

They ordered, and Iris sat with her hands folded lightly on the table, looking at Jonathan's handsome features. *I wonder if his daughter looks like him. She's probably as beautiful as he is handsome.*

Jonathan started. "Iris, I need to apologize."

Iris was ready with a reply. "For what? Forgetting to tell me that you were married and have a daughter?"

Jonathan's face registered shock, and his jaw hung slack.

"How did you know about..." he breathed, unable to finish the sentence.

"What? How did I know about your divorce over your extramarital affair with Zuma Harris?"

Jonathan's mouth dropped completely open, and his eyes stretched wide.

"Who told you that?" he whispered in a voice that was barely audible above the clinking of silverware and talking around them.

"Does it matter?" Iris asked.

Iris smiled at the server as she placed bread, soup, and salads on

222

the table. Dipping a piece of sour dough bread in the creamy orange sauce and taking a bite, Iris said, "This is delicious. You should try some."

Jonathan ignored her reference to the food and answered her question. "Yes, Iris, it does."

"What matters to me is that *you* didn't tell me," Iris said, showing a little of her real emotions for the first time.

She picked up her fork and speared a slice of cucumber. Chewing, she noticed that he hadn't touched any of his food. Getting her emotions under control again, she said, "Your cream of crab soup is getting cold."

"Fuck the soup!" he hissed, shoving the bowl to the side, causing white cream to slosh over the edge onto the table.

"Missionary or doggy-style?"

"*What?*" Jonathan said, his green eyes flashing.

"You said 'fuck the soup,' so I'm asking you how you like it. Missionary or doggy-style? Zuma seems to think you prefer doggy-style and, after our last couple of — you know — I'd have to say that she's right." Iris continued to munch on the food in front of her.

Jonathan was so stunned, he couldn't immediately respond.

Iris finished her salad and innocently asked, "Aren't you hungry?" as she surveyed his untouched food.

Finally recovering, Jonathan retorted. "You seem to think this is pretty damn funny. I'm obviously wasting my time," he said in a low voice. He opened his billfold to pull out a credit card and drop it on the messy table. Craning his neck, he searched for their server.

Iris leaned across the table, bringing her face inches from his. In a pinched, even voice, she said, "No, Jonathan. I didn't think it was funny to walk into your office and hear you calling someone I don't know 'honey' and 'baby.' It was even harder to hear from my mentor, someone who *shouldn't* know your personal business, that you were gone for the last two days on a vacation with your ex-wife and daughter — neither of whom I even knew existed. I was definitely not laughing when I found out that you cheated on your wife and the mother of your child with the very woman you've pretended not to know that well on a personal level. No, I don't think this is funny, but I *am* tired of being the butt of Zuma's jokes."

Iris sat back, looking at Jonathan. She waited for him to speak. To challenge anything she'd said. She wished he would say it was all a lie. But he sat silent, simply looking at her with an unreadable expression.

"Just as I thought. You have nothing to say," she whispered, shaking her head sadly.

Jonathan gestured with his hands as he said, "Iris, I tried to tell you. I was talking to my daughter that Friday when you overheard my conversation."

Iris put up her hand. "Save it for someone who cares. Thanks for lunch, it was delicious."

She stood and walked to the counter in the lobby to request a taxi. After a few minutes, Jonathan caught up to her.

"Iris, there's still more I have to tell you. You don't have all the facts."

Looking him dead in the eye, Iris said, "Thank you, but I'm not interested. Would you like to share a ride back to work?"

"You can just throw us away that easily?"

"I didn't throw us away, Jonathan. With your secrets, you made sure there was no *us* to begin with," Iris said bitterly.

When he didn't respond, Iris sighed resignedly. "Don't make the last few weeks of my internship difficult, Jonathan. I have to work with both you and Zuma to finish this internship and get the hell out of here. Just let it go, okay?"

Jonathan let his eyes roam over her face. A cab pulled up in front, and the man behind the counter waved for their attention. Iris gave Jonathan a small, sad smile before turning and walking down the stairs to the car waiting below.

Chapter Sixty

ZUMA GREETED JOHN HERNANDEZ in the lobby of the building. Pleased that his looks did indeed match his voice, Zuma put a little more into her effusive greeting and sexy sway to the elevators.

"We're so glad you could make it to speak with us, Mr. Hernandez. How was your trip?"

"Very smooth, thank you."

"Did you have any problems finding the car we sent for you?"

"Not at all."

Zuma continued the chatty small talk as they alighted on the twelfth floor. "Can I offer you some coffee or tea?"

"Some water would be fantastic, thanks."

Zuma picked up the receiver from a phone resting on a bare table along the wall of the boardroom. She spoke briefly and quietly before replacing the handle and turning back to Mr. Hernandez.

"Please relax. The other members of our marketing executive team will be in shortly. Excuse me while I make a few calls."

"Please," he said gesturing to the phone.

Opening his brief case, he pulled out a stack of informational packets before propping a portable flip chart on the end of the boardroom table.

A secretary came into the room with a basket of bottled waters, soda, and an assortment of cookies. As she exited, Bob and Steven Searson entered together. Zuma quickly ended her phone conversation and moved to the three men. Introducing everyone, she assumed instant control of the meeting and moved to the head of the table.

"Where's Iris?" asked Steven as Zuma prepared to start the meeting.

"I don't know, I told her the meeting was at one o'clock. She's often late," she lied with an apologetic shrug.

At that exact moment, Iris walked into the reception area of the marketing floor. Betty stared at her agog.

"Girl, what are you doing here?"

Taken aback, Iris asked, "What do you mean? Where should I be?"

"Zuma scheduled the twelfth-floor boardroom for a meeting at one o'clock with Bob and Steven Searson. You were listed as one of the attendees."

Iris spoke between gritted teeth. "She told me the meeting was at *two* o'clock."

Rolling her eyes, Betty came from behind the desk and pushed Iris back toward the elevators. "Worry about that shit later. Get your butt downstairs."

On the twelfth floor, Iris took a deep breath as she gripped the handle to the boardroom door. Exhaling, she turned the knob and pushed the door open. Four faces turned in unison to look at her. Zuma's was a smirk of success. She stood as Iris walked in.

"Mr. Hernandez, please meet our summer intern, Iris Pe—"

Before she could finish, Iris and Mr. Hernandez were embracing and chatting rapidly in Spanish. They paused to kiss each other on both cheeks. Zuma stood dumbfounded, her mouth hanging open.

Steven, the first to recover, said, "I take it you two have already met?"

"Oh, I'm sorry!" Iris said, flustered. "Juan and I have known each other for *years*! I'm just so surprised to see him here."

"I wasn't aware that you spoke Spanish, Iris," Steven said.

Mr. Hernandez and Iris looked at each other, laughing. Zuma noticed they were still holding hands.

"I *am* Spanish, Mr. Searson." The room fell silent as Mr. Hernandez moved over a seat and offered Iris his.

Iris turned to Steven and Bob saying, "I apologize for my tardiness. Zuma emailed me that the meeting was at two o'clock. Luckily for me, Shearing has a talented and thorough secretarial team." Iris smiled in Zuma's direction and was ecstatic to see her jaw still hanging slack.

Turning back to her friend, Iris said, "Please, don't let me interrupt. Continue and I'll catch up."

"Well, if I'd known you had Iris working with you on this project, I would have prepared a much different presentation for you today," Mr. Hernandez said, smiling at Steven and Bob. Iris dropped her head modestly.

"What do you mean?" Bob asked.

"Didn't Iris tell you she worked as an account executive for International Communications?"

As Zuma squinted at Iris in anger, Steven and Bob looked at her with renewed interest. Steven spoke first.

"Why, no! Iris why didn't you say something?"

"I did. I prepared the proposal for you," she said, pointing to the open binder resting in front of him.

Bob glanced quickly at Zuma, but her eyes were glued to Iris's face, and an odd look had settled on her features.

For the remainder of the meeting, Mr. Hernandez presented the services International Communications offered to big businesses hoping to penetrate American Spanish-speaking communities. He often deferred to Iris for her opinion, and the two presented like they'd been working together for years. Zuma sat alone, fuming at the head of the long table, as the other four talked across it like she wasn't there.

"Ladies, gentlemen, as much as I would love to stay and promote my company more, I must prepare to make my departing flight."

"Of course," said Steven, standing and walking around the table to take Mr. Hernandez's hand firmly in his own.

After shaking Steven's hand, Mr. Hernandez moved to shake Bob's hand next, but instead of moving to Zuma, he turned his attention to gathering his presentation materials. Zuma watched as Steven reached out for Iris's hand and grasped it firmly. Bob followed closely behind him, repeating the gesture.

Standing in the middle of the small group, Steven said, "Thank you again for coming, Mr. Hernandez. We'll definitely be in touch with you in the next couple of weeks. Have a safe trip back."

He clapped the Spanish man on the back before walking over to Zuma and quietly saying, "Please show Mr. Hernandez out and make an appointment to meet with me as soon as possible."

Not waiting for a response, he walked out the door with Bob close on his heels.

As she turned back to Mr. Hernandez, Zuma watched in awe as Iris rattled off a sentence in Spanish, gesturing with her face and hands. The man in front of her threw back his head and laughed at whatever she'd just said. Noticing Zuma watching them, they quickly reverted to English.

"Iris, please tell your father to drop by sometime. We miss him around the office."

"I will. And give my love to the girls."

Iris carried his flip chart as they walked slowly toward Zuma standing at the door.

"Are you coming to the national meeting in Miami?" he asked Iris.

"I haven't decided yet."

"Your family would have a fit if you missed that meeting, Iris," he said, laughing.

"I know. I guess I better make plans to attend, huh?"

They both laughed at an apparent inside joke as they walked behind Zuma to the elevators. They continued conversing comfortably on the ride down to the lobby. To Zuma's horror, Iris stopped at the security desk and introduced Mr. Hernandez to Will. Strangely, the Spanish man took Will's hand, smiled at him, and spoke genuinely.

Finishing the interchange, he stepped to Zuma. "Thank you," he said curtly, ignoring her outstretched hand.

Turning back to Iris, he gave her a tight hug, and they kissed on both cheeks again. Lowering his voice, he asked Iris something in Spanish, and they both glanced at Zuma before Iris responded. He nodded with a grave look and squeezed her hands before moving through the glass doors and down the walkway to the black town car waiting at the curb.

"See you, Will," Iris said, smiling brightly at the security guard as she walked past Zuma to the elevator.

Zuma watched her step into the elevator and push a button on the wall as the doors slid shut. Turning back, she was pissed to see Will chuckling at her and shaking his head.

Chapter Sixty-One

"ZUMA, THERE'S NOTHING I CAN DO," Bob said, shaking his head resolutely. "You claimed her work was yours."

Zuma paced back and forth in front of Bob's desk. "How was I supposed to know she used to work for the company?"

"You could have asked her," he said, watching her move from one side of the office to the other.

"I did! She lied to me," Zuma whined, throwing her hands in the air.

Bob rapped the knuckles of his fist on the table, making Zuma stop mid-stride. "Why do you dislike her so much?" he asked, squinting curiously at Zuma as though seeing her for the first time.

Zuma was flustered by his question. "Wh-what do you mean? I don't dislike her," she stammered.

"Then why are you making it so difficult for her to succeed? Rick has worked closely with her for the last two weeks, and their project is off to a fantastic start. Is there something personal between the two of *you* I don't know about?"

Unable to answer his questions, Zuma looked at her watch and said,

"I have to go. I have a meeting."

Bob watched her retreating back.

Walking toward the elevators, she replayed their conversation in her head.

"Why do you dislike her so much?" *How could he ask me that? I don't dislike her. I tried to give her a chance, and she just took advantage of it. Lying to me about her background. Sneaking behind my back and submitting proposals to my bosses. Even sleeping around with co-workers. Someone should ask her why does she dislike me. Sneaky bitch. She can hang up getting a good review from me. She must be crazy trying to make me look bad.*

Stepping outside into the hot summer air, she flipped open her cell phone and dialed a number she knew by heart. He was the only one who could calm her down.

Chapter Sixty-Two

BACK IN HER APARTMENT, Iris couldn't decide who to call first. There was so much to tell.

"Hi Mom, it's Iris."

Laughing, her mother replied, "I know who it is, Iris. You sound a hundred percent better than the last time we spoke."

"I feel better."

"Want to tell me what's been going on?"

Iris gave her mother the full report on Zuma, revising the parts that included Jonathan. When Iris got to the part with Juan Hernandez at the meeting, her mother called in the background to her husband to pick up the upstairs phone. The three of them laughed together as Iris replayed the scenes and described Zuma's facial expressions.

After her father had hung up, her mother said, "Iris, I know there's something else you're not telling me."

Iris sighed, looking around the room for the right response. "You're right, Mom. There was a guy I was seeing. But I'm over it and him, and I really don't feel like talking about him right now."

"Okay," her mother said tenderly.

"Well, I'm gonna go, Mom. I want to call Rey and check on him.

How is his mom doing? Do you ever see her?"

"I only see her between trips. She stays on the go. Which reminds me, are you coming home for the fourth?"

"Oh! I almost forgot to tell you, I'm going to Jamaica."

"With Rey and your friends?"

Ignoring the "and your friends" part of the question, Iris answered, "Yeah. I think we need to get away."

"Call me before you leave, okay?"

"Alright. Give Papa my love. Night."

"Goodnight, baby."

After hanging up with her mother, Iris went into the kitchen and dug around in a cabinet until she found a bag of popcorn. She tossed it in the microwave and dialed Rey's number while she waited for it to pop.

"Hey, boy," she said, when he answered.

"Whassup, girl?"

We're back to normal. It's like Memorial Day never happened.

"How much time do you have?"

"Aw, shit. I know what that question means. Hold on."

He clicked over and was gone for almost two minutes. Iris tucked the phone in the crook of her neck while she took her popcorn out of the microwave and ripped the bag open. The steam came up, burning her fingers. She poured it into a bowl and, just as she was about to hang up, Rey came back on the line.

"Damn, man. I was about to hang up on your ass," Iris said, sucking on her burned fingers.

"Sorry, Eb— Iris."

Iris pulled her fingers from her mouth. "Who did you just call me?"

234

"Iris," Rey replied innocently.

"No, you were about to say another name."

"Girl, stop buggin' and tell me what's up."

Pushing her irritation back, Iris delved into the Zuma saga for a second time. Again, editing out any and all references to Jonathan.

As she came to the end, Rey said, "What the *fuck* is wrong with that trick you work for?"

Iris laughed out loud.

Rey continued fussing. "No, seriously. She's a fuckin' head job. Watch your back, fa real. I'm not playin', Iris. I do *not* want to have to come crackin' heads down there!"

The more he said, the harder Iris laughed. She knew he was dead serious, but just the way he said things always tripped her out. It was kind of like talking to the rapper, DMX.

"Why are you laughing, cuz? I'm for real!" Rey said, getting more intense with each comment.

"I know. That's why I'm laughing," Iris said between giggles.

"Damn! Well, at least I know you deserve the Jamaica trip."

"I know that's right. I can't wait. Five days may not be long enough."

"Shit. In five days, we'll be fighting again, and you'll be happy to get back to that nut job you work for."

They laughed together, then Iris heard a break in the phone line. Rey asked her to hold again.

Coming back on the line, he said, "Yo, Iris, I gotta go."

"Okay. I'll see you in a coupla' days."

"I'll call you before our flights pull out to confirm everything, okay?"

"Cool."

"Aight. Peace," he said and disconnected.

Curiosity ate at her. *What name was he about to call me? Is it the person who keeps calling him?*

It has to be a woman, right? Who else would he hang up on me for? It could be one of his brothers or mom. But wouldn't he just tell me it was one of them instead of just saying he had to go?

Still wondering, she dialed a '305' number from memory and waited.

"Halo," came Sonja's voice through the line.

"*Girl*, wait until I tell you what's been going on…"

Sonja was the one person who could hear the *whole* story. Uncut.

Chapter Sixty-Three

Thursday, June 28

IRIS DIDN'T KNOW WHAT TO expect when she entered the building the next morning. She stopped at Betty's desk and deposited a bag with a hot muffin in it.

"If you don't tell me what's going on..." Betty whispered between clenched teeth as she peeked in the bag.

Iris laughed and leaned over the desk. "I can't tell you anything in this building. Lunch?"

"You got it. You know I only get forty-five minutes, so don't play."

Iris nodded and waved as she moved to her cubicle. When Zuma came in, she walked past Betty without a word or look. Betty smiled to herself.

Iris saw the light go on in Zuma's office, but she didn't acknowledge the other woman's presence as she pulled together the numbers she'd gathered for Rick to present to the finance department.

When the phone rang, she picked it up immediately. "Good morning, Iris Pena speaking."

"Iris, good morning. This is Steven Searson. How are you today?"

"Fine, thank you. And you?"

"I'm great. I just wanted to call and personally tell you what a great job I thought you did — both on the initial presentation you provided to me last week and with the tremendous effort you made yesterday with the representative from International Communications. I am truly impressed with your knowledge, background, and experience."

Iris was astonished and rendered temporarily speechless. Quickly gathering her wits, she replied with a simple, "Thank you, Mr. Searson."

"You're welcome. I know you have a project going on with Rick York and his team right now, but after the holiday, I'd like to schedule a meeting with you. There are a few things I'd like to discuss before the end of your internship with us."

'Of course," she answered.

"Just have Betty make the arrangements. She'll know how to handle it. Have a good day and, if I don't speak with you, a great holiday as well."

"Thank you. You too."

Now this *is how a graduate internship is supposed to be,* Iris thought, as she turned on her computer.

Down the hall, Zuma was searching her email for any word from Bob. Nothing. She checked her voice messages. Nothing. She dialed his extension and waited while the phone rang several times. Nancy, his administrative assistant, answered on the fifth ring.

"Bob O'Brien's office, Nancy speaking."

"Hi, Nancy, this is Zuma. Is he in?"

"Sorry, Zuma, he's in with Mr. Searson and Mrs. Castor right now. Do you want his voicemail, or do you want to leave a note with me?"

Zuma left a brief message on his voicemail, then sat turning things over in her mind.

The CMO and HR manager again? I thought he said his meeting with them was last Tuesday. He never did tell me what happened. Maybe they moved it to today.

Zuma tried to focus on the work on her desk, but she couldn't stop looking at the clock. 10:05 a.m. *He should be done with the meeting by now. Why hasn't he called me back, yet?*

Zuma picked up the phone and put it to her ear, listening for a tone. The phone was definitely working. She sent herself a test email from her personal Hotmail account. Tapping her nails on the desk, she waited to see if the email came through. Thirty seconds later, "test" appeared in the inbox of her office email. It looked like email was working, too.

Why hadn't he contacted her? This wasn't good. When the phone finally rang, she snatched the receiver from the cradle, not allowing the ring to die before putting it to her ear.

"Zuma Harris."

"Good morning, Zuma. I noticed that you aren't on my schedule for today." Steven Searson waited for a reply.

Zuma's mouth worked like a guppy as her brain scrambled for the appropriate words.

"Zuma? Are you there?"

"Sorry, yes. I was just checking my PDA," she stammered.

Silence.

"If you're free now, please come to my office."

There was no mistaking the directive.

"Sure. I'll be right up," she replied.

Shit. Bob's meeting is obviously over. Why hasn't he called me?

Zuma dialed Bob's extension again. When Nancy answered after several rings, Zuma pushed the hook with her finger and replaced the receiver carefully in the base. Her eyes flicked from side to side as she tried to figure out her next course of action. Rising slowly, she checked her image in the mirror behind the door. Unable to stall any longer, she left the office and walked down the hall, past Betty's desk, to the elevator beyond.

When the elevator doors opened on the higher level floor, Zuma walked as calmly as possible to the reception desk guarding the way to the chief executive offices. She clasped her hands tightly to conceal the nervous shaking.

A well-dressed blond woman in her late forties or early fifties looked up from behind the desk with an unreadable expression and something that was not quite a smile. "Ms. Harris, please be seated. I'll call you when Mr. Searson is ready."

Zuma sat primly on the edge of one of the chairs lining the wall of the reception area. Thinking of how calm and nonchalant Iris always looked seated across from her, Zuma scooted back in the seat and tried to cross her legs, but the short, tight suit skirt was restrictive and revealing. Her feet, dangling at the end of short legs, couldn't reach the floor. The effect obviously wasn't the same, as indicated by the receptionist's odd glance in her direction. She frowned for a fleeting moment at Zuma's exposed legs before dropping her gaze to something more important on her desk.

Zuma readjusted her position as the phone buzzed on the reception desk. After listening for a few moments, the receptionist hung up and looked at Zuma with the non-smile smile. "Mr. Searson will see you now." Then, pressing a button under the lip of the desk, she unlocked the door that led to the offices beyond.

Zuma rose with as much respect as she could muster. She wondered if she was being paranoid as she asked herself, *Why is she looking at me like that? Like she knows something negative about me.*

She continued the silent conversation with herself as she padded past private secretarial cubicles placed across from spacious, windowed offices lining the perimeter of the floor. She stopped when she arrived at the third door on the right. Knocking lightly, she waited nervously while Steven Searson arranged some papers on his desk before rising and walking to open the closed door.

She smiled professionally, but was at a loss for words. Instead of attempting small talk, she perched on the front edge of one of the chairs in front of his desk and folded her trembling hands in her lap. Moisture built in her armpits and along her back, making her silk shirt cling to her uncomfortably.

Not wasting any time, Steven leaned on the desk and propped himself up on his elbows, crossing his forearms on the glossy wood surface.

"Zuma, I believe there are always two sides to a story. Sometimes, three or four," he shrugged with a smile. "I called you here to find out your side of a pretty intricate story." He paused without moving or breaking eye contact.

"Two weeks ago, I received one of the most thorough and professional marketing proposals ever submitted from a Shearing employee. Interestingly, the author wasn't an employee, but a college intern. It was later communicated to me that you, not the intern, had actually gathered the information disclosed within. However, I was embarrassed, to say the least, when on yesterday I believe I discovered *that* was not true." He stopped here, and lifted his hands, clasping them to form a fist under his chin. "How about if you enlighten me."

Damn, damn, damn.

Attempting to match his cool demeanor, Zuma remained expressionless and immobile as she responded with brief statements.

"Iris Pena came to us in early May, during the height of the Pdata rollout. Being very involved in that marketing campaign, I devised a project for Ms. Pena to keep her busy but to also give her real hands-on experience in marketing segmentation. Each Friday, I met with Ms. Pena to consider her progress and offer tips and techniques for compiling statistics. For two weeks, I was on vacation and away at a conference, but during that time, I suggested she put the research we'd done together into a proposal format for us to present together in August. I'd planned to help her with the proposal upon my return from New York, but when I arrived in the office the following Tuesday, she had already completed the proposal, made copies, and distributed it to you and Bob. I didn't even receive a copy until Wednesday."

She stopped talking, but maintained their eye contact. His expression was unreadable, but Zuma was confident in the message she'd delivered. Everything she'd said was actually true. Well, almost everything.

He sat back in his chair and rocked smoothly for a few seconds. "So you're telling me that she purposely went over your head with the proposal while you were away."

Zuma nodded, "Yes."

"Why?"

"I can't answer that. You'd have to ask her that question."

"Believe me, I plan to."

He stood and walked around the desk to take the knob of the door. Zuma took the cue and stood also.

"Please prepare a preliminary internship evaluation and send it to Margie in HR with a copy to me. Thanks." Opening the door, he stood, waiting for her to exit. As she stepped out, he closed it firmly behind her. Zuma let out the breath she'd been holding.

"Have a nice day, Ms. Harris," the blonde receptionist said as Zuma made her way shakily to the elevator. Zuma couldn't tell, but it seemed like the woman was mocking her in some way. *I'm being paranoid.*

Once in her office, she checked her email and voice messages again. Still nothing from Bob. Sucking up her pride, she dialed his extension and when Nancy answered, she said, "Hi, Nancy. It's Zuma again. Is

Bob around?"

"He is, Ms. Harris, but he's not available at this moment. Would you like his voicemail?"

"Yes, thank you."

When the computerized greeting ended, Zuma said, "Bob, it's me. Give me a call, please, and let me know how your meeting with Margie and Steven went last week and this morning? Thanks."

She hung up and stared, unseeingly, at the view from her office window.

Chapter Sixty-Four

"IRIS, YOU'VE TURNED THIS company upside down. I don't know what went down yesterday, but I've got to tell you what the admin from executive offices told me this morning." Betty was busting to gossip with Iris as they walked to a deli on the corner and queued up at the order counter.

"Not yet, Betty," Iris said anxiously. "We only have thirty-five minutes left, and we have to go in order for everything to make sense."

As Iris started to speak, Betty stopped her with a little shake of her head, holding up her hand. "You never know who's listening," she said, looking around at the various people waiting in line to place their order.

With a huff and her hand akimbo, Iris said, "If we don't talk now, then we'll definitely run out of time."

"Okay, okay. But you have to whisper, and keep your eye out for anyone who appears to be listening," Betty said cautiously.

"You're crazy."

"No, I'm serious."

Iris bent close to Betty's ear and whispered in rushed sentences.

Periodically, Betty leaned back to look in Iris's face with a "What?" or "No she didn't!" or "Get outta here!" By the time Iris had finished her part, they were at the front of the line and took a break from gossiping to order sandwiches.

Outside was unbearably hot and humid, but the women were tired of whispering and looking over their shoulders, so they found a shaded bench in the nearby War Memorial and sat watching the chess players silently maneuvering in the heat.

"Okay, so here's what Linda called and told me this morning," Betty started.

"Who's Linda?" Iris asked.

"Any name I say is a secretary, receptionist or administrative assistant to someone. Just follow me and don't interrupt."

"Okay, okay," Iris agreed, biting into her sandwich.

"Linda called me and said that Mrs. Castor from human resources and Mr. Searson had scheduled a meeting with Bob O'Brien last week, but the U.P.Ex deal pushed everything back to this week. Everything you said went down yesterday, so this morning, Mrs. Castor and Mr. Searson put themselves on Bob's schedule."

"What?" Iris interjected.

"Yes, honey. Apparently, they wanted to offer him a package."

"A package?"

"Sometimes when a company is being downsized, restructured, or merging, it's desirable to decrease the human resource expenses, so early-out packages are offered to high level executives and the departments are streamlined."

She stopped to take a bite of her sandwich, and they both sat chewing for a few seconds.

"Okay, where was I?" Betty asked, swallowing quickly.

"They offered Bob a package," Iris reminded her.

"Right. They offered him a package and all the other vice presidents, too. Whoever sticks around will be reassigned. From there, they will start the process all over again with the directors and finally make a decision about the managers and non-exempt employees."

"Wow. So what did Bob decide?"

"Nancy says he called his wife and talked to her for awhile before leaving for an early lunch."

Iris shook her head as she chewed her sandwich. *He has a wife and he's messin' around with Zuma's nasty butt.*

Swallowing, Betty continued. "But that's not it, girl."

"There's more?"

"There's always more. Linda told me that Mr. Searson called Zuma *personally* after the meeting with Bob and *made* her come to his office for a meeting. He apparently had asked her on Wednesday to make an appointment with him this week, and she didn't follow up, so he called her and made her see him!"

"Stop it!" Iris said in shock.

"It's true."

"So what happened?"

"Linda couldn't hear, but when she walked past the office, she said Zuma was perched on the edge of her chair like a stone statue, and when the meeting was over, she looked like someone had killed her cat."

At first, Iris smiled gleefully, but slowly, the smile faded.

"What's wrong with you?" Betty asked.

"Betty, I'm not a hater."

"What are you talking about?" Betty responded, confused.

"Listen. I don't like the things Zuma did to me, and I don't like how she treats people, but I'm also not the type of person that enjoys someone else's pain. Even if it *is* deserved. I think I feel sorry for her."

Iris said sadly.

Betty coughed, choking on her sandwich. "Iris, you're too softhearted to work at Shearing. Zuma would stab you in the chest and smile at you as you fell, bleeding to your death. And you talkin' about 'I feel sorry for her'." Betty mimicked Iris's voice.

"You may be right. But acting like her doesn't make me the better woman."

Betty didn't answer.

"My parents taught my brother and me right from wrong and how to run a successful business with integrity and ethics. Not every company has to be full of corruption and deceit. A company becomes that way when it allows bad people like Zuma to grow and infect its operations."

Betty nodded thoughtfully before saying, "I can appreciate that. But right now, you're working for an infected company. If you want to leave healthy, you better watch your back, because that woman is out to get you. That's a fact."

With those final words, Betty balled up the paper from her sandwich, tucked it in the brown bag it came in, and said, "Let's go. I can't be late."

* * *

For the rest of the week, things were relatively quiet on all fronts. Iris and Jim met with Rick and Jonathan to deliver the final numbers on their tween research. Zuma sat sullenly in her office, participating on conference calls and sending emails, while still waiting for any word from Bob. Betty continued making and receiving phone calls on the secretarial hotline while efficiently typing memos, letters, and reports.

By five o'clock on Friday, Iris had packed up her desk and was ready to leave all the drama behind. She called down to the security desk and had Will arrange a taxi for her trip to the airport. Before leaving, she popped her head in Jim and Barbara's offices to wish them a good and safe holiday.

Walking toward the exit, she glanced in the direction of Zuma's office and caught a chill when she saw Zuma's cat eyes watching her. With a shake of her head — pity or disgust, Iris didn't know which she felt more — she continued walking. She stepped behind Betty's desk, where the secretary was also packing up to leave. Hugging the older woman, Iris whispered, "Thank you for everything, Betty. I don't know what I would have done without you."

Betty was too choked up to say anything, so she just patted Iris on the back and nodded with a smile.

Together, they walked to the bank of elevators, completely unaware of the fire in Zuma's eyes as she watched them disappear.

Chapter Sixty-Five

"REY," IRIS SING-SONGED into the phone.

"I-ris, I-ris," he rapped back.

They laughed together.

"When does your flight depart?" Iris asked.

"Six forty-five. What about you?"

"Seven fifteen."

"Cool, I'll wait for you at the Caribe House reservations desk."

After hanging up, Iris settled back in the seat to watch the bumper-to-bumper traffic stopping and starting through the taxi's window. She began singing one of Bob Marley's hits quietly to herself.

A few short hours later, a pre-recorded voice with a lilting West Indian accent directed everyone to put up their tray tables and bring their seats to the full, upright position. Iris rested her chin on her hand and glimpsed at the lights of resorts and hotels along the beach reflected in the vast blackness of the ocean below. When it looked like the plane was about to land in the dark water, a row of lights suddenly appeared, and Iris could make out the figures of palm trees swaying in the breeze along the sides of the runway.

She fought through the long line in customs, searched for her luggage on the baggage claim carousel, and waited in another slow-moving line to clear her bags. Finally, she passed down a short, wide hallway and was directed to the Caribe House reservations desk at the end of the building. Just as she was about to give her name to a thin Jamaican man wearing a purple and green shirt with "Alex" printed on a silver name tag, she felt a warm hand on her neck.

"Rey," she breathed with exhaustion, falling into his embrace.

"You look tired as hell," he laughed, hugging and holding her up at the same time. "Alex, whassup?" he said to the man at the counter.

"Eh Mon. Whagwan? Welcome back, Mr. Hargrave," Alex replied.

Another man in a similar uniform took their bags and gestured for them to follow him through a doorway to a row of white minibuses waiting in a lot. Even though it was hot, a cool breeze blew over them.

"I thought it would feel like Miami at this time of the year," Iris said with a yawn.

"Nothing feels like Miami but Miami," Rey answered with a yawn of his own.

They climbed into the cramped bus and fell across individual seats. The man moved into the driver's seat on the right side and looked in the mirror at the two people laid out in the back. His usual question of "Is this your first time in Jamaica?" would have to go unanswered tonight.

Chapter Sixty-Six

ZUMA TIPPED THE wine bottle completely over, letting the last drops creep out before throwing it on top of two other empty ones in the trash. The liquid sloshed around in the wine glass as she snatched it from the counter and retraced her steps to the sofa.

Lighting up another cigarette, she squinted through the smoke and darkness, seeing nothing. She took a sip of the wine, letting the taste linger in her mouth before swallowing. Ashes from the cigarette dropped onto the floor as she brought the stick to her lips and sucked until her cheeks creased inwardly. Smoke escaped through her mouth and nose and danced around her face.

How could I fuck everything up so badly?

Zuma mentally rewound the tape of time and pushed play again. She kept revisiting everything that had happened since Iris arrived in May, but she still couldn't find where she'd messed up.

Drunk and out of cigarettes, she stumbled to the kitchen, spilling red wine on the white carpet, and began rummaging in a drawer until she found the medicine bottle she was looking for. She struggled with the child-proof top until it popped open, spilling small white pills over the counter and floor. Zuma dropped to her knees and scooped several pills off the floor and into her mouth, swallowing them dry.

Crawling back to the living room, she collapsed onto the sofa. Soon she was drifting into a fitful sleep where dreams and memories blended into one.

* * *

"Where's my mama?" Zuma wailed. "Mama! Mama!" she screamed out.

The gurney was being wheeled briskly through a cold, white corridor.

"You've got to stay quiet. Lay back now," one of the nurses directed as she dragged a pole with bags of liquid attached by hooks alongside the gurney.

"My baby. What about my baby?" Zuma asked, trying unsuccessfully to move her hands to her round abdomen.

"Shh," whispered another nurse as she placed a clear mask over Zuma's nose and mouth.

"Where's my mama? What about my baby?" Zuma whimpered into the plastic mask. Eventually her eyes fluttered shut.

"She's out, Doctor," the nurse said as the surgeon prepared to cut.

Chapter Sixty-Seven

Saturday, June 30

SOFT ROOTS REGGAE STREAMED through the open balcony doors. Iris turned her head slowly and looked around the sunny room. It was simply decorated in peach and cream with pretty rattan and bamboo furniture. A television was resting inside a bamboo entertainment center, and a glass-top desk with a wide-backed chair tucked underneath stood next to it. Sitting up, she noticed a cd player with a radio resting on a long shelf attached to the head of the king-sized bed.

Iris jumped when she heard a voice on the other side of the open glass door yell, "Whassup man?"

Iris called out, "Rey? Are you out there?" She pulled the covers up to her chin.

Poking his head through the opening, he looked at her balled up in the bed.

"Of course. Who'd you expect to be on the balcony?" His head disappeared back outside.

Iris heard a faint voice with a Jamaican accent and, then, Rey shouting again. "Naw, man. I just got in last night."

She hung her legs over the side of the bed and scratched her hair.

"You look like shit," Rey said, walking from the patio through the suite and into the adjoining room.

"Good morning to you, too," Iris mumbled.

Shuffling to the bathroom, she brushed her teeth and washed her face. Taking some water in her palm, she attempted to pull her fingers through matted tangles of hair.

"Bad hair day?" Rey asked, peeking his head through the open doorway.

"Two words. Shut up."

Iris closed the door and took a long, cool shower. She pulled a brush through her hair as she dried it with the hotel blow dryer hanging from the wall. Smearing sunscreen all over her face and body, she wrapped herself in a towel and walked back to the bedroom.

"Rey?" she shouted out to the other room where the television was blaring.

"Yeah."

"What's the plan for this morning?" she asked, rummaging through the clothes mixed carelessly in the case.

Coming to stand in the doorway to her bedroom, he answered, "Breakfast for sure. My boy, Bobby, runs the jet skis, and he said we can' get one around eleven o'clock." He disappeared again.

Iris opted for a thong bikini and matching top with a long sarong, which she wrapped behind her and crisscrossed across her chest, tying it in a knot to create a dress.

Iris stepped out into the sitting room where Rey, wearing brown leather slip-ons, had his feet propped up on a low, glass-top bamboo table. One hand held the television remote and the other was propped behind his head.

"Are you finally ready, Cinderella?" he asked, without looking up from the TV screen.

Fluttering her lashes at him, she walked out the door, leaving him to catch up. Looking over the rail to the street below, Iris watched cars speeding dangerously along the busy Hip Strip, beeping at each other and pedestrians fool hardy enough to be in the narrow street.

An old man with matted, dirty dreadlocks was washing cars parked in spots along the street. The black, yellow, and green of his tattered tank top were faded and barely discernible. The sun glistened on the perspiration beaded on his black skin. Though he was old, years of hard work and hard living made the muscles of his arms, shoulders, and back enviable.

Rey caught up to her and cupped his hands around his mouth to shout, "Roy!" to the old man on the street.

The man, who'd been stooping to wash the wheels of a Toyota, looked up. "Eh bwai! When ya get in?"

"Last night."

"Me soon check ya," the man yelled back with a wave and a toothless smile, before stooping back to his work.

Raymond Hargrave knows everyone in every country in the world. Even old men, living in the streets and washing cars for a living. Iris shook her head as she followed him down the winding staircase, through the marble-tiled lobby, and into the open dining area.

Several guests were already seated around the pool, eating fruit, eggs, and bacon.

"Oh my God! Look what the wind blew in. Whagwan, Ras?" A thick, muscular young man with a smooth, dark complexion slapped Rey's hand and gave him the Black man hug.

"Whassup, man?"

"The same ol' same ol.' So what's the deal this time? How long you here?"

Rey gestured to Iris who was gazing at the clear blue of the pool.

"My girl, Iris, and I are on vacation for a few days. So, you know what's up."

"Right. Parties. There's a party at the Pier tonight, and a Baddest Wine contest at the Casino tomorrow night. Margaritaville is always an option for good music and drinks."

"My man," Rey said, slapping his hand again.

"Aight, Ras," he said to Rey. He smiled and winked at Iris as he passed.

They moved into the air-conditioned dining room and selected fruit and breakfast food from the buffet. Carrying their plates outside and down the steps, they chose a table in the shade near the outdoor bar.

"Why do they call you Ras?" Iris asked, sticking a fork in the pineapples and strawberries on her plate.

Shaking salt and pepper on his eggs, he said, "It's a short name for Rastafarian."

"You're not a Rastafarian," Iris said, confused.

"No, but I have long dreadlocks, so a lot of people refer to me as Ras."

As though proving his point, a short, light-skinned man wearing khaki shorts and a yellow shirt walked up to the table. He put his full plate of food at an empty spot on the table saying, "I heard you were back, Ras. Whassup?"

The two men brought their fists together and nodded slightly to one another as the young guy walked to the bar for a drink. To Iris, it was like they were communicating without saying very much. *How does everyone know he's here? Is this guy just going to sit and eat with us without being invited?*

Reading Iris's mind, Rey leaned toward her and said, "Miquel's part of the entertainment staff. They have to sit and eat with the guests during every meal."

How does he always know what I'm thinking?

"Your face reads like a book."

Asshole. Read that.

"I know you're saying something smart about me in your head, but it's okay. I still love you." He grinned at her.

She back-handed him in the arm. Miguel came from the bar and sat down.

As they made small talk, a few Caucasian couples began spreading towels on the lounge chairs around the pool and slathering sun tan lotion on each other. On the other side of the pool, a Jamaican woman was braiding a thin white girl's hair, applying brightly colored beads to the end.

Giving Rey another handshake, Miguel stood and promised to see them later. He crossed the pool deck, shouting a greeting to two white guys drinking Red Stripes for breakfast, and stepped up on a stage covered with instruments and stereo equipment. Picking up a microphone and pushing some buttons on a large mixer, his proper West Indian accent came across the terrace announcing the start of a drinking game.

"They start early, don't they?" Iris asked.

"This is vacation in Jamaica. It's never too early to start drinking." Rey stood and stretched. "Come on. Let's see if my boy, Bobby, is on the beach yet."

Iris followed him along a path and down some steps to a beach lined with lounge chairs and random sunbathers. Several Jamaican men were standing and sitting around the steps of a white building with the words "Water Sports" printed above the open window. As usual, they all recognized Rey and gave him love. He introduced Iris, and she felt naked as they stared at her thick, brown legs sticking out from the bottom of the sarong.

A man, slightly older than the rest, with a big belly hanging over the edge of his red swim trunks spoke in quick Patois to Rey. Rey answered in kind, then he beckoned for Iris to follow him. Several sets of eyes followed her progress through the sand to the pier where two boats were docked, and three jet skis sat on the sand.

"Take off your wrap," Rey directed, as he chose a jet ski.

I cannot take this off in front of those guys. I won't, Iris thought self-consciously.

When Rey looked back and saw her still standing wrapped in the bright fabric, he put his hand up in consternation. "What are you waiting for, Iris?"

She tipped into the water up to her knees and whispered loudly enough for him to hear over the engine of the machine. "I'm too embarrassed."

He looked her blankly. "What are you talking about? You've been half-naked in Miami, LA, and Mexico and topless in Spain! What's the issue?"

"No one in those cities was looking at me like *they* are," she hissed, pointing her thumb over her shoulder to the men waiting to see what she had to offer.

Rey threw back his head in laughter before shouting something in Patois to Bobby and sliding off the jet ski. As Bobby took the handle of the running vehicle, Rey reached for Iris's hand and tugged her gently to his chest. Then, in a single movement, he dunked her in the ocean.

Spluttering and coughing, she popped up swinging. "Are you *crazy*?"

"Now can we go?"

Iris slapped him hard on the arm. "You are insane." She muttered as she tugged at the wet knot of fabric on her chest. Peeling off the material sticking to her body, Iris balled up the sarong and tossed it on a step of the pier. Dipping her head under the clear water, she came up smoothing back her hair and climbed up behind Rey to straddle the vibrating jet ski.

"Goddamn!" she heard one of the men mutter as she tucked in close to Rey and wrapped her arms around his tight midsection.

When they had pulled away from the beach, Iris glanced back and saw the guys dapping each other up and falling over themselves in the sand. One was holding his heart, and another was on his knees in the sand reaching out to her.

Suddenly, Rey gunned the engine, and the guys on the beach turned into stick figures as they sped over the water, creating a wide arch around the pier and the resort's private beach. Iris laid her head on his warm, muscular back and watched the bright colors around them blend and swirl together as he spun and turned expertly in circles, sometimes fishtailing playfully to make her squeal. She admired the breathtaking view of a mountain stretching to the clouds beyond the twin towers of a resort in the distance.

Five days won't be long enough for me to get used to this.

Chapter Sixty-Eight

ZUMA AWOKE ON HER BACK, hanging half on and half off the edge of the couch in the living room. A trail of drool had dried on her cheek, and the uncomfortable puffiness around her eyes indicated she'd been crying in her sleep again. Touching the area beneath her eyes, she felt the dry spots where tears had evaporated on her cheeks.

Her mouth tasted like cotton, and her attempt to swallow was fruitless. She wrinkled her nose at the stench of stale cigarettes and bad breath emanating from her lips. As she tried to sit up, a feeling of pressure pulsated in her head. Lying back on the soft fabric of the sofa, she closed her eyes to rest, but thoughts and images immediately took off in a sprint through her mind.

Visions of the hospital, memories of her mother's cries. A sharp pain ripped through her abdomen, causing her to double over and hug herself. The pain disappeared as quickly as it had come, a figment of her imagination, a reminder of history. She whimpered and squeezed her eyes tightly together to push the images and recollections away.

Leave me alone. Leave me alone.

A noise far away made her relax the muscles in her face and listen. There it was again — music. No, ringing. The phone. Zuma opened her eyes in a daze, but the room was spinning, and she quickly shut them again. Points of light flashed behind her closed lids as the ringing ceased.

Something's wrong with me.

Zuma fought to sit up, but fell weakly to the floor amid cigarette butts and the red stains of spilled wine. A pain shot through her stomach again, but this time it didn't disappear. She gagged once before regurgitating on the thick white carpeting. The muscles in her face and neck strained as her body fought to release the impurities inside. Beads of perspiration covered her forehead and nose as she dry-heaved, struggling to keep from falling in the blood-red mess on the floor.

Eventually, her body stopped straining, and she leaned, trembling, back on the base of the long leather chair. Stiff hair stood out from her head, like wild straws of hay, while loose strands around her face stuck to her damp forehead. Tears flowed freely down her sallow cheeks, dripping from her chin to her chest that was rising and falling with each unsteady breath. The phone rang again as Zuma sat perspiring and shivering in a pool of urine and vomit.

Chapter Sixty-Nine

REY BROUGHT THE JET SKI back to shore, and Iris dived off the side into the water to avoid pointing her bare behind in the direction of the men waiting on the beach.

As she swam up on the sand and sat in the shallow water, Rey shouted something to Bobby. Nodding his head, the fat Jamaican trudged slowly through the sand to the Water Sports window and reached through to grab a colorful board and a life vest. He carried them out to the water and tossed the vest to Rey before placing the board flat on the water and pushing it gently in Rey's direction.

Rey fastened the vest over his muscular chest and flat stomach, then dropped into the shallow water to strap his feet to the surface of the board. Bobby unraveled a long rope with a handle on the end and bent over the back of the jet ski, twisting and tying, until the long string was attached. He climbed onto the rumbling vehicle as Rey grabbed the plastic handle. Bobby, looking over his shoulder at Rey, nodded once. Rey gave him a thumbs up in response. Gunning the motor, Bobby took off, and Rey shot up out of the water, skiing sideways on the board. His long dreadlocks flew out behind him as the muscles in his arms and shoulders flexed in the sunlight.

Iris watched him admiringly. *Sonja's right. He's fine as hell.*

Feeling the salt drying on her skin and in her hair, Iris stood and walked to the Water Sports window.

"Excuse me," she said to a light-skinned boy with hazel eyes behind the counter. "Where are the outdoor showers?"

He didn't speak as he casually pointed to the back of the building.

"Thanks," Iris said dryly.

There was no way to avoid the scrutiny of the group that had grown in the thirty minutes since Rey had dunked her. She smiled nervously and kept her eyes on the ground as she walked past as quickly as possible, trying not to let her butt jiggle.

"Princess," One called out to her.

She turned to him and raised her brows in response.

"You wi Ras?"

Not sure of the answer, she nodded her head awkwardly and kept moving to her destination. Iris knew every eye was on her ass. Her face was burning with embarrassment by the time she made it around the side of the building and found the three shower heads in back.

Taking her time, she stood under the cool spray and let the water run through her hair, over her face, and down her body. Enjoying the sensation, she closed her eyes and stood swaying back and forth in the stream of water. Eventually, she reached up and smoothed her hair back from her face before wiping water from her closed eyes. With her eyes still shut, she reached in the direction of the knob and groped around until she found it, turning off the water.

Running cool hands over her eyes one last time, she blinked them open and sharply sucked in her breath at the sight of the light-skinned boy from the counter standing a foot away.

"Shit, you scared me!" Iris spluttered, clutching at her heart.

Looking sleepily out of his hazel eyes, he simply handed her a thick, cream-colored towel and walked away when she took it. Iris shook her head, wrapping the warm towel under her arms, and tucked it in at her breast.

More confident, now that she was covered, she walked leisurely to an area with lounge chairs strewn along the beach. She chose one in the shade of a low-hanging tree and propped the back up slightly so she could watch Rey skimming over the sparkling water behind the powerful jet ski.

His chocolate skin glistened in the sunlight, and the muscles of his legs flexed as he dipped and changed directions in and out of the wake behind the jet ski. She could see the muscles of his forearms and shoulders flex as he held the handle firmly in his hands.

A combination of the heat, sun, and sounds of water washing up on the beach lulled Iris into a light sleep. She was vaguely aware of men speaking low in their native version of English and the faint melody of reggae playing in the background.

It was hard to come back to reality when she felt drops of cool water on her arms and face. Still half asleep, she swiped at the drops as they trickled down the smooth curves of her cheeks. She groaned softly, scratching at the tickling sensation moving down her arm. Slowly, she peeled her eyes apart and looked up at a blurry, dark form. Blinking, she tried hard to wake up. A familiar laugh came from the fuzzy shape above her. Rey shook more water from his locs, creating a shower on Iris's exposed upper body.

"Stop it, Rey. Damn," she mumbled groggily.

"You sleep too much," he laughed.

"I know you're not talking."

"I wake up late, but once I'm up, I'm up. *You* on the other hand, wake up early, but sleep from noon to the next morning."

A heavyset Jamaican woman in a green formal security uniform and cap walked up. Ignoring Iris, she spoke in Patois to Rey. Iris picked up on some of what she said. Like everyone else, she was welcoming him back.

Iris rolled her eyes at the slight from the woman and laid back down on the chair. She watched drops of water fall from the tips of Rey's locks, creating trails over and around the muscles of his chest, arms, and back. The ones on his back seemed to be sneaking into the waist of his brightly colored board shorts, sitting low on his hips. Just as she was about to let her gaze wander a little further down, Rey turned and put a firm grip on her arm.

Checking herself, she let Rey introduce her to the woman, but the female security guard's attitude changed, and she walked away with a hater look only another woman would recognize and understand.

"She's not someone you feel like dealing with, huh?" Iris asked, grinning at him.

"What?" Rey asked, confused.

"You heard me."

"Why'd you say that?"

"You've never introduced me to another woman in your life," Iris said nonchalantly, stretching and kicking her legs over the edge of the chair.

Rey's face was unreadable as he looked at her.

The rest of the day was full of activities. Rey and Iris played pool volleyball, toured the island on a sleek, white speedboat, and parasailed. While Rey played a few rounds of dominoes, Iris slept in a hammock hanging between two palm trees, shaded by wide fronds.

By eight o'clock, they were back in the suite, getting ready for dinner. Rey dressed in loose jeans and a polo-style shirt with tight, short sleeves that hugged his biceps. Iris donned a long silk wrap riding low on her hips and a tiny crop top that revealed her chiseled stomach muscles.

They checked each other out, and both nodded approvingly. As they walked out the door into the breezy night air, Rey said, "I see why those brothers were all over you."

Iris stopped short. "Excuse me?"

"What? You think I'm blind?" Rey replied, laughing.

Iris walked on. "They act like they haven't seen a black woman before," she grumbled.

"They don't see one like you very often."

"What do you mean, like me?"

"You're not the average black woman, Iris."

Iris turned to look at him.

"Hey, not that I'm looking or anything. I'm just telling you what *they're* thinking."

Walking into the crowded outdoor dining area, they found an empty table between the stage and the pool. A band was performing jazz renditions of popular reggae favorites. Colored lights cast a red glow in the pool beyond.

They ate and watched a show put on by the entertainment staff. The performances of singing, dancing, and acting ended with a fashion show. When the performers finally stood along the edges of the stage in colorful garb from the gift shop, Miguel spoke into the microphone, announcing the final activities of the evening — a pajama party in the disco and karaoke in the piano bar.

Rey turned to Iris with a look that said, *"We will not be participating in those activities."*

Coming behind her, he pulled out her chair for her to stand. Taking her hand, he led her down a sandy path to the beach and rolled up the legs of his jeans while he waited for her to remove her heels. They walked silently through the sand and shallow water. Periodically, he stooped to show her a school of fish or a jellyfish just under the water's surface, glowing in the moonlight. When they reached the end of the beach, Rey perched on a low stone while Iris rested on the sand. They sat in a comfortable silence, each lost in their own thoughts.

After a few moments of listening to the waves, Rey said, "Thanks for coming with me, Iris. I needed to relax with someone like family, but just not family, this week."

Iris nodded her understanding. Sometimes family was too much to deal with, and simple acquaintances required too much thought and attention. Iris fit right in the middle.

"Thanks for inviting me," she said softly.

Rey gazed seriously toward the dark water. "You know, sometimes it doesn't seem like Pop's gone, and then I go to the house and it's so obvious, I can't stay. I know why Mama's flying around like she is."

His statement didn't require a response, and Iris nodded, feeling his pain in the darkness.

"I miss him. *Damn*, I miss him." Rey's voice cracked with emotion.

Iris rose from the sand and cradled his head against her abdomen. She rocked him gently as his tears fell silently against her skin.

Chapter Seventy

ZUMA STRAINED TO PULL HERSELF up from the mess on the floor. The room was dark, and the only illumination was from the moon shining through the glass back doors. Swaying weakly, she dropped to her knees and crawled to the stairs. Using the rail, she dragged herself up the steps and crawled from the top of the stairway to her bedroom.

Reaching for the phone on the vanity, she dialed a number from memory. When she heard an answer, she whispered in a raspy voice, "Please help me. I need you." She passed out on the floor, letting the phone slip from her fingers.

An hour later, a man dug around the flower pot near the front door until he felt the front-door key. Letting himself into the house, he called out Zuma's name. Moving from room to room, he finally found her sprawled out near the dresser in her bedroom. He quickly checked her vitals to make sure she was safe. Her pulse was faint, but steady. He moved through the darkness to the garden bathroom and began running hot water into the jacuzzi bath.

Back in the bedroom, he struggled to pick up Zuma's limp form. Carrying her into the bathroom, he undressed her like a nurse in a hospital and carefully placed her in the tub. He rinsed the mess from her face and scooped water over her matted hair.

Feeling the warm water on her face and head, she woke from her stupor. Her eyes met his and they shared an unspoken communication. Hers, grateful and appreciative. His, concerned and caring.

He handed her a wash cloth and her bath soap, before turning his back to allow her to bathe in privacy. He refused to leave in case she slipped or passed out in the tub.

When she had finished, he bent to help her out of the tub and pressed the release, letting the water drain out. As she sat on the edge of the wide tub, he wrapped her in a thick bath sheet and rubbed her arms and back.

"Come on, dear," he said, guiding her from the tub to the double sinks across the spacious bathroom.

He pulled the single toothbrush from the ceramic holder on the counter and rinsed it before putting some toothpaste on the bristles. "Can you hold it?"

Zuma shook her head weakly. Holding her up with his left arm, he brushed her teeth with his right hand. "Spit," he directed. Filling one of the paper cups on the counter with water, he held it to her lips so she could sip and rinse.

After dabbing her mouth with a hand towel hanging in a loop on the wall, he half carried, half guided her through the dressing room to the bedroom beyond. He propped her on the edge of the bed and pulled all of the decorative pillows off, tossing them to the floor. He lifted back the comforter and top sheet and let her fall back.

Moving to the dresser, he pulled open random drawers, searching through the lace and sheer silk until he found the most decent thing he could to cover her for sleep. Pulling the top over her head and fighting to get her arms through the holes, he paused to wipe perspiration from his brow. He put her tiny feet through the holes of the satiny pajama shorts and tugged and pulled until they covered her private area.

Covering her with only the sheet, he looked down at her flushed face and shook his head.

What must this poor girl have been through to make her like this?

Rolling down his shirtsleeves, he walked to the guest bedroom across the hall and lay on top of the spread to wait for sunrise and the inevitable conversation that lay ahead.

Chapter Seventy-One

Sunday, July 1

IT WAS A LITTLE AFTER MIDNIGHT when Rey and Iris flagged down a taxi to take them into downtown Montego Bay. They rode slowly past a line of scantily clad women and young Jamaican men waiting outside the club at the pier. When the car stopped, Rey handed the driver two Jamaican bills, bumped the man's fist, and they alighted into the humid night air.

Iris followed Rey past the waiting people to the entrance where he gave the security guard a shake and shoulder bump. They were ushered inside and immediately began jockeying for space in the crowded, dark room. Rey navigated them to the bar and shouted above the noise to be heard by the bartender. A minute later, he handed a cup with something fruity and alcoholic in it to Iris.

"Stay here. I'll be back," he yelled into her ear.

She nodded, sipping her drink, as she watched him disappear into the crowd toward the DJ booth. Couples were gyrating and rubbing against one another to the beat pounding through the walls and floor. A girl dropped to her hands and kicked up her legs as a lanky man grabbed her hips and mimicked anal sex in rhythm with the driving bass.

Rey stepped down from the DJ booth and fought to push back though the crowd. He beckoned for Iris to join him on the dance floor. When she finally made her way through the mayhem, Rey stepped behind her and guided her hips in time with his. She closed her eyes and danced in rhythm with his body.

Suddenly, the DJ stopped the song and spoke in Patois into the microphone. The music came back on a split second before being stopped again as the DJ said something else. Even though she couldn't understand all of what the man wearing a floppy blue Kangol said, Iris recognized Rey's name and jumped when several people started barking like dogs around them. A few men bumped fists with Rey, and the DJ smiled and nodded in their direction.

As the music resumed, the DJ said, "Dis is fa di lady called I-ris."

A beat, slower than the dancehall that had been playing, pulsated through the speakers, and an artist with a Jamaican accent began speaking in Spanish. The people on the dance floor responded with shouts, pointing their fingers in the air.

"Reggaeton!" The DJ growled to more shouts of pleasure from the crowd.

Iris spun around to face Rey and pulled his head close so she could shout in his ear. "Rey, it's a Spanish dancehall song!"

He nodded and said, "It's called reggaeton. I thought you'd like it."

Pulling her close, Rey wound his hips expertly to the rhythm of the music. Iris pressed against him, letting his movements guide her. The strobing lights, the heat, the heavy beat, and Rey's hard body against hers were all perfect. She swayed her hips in a slow wine, as if in a trance.

After a few reggaeton songs, the DJ created a combination of siren and gunshot sound effects before changing the style of music to hip hop. Rey and Iris changed their moves to match the gritty rhythms, raising their arms and yelling when the DJ gave a shout out to New

York.

Eventually, the music changed to top 40 pop, and they surrendered the floor to others pressing in around them. Rey led Iris from the dance floor to a stairway in the back. At the top, he stopped and pointed to the restrooms. Feeling sweat dripping down her bare back, she nodded and moved in the direction of the ladies' room. When she emerged, he was waiting with his damp shirt unbuttoned and hanging from his broad shoulders. She tried, unsuccessfully, not to look at the ripped abdominal muscles resting beneath the curves of his muscular chest.

Unaware of her gaze, he asked, "Want something to drink?" and took her hand to guide her up another short flight of steps to an open patio on the roof of the club.

"Water..." Iris pretended to croak, sitting on an empty stool at the bar.

Even though the beat from the speakers below vibrated beneath their feet, Iris could clearly hear the rich, melodic voice of a tall Rastafarian with heavy dreadlocks singing into a microphone on a small stage across the roof. Iris felt herself rocking gently to his rhythm.

Rey placed a sweating bottle of water before her on a napkin and turned up a dark bottle of Guinness to his mouth. After a few minutes, he picked up her bottle and motioned with his head for her to follow him.

Along a rail, away from the lights of the bar and stage, were small tables and plastic chairs. Rey placed their drinks on one of the tables and pulled two chairs to the rail. Iris sat in one and turned to look into the darkness.

Her breath caught when she looked out at the view over the ocean, lit with blinking lights from hotels and restaurants along the island's edge. A cruise ship was docked at the pier, and a row of colored lights outlined its hulking, white frame. Looking directly down, Iris could see rocks and large fish swimming beneath the surface of the clear water, illuminated by the lights from the club. Lifting her eyes, she saw the dark backdrop of mountains rising behind the hotels, sporadic lights from hillside homes winking from their shadows.

"Are you going to drink this?" Rey asked, pointing to her water and breaking into her thoughts.

Still mesmerized by the surrounding beauty, Iris picked up the bottle and sipped without answering. The cool liquid trickled down her throat, giving her a chill.

"Are you cold?" Rey asked.

Still silent, Iris shook her head slowly. She didn't want to disturb the perfection of the moment.

After a minute, he said, "It's almost three in the morning. Ready to bounce?"

Reluctantly, Iris nodded and put the cap on her bottle. She stood and followed Rey down a narrow and steep set of stairs on the opposite side of the roof. Fighting through the crowd to make their way to the exit, Iris turned to see some young girls shaking their butts on a roped stage while the DJ asked the crowd to pick their favorite. A cameraman holding a heavy Sony camera with "MTV" imprinted on the side attempted to remain steady amid jostling people screaming, shouting, and barking for their favorites.

Leaving the mayhem behind, Iris and Rey slipped out the door and onto the crowded sidewalk. Rey spoke to a couple of people as they passed, but the crowd was soon left behind.

They walked slowly, and he grew quiet looking up at the sky. Iris followed his gaze and marveled at how clear it was to see hundreds of stars twinkling in the night. "You can't even *see* the stars in New York," she whispered. Rey grunted in agreement. They found an empty taxi and hopped in, fighting sleep, as it sped through the narrow, winding streets.

At the resort, they rode the elevator to the top floor and walked wearily to their suite. Unlocking the door, Rey stood back to let Iris enter first. As he closed the door behind them, he groped for the light switch on the wall, but Iris grabbed his hand before it reached.

"What's up?" Rey asked in a tired voice.

Instead of answering him, Iris pulled his hand to her face and softly kissed his open palm. When he didn't move, she stepped closer and kissed his neck, savoring the salty flavor on her tongue. Closing her eyes, she tilted her head back to kiss his lips, but was shocked by a firm hand on her shoulder. Opening her eyes, she tried unsuccessfully to see his face in the darkness.

"What?" she asked, confused.

"That's what I wanna know — what?"

The seriousness of his tone made Iris take a step back, still trying to see him in the dark. She didn't have to struggle for long, as Rey snapped on the lights, causing them both to blink and squint in the sudden brightness.

"What's up, Iris?" Rey repeated in irritation.

Iris was caught off guard. She thought he wanted her as much as she wanted him and was speechless with confusion. How could she put into words what she thought was understood?

Rey closed his eyes momentarily and took a breath. He brushed past her to sit on the arm of the sofa behind her.

"Look, you're confusing me," he said, looking at her back. "When I kissed you a month ago in New York, you kissed me back, then pushed me away. When I told you I was in love with you, you laughed at me and told me you didn't feel the same way. We agreed weeks ago that we were better off as friends."

Iris stood facing the door with her back to him, absorbing his words. He was right, and she'd just embarrassed herself. Again. As the silence drew out, she finally turned around and faced him.

"You're right. I did do all those things. But now, we're here. Alone in Jamaica," she said, moving toward him, "and I want you." She finished in a whisper, stepping between his parted knees, looking down on his thick hair.

Lifting her hands, she dug them deep into the ropes of his locks and pulled his face gently to her stomach where he had cried tears of pain earlier in the evening.

"I want you," she whispered again, dropping to her knees in front of him, letting her gaze roam over the muscles of his chest and abdomen.

"I want you," she continued to whisper, as she looked up at the lashes curling from his closed eyes.

"I want you," she said, even softer, as she stared at his full lips.

She repeated the phrase, as she placed her hands inside the opening of his shirt and pushed it, gently, from his shoulders. She let her hands linger on the curves of his back, then slowly rubbed them down his chest and over the ripples of his abdomen. She felt him tremble beneath her touch. The dark skin of his face was smooth, and she reached up to touch his cheek with the palm of one hand. Her fingers caressed his curved brow as she leaned into him.

Her kisses were so faint on his face, he almost didn't feel them. Why was she doing this to him? He had finally pushed his feelings for her to a place where he couldn't be hurt. He was moving on and had found someone else to share this feelings, thoughts, and aspirations. Now, here was Iris — his other half and an old dream — telling him that she wanted him. As much as he wanted to push her away and not let her hurt him again, he couldn't avoid the feelings he'd put on a shelf in the back of his heart and mind.

Please stop. Don't do this to me, Iris. Please. Rey silently pleaded with her, as he slipped from the arm of the chair and let his arms move around her. *Please leave me alone.*

He felt her lips on his and couldn't stop his tongue from escaping to taste her. He saw Ebony Crenshaw's face in his mind, but only one name was ringing in his ears.

Iris. Iris. Iris.

Chapter Seventy-Two

ZUMA GROANED AS SUNLIGHT filtered through the closed blinds of her bedroom. Soreness radiated from her stomach up to her throat. She tried to lick her lips, but her tongue felt swollen and stuck in her mouth. Shifting in the bed, she felt soft fabric moving against her skin, and she lifted the satin sheet to see a pink pajama set she hadn't worn in years covering her body.

She frowned in confusion, trying to remember why and how she'd put on the outdated silk. Suddenly, she tensed and lay stiff, listening. There was a noise in the kitchen. Sniffing, she smelled the aroma of coffee and food.

A memory of being bathed flashed behind her eyes. Someone brushing her teeth. Fragments of the night before came to her. She closed her eyes and lay still on the pillow. She heard soft footsteps on the stairs and slowly opened her eyes to see the older man walk slowly into the room with a tray of toast and a steaming cup of coffee.

Elijah Pharrell. The kind gentleman from her flight from Cape Cod. As she watched him fussing over the food and coffee, she thought about the first time she'd called him and disconnected without leaving a message. She was glad that she'd been strong enough to call him back and let him help her. The licensed social worker had listened patiently to her that day and any time she called him afterward. He always offered support and never judged her actions or decisions. But what was he doing here?

"So, you survived." He smiled at her and sat on the edge of the bed, peering into her face. He placed his hand on her forehead like a worried mother with a sick child. "Well, you're looking better and are obviously stronger than last night."

She opened her mouth to speak, but the dryness in her throat and the glue in her mouth prevented anything from coming out.

"I think you need some water," he said, rising and moving out the door.

Zuma didn't want him to leave, but she couldn't speak and was too weak to pull him back. Within minutes, he returned holding a tall glass with a straw sticking out.

"Here, sip this." He held the glass in front of her and put the straw to her lips.

The straw stuck to the film on her lips, and the water tasted nasty in her mouth, but the parched feeling was being washed away. She sipped slowly for a few moments then lay back on the pillow and whispered, "Thank you."

"You're welcome, young lady." He sat holding the glass, looking at her with concern.

Eventually, she was thirsty again and lifted her head for the straw. He sat quietly with her until the water was gone, and she'd managed to choke down a bite of the toast.

"Feeling better?" he asked. She nodded her head and looked gratefully at him. "Why are you here?"

He raised his eyebrows and said, "Because you called and asked me to come."

Zuma frowned, obviously not remembering.

"Why did you do that for me?"

"Because I think you need someone," he said softly, holding her gaze.

Hurting with the truth of how alone she was, Zuma closed her eyes, trying to fight back tears.

Chapter Seventy-Three

IRIS COULDN'T REMEMBER EVER having this feeling before. The sun was just starting to shine, and the sound of waves washing up on the beach could be heard through the open balcony doors. A warm breeze blew through the room as Iris rested one arm on top of the single sheet covering her and Rey on the bed.

Propping her elbow on the pillow and resting her head on her hand, she watched him snoring peacefully beside her. His dark lashes curled up from his cheeks, while a few dreadlocks hung across his face. The rest were splayed around his head on the pillow.

His full lips were slightly parted, and Iris remembered kissing and biting them. She moved her legs around as she thought about him licking the inside of her thighs, kissing her down below. Pulling her eyes from his mouth, she looked at the smooth skin of his neck and shoulders, the definition of his muscles, twitching slightly as another breeze blew into the room. Her eyes wandered down to the tent of the sheet over his groin, and she ran her tongue over her lips, remembering.

As though he felt her watching him, he stirred a little and opened his eyes. Iris smiled at him, and the dimple waved, "Good morning."

Her tousled hair framed a face that was bright and shining, and Rey thought she was prettier than he'd ever seen her before.

To Iris's surprise, he didn't return her smile. Instead, he slowly closed his eyes and lay still. Iris leaned forward and trailed kisses from his forehead down his nose. When she got to his lips, she realized he wasn't responding and pulled back with a frown.

He didn't have to say a word for her to feel the regret emanating from him. A dullness settled around her face and, when Rey finally opened his eyes, her radiant glow had completely dissipated.

Shaking his head, he rolled to the side of the bed and, pulling his hair from his face, sat silently on the edge. Iris looked at his smooth, brown back and remembered the muscles of his upper body flexing as he made love to her just hours before. He stood, and her eyes followed the beauty of his naked body with a combination of desire and hurt as he silently walked out the door.

Chapter Seventy-Four

ELIJAH WAS SITTING IN A DEEP, cushioned armchair in a corner of the bedroom when Zuma awoke from her fitful nap. Their gazes met, but neither said a word. Elijah was waiting patiently for her to speak. She knew she had no other choice but to explain the medicine bottle he held in his hand. She forced herself into a sitting position, and Elijah sat back, looking at her encouragingly.

Zuma sighed and rolled her eyes upward. *Where do I begin?* Hot tears built in her eyes, blurring Elijah's image in her vision. His quiet presence and patient acceptance spurred her to speak.

She told him about her childhood as a cherished and spoiled only child. How her beauty had made other girls hate her and older men desire her. Through tears and snuffling, she described her love affair with her community college teacher, Professor Simons. She explained how he'd resigned from the school and moved away when he found out Zuma was pregnant with his baby. Blowing her nose and gripping the tissue, she poured out the truth about the baby that died in childbirth and the emergency hysterectomy she'd undergone at eighteen years old to save her life. She cried with shame when she recounted how her parents had legally changed her name from

Zumatha Harrison to Zuma Harris and moved her up to Maryland to live with a relative. Her parents had endured the embarrassment of all the townspeople talking about their only daughter, until they were eventually able to retire and move to Florida.

Hours later, purged and unable to continue, she crawled under the sheets, clutching several wet tissues to her chest. Elijah rose to sit on the edge of the bed and tenderly rubbed her back until she cried herself to sleep.

Chapter Seventy-Five

IRIS WAITED UNTIL REY HAD showered and left the suite before coming out of her room. Staring in the mirror over the bathroom sink, she realized the mistake she'd made. How was she going to spend the next three days with him? *I'm so damn stupid.*

Downstairs, Rey sat alone at a table in the empty dining room absently mixing the popular Jamaican dish, ackee and saltfish, with a fork on his plate. He stared gloomily out the window at couples mingling on the pool deck. Everyone looked so fucking happy to be together.

What was he thinking bringing Iris here? He'd planted the seed in her head back in May, and it was inevitable that she'd eventually want to get together. Why couldn't he stop her this morning? Why couldn't he stop himself?

He gave up trying to eat. Instead, he sipped his soursop juice, one of his favorite island fruit drinks. Setting the glass down, he closed his eyes and remembered lifting Iris up to sit on his shoulders, while he licked, sucked, and kissed the heat of her clit. He shook his head to dispel the memory, but his mind ignored the command and, instead, moved to the memory of her straddling his lap, staring into his eyes, as she rode him, strong and steady. Opening his eyes, he slammed his fist on the table, making the glass and silverware jump and clang.

Finally making her way to the dining room, Iris spied him hunched over the table, the muscles in his jaw moving as he ground his teeth behind pinched lips. The same lips that were so soft and gentle earlier that morning. As she shifted from foot to foot, debating whether to approach the table, he suddenly stood and turned to walk out, stopping when he saw her standing like a scared rabbit in the doorway. The muscles in his face continued working as their eyes made contact, but the murderous look on his face softened.

Eventually, Rey stepped toward her and said, "We need to talk."

Nodding, she followed him out the door and down a private walk with a sign reading "Employees Only" on the bordering lawn. As he came to the end of the sidewalk, Iris noticed a little dirt path leading to a grassy knoll overlooking the resort's section of the beach. Iris wondered how many members of the staff had sat here and watched the sunbathers at the bottom of the hill, ignorant of the lascivious stares from above. She wondered how Rey knew about this spot.

He dropped onto a worn section in the grass and gestured for Iris to join him. They sat without speaking for several minutes. Rey wrapped his arms around his bent knees while Iris sat Indian-style, with her shoulders rounded forward and her elbows resting on her thighs.

For awhile, Iris forgot that they were there to have a serious conversation. A group was playing volleyball and laughing or cheering with each missed or made shot. Two women lay topless on a huge inner tube floating in the ocean. A man rubbed suntan oil on the shoulders and back of his female partner, resting on a lounge chair near the water's edge. Iris's face softened as she watched them moving and interacting without any knowledge that she was looking at them from a secret spot behind the trees. When Rey finally spoke, it startled her.

"Iris, I love you," he started. Iris's face showed obvious relief, and she opened her mouth to speak, but he raised his hand, silencing her. "What happened this morning was a mistake," he said, before she could interrupt.

With her mouth still open, Iris tilted her head to the side and squinted her eyes at him. "What do you mean a mistake?"

"I mean, it shouldn't have happened."

"Why not? You said you're in love with me, and I'm attracted to you, so what's—"

"That's it!" he said, interrupting her and slapping his hand on his knee. "I was in love with you, but you're only *attracted* to me."

Iris didn't miss the "was" in his statement.

Looking out over the water, Rey said wistfully, "You know, when we were kids, I thought you were the coolest, prettiest, smartest girl I knew. You spoke two languages. You were cool with all the boys in the hood. And every girl in our class was jealous of you." He smiled at the memory and twisted his head to look at her for a moment, then turned back to the ocean.

"I wanted to take you to prom, but that damn Michael Brown asked you, and you and every other girl in the class thought he was the bomb or some shit like that." He waved his hands in the air to emphasize his point. Hugging his knees again, he added softly, "But I wouldn't have had the guts to ask you anyway, because I knew you weren't feeling me like that."

Iris followed his gaze to the water. She regretted ever using those words as she listened to him speak. She plucked a blade of grass and played with it while he continued.

"The only reason I applied and went to FAMU was because you were going there, and I *had* to be around you — see you every day, talk to you, hear you laugh. I couldn't imagine living life without you around me." He paused to look down at his feet and toes resting in the grass.

"When Raj and I started the company, you were the first one to believe in us and see my vision and know it could be what I said it would be." He turned to face her and forced her to meet his stare.

"The reason I've never introduced you to any of those women you're always talkin' about, is because they don't deserve to know you. Someone would have to have my respect to be introduced to you."

Iris was totally confused. If all of this was true, then why was their lovemaking a mistake?

"Rey, I had no idea..."

Rey closed his eyes and shook his head hard silencing her. "Lemme finish, Iris."

She took a breath and looked down at her hands.

He continued. "When I finally got the nerve to show you, tell you, how I felt, it hurt — I mean really hurt — when you turned away from me. And regardless of the reason, for you to laugh at my feelings was too much for my ego to handle. The only reason you're attracted to me now is because I told you how I felt about you. If I'd never made a move, you'd still see me as your brother. What happened this morning was lust, not love. And I love you too much to allow that to be a part of my image of you."

He stopped and let his eyes roam over her face. When Iris didn't speak, he looked down at his feet and flicked at an ant ambling over his toe. Iris was too emotional to say anything, so she sat in silence and watched a couple kiss one another in the shallow water below.

"I love you too much to be with you like that," Rey said softly.

Finally, Iris spoke. "I don't think you'll ever understand why I turned away from you that night in City Island, and I can never apologize enough for what happened at the train station. But you could at least give us a chance."

Rey shook his head. "No, I can't."

"Why not?" Iris asked, confused.

"Because, there's someone else."

"What do you mean someone else? A month ago you were telling me you were in love with me."

Rey didn't miss the irritation in her tone. He cleared his throat and said, "I recently met someone that shares my interests and ambitions."

"And now you're in love with her?" Iris asked incredulously.

Rey shook his head. It was harder than he thought it would be to explain how he was feeling.

"No, I didn't say that. What I'm saying is that I know I can't be with you like that, so I'm allowing myself to get to know other people. I'm not lookin' to get married, I just want to be with someone that shares my values, interests, and desires. For once, I'm making time for something and someone besides TravelWise, my family, and… you."

Iris was hurt, jealous, and pissed at herself, all at once. Unable to continue the conversation, she stood and dusted off the seat of her shorts. Rey remained motionless, gazing through the trees. Iris took a last glimpse at the dreadlocks hanging down his back, then turned and followed the dirt path back to the resort.

Chapter Seventy-Six

ELIJAH AND ZUMA SAT IN PATIO chairs on the back deck. He thought the fresh air would do her good. The sun was starting to set, and the sky was turning beautiful shades of fuchsia and orange.

"What are your nightmares about?" Elijah asked.

Zuma hesitated, then said, "The baby. The pain. The loss." She spoke in short, dull statements. Her usually pretty face was jaundiced, and her earlier outpouring had left her emotionless.

"If this all happened so long ago, why is it all coming back to you now? Did something happen recently?"

With a bland expression, Zuma nodded as though in a trance.

"Do you want to talk about it?" he asked her.

Zuma turned to face him, and he saw the weariness and strain of the last two days on her features. Instead of answering him, she turned away to look out at the darkening sky.

Elijah realized she wasn't going to reveal anything else for now, and he decided she was well enough to be left alone. He rose from the chair and patted her on the shoulder.

"Well, dear. I'm going to leave you to do some thinking on your own. You know my number if you want to talk."

Fearing being alone with herself, Zuma stood swiftly and grabbed his hand. "Please, don't go yet."

He saw the pleading look in her eyes and resumed his seat. "Is there something else you need to say?"

Zuma started with a heavy sigh. "There's this girl. Her name is Iris Pena..."

Chapter Seventy-Seven

IRIS LAID THE LAST FOLDED garment in her suitcase and looked around the room to make sure she hadn't forgotten anything.

As she kneeled on the floor to check under the bed, she heard the front door to the suite open and close. She stood, dusting off her hands and knees, then lowered the suitcase to the floor and wheeled it into the front room.

Rey sat, leaning back on the couch, and looked up at her when she entered the room. He didn't speak or move as he watched her prop the suitcase against the wall by the door.

"I was able to get on the last flight out tonight," Iris said quietly.

Secretly hoping he would ask her stay, Iris's heart sank when he simply nodded.

She blinked back quickly-forming tears and ran to the bathroom. For the second time during the trip, Rey felt hot tears piercing his own eyes and, unwilling to let her see his emotion, moved to his room, gently closing the door behind him.

Eventually, she knocked on the closed door, and her muffled voice told him she was leaving. He didn't respond. He knew she was waiting on the other side, but he also knew she'd eventually walk away.

Chapter Seventy-Eight

"I DON'T KNOW WHAT IT IS ABOUT HER, but everyone just seems to fall in love with her," Zuma said, stopping to blow a stream of cigarette smoke into the night air. "The secretary, the security guard, my staff, my bosses. Everyone." She paused again to take a pull on the cigarette.

"She's tall. Beautiful. And very smart." Zuma paused, and Elijah watched as her mouth turned up into a half-grin. "I think I hated her from the moment she walked into my office."

"Were you jealous?" Elijah asked.

Zuma nodded reluctantly, hating to admit it.

"It was obvious that she wasn't a regular college intern. She spoke differently, dressed differently, and carried herself with more confidence than any woman in the whole damn building. Even though she told me she hadn't interned anywhere before, I *knew* she'd been exposed somewhere, somehow. I could feel it."

"And had she?" Elijah questioned.

Zuma harrumphed, rolling her eyes. "She worked as an account executive at an international marketing firm in New York."

Painfully, Zuma described the embarrassing meeting with John Hernandez. She recalled Iris calling him Juan. The humiliation was still fresh, and Elijah watched as Zuma's face contorted with anger and colored as she spoke.

When she finished, he said, "Maybe you should take a break from talking and get something to eat."

Zuma watched him stifle a yawn and looked over his rumpled shirt and slacks. The poor man hadn't slept, eaten, or showered since he'd arrived. And here he was helping her — a lonely, selfish bitch.

"Uh, yes," she said, getting to her feet. She slid open the glass door and stepped in, waiting for him to follow, before closing and locking the door behind them. Not wanting him to leave, but attempting to regain some dignity, she led him to the front door. Opening the door, she looked sincerely into his eyes.

"Elijah, I can never thank you enough for what you've done. No one, except my mother and father, has ever been this kind to me."

Feeling sorry for her, he smiled and said, "Anytime you need someone to listen or just be here, call. I'll check on you tomorrow." He patted her shoulder and stepped through the open doorway.

Closing the door behind him, Zuma sighed when she realized she was alone and didn't like the person she was with.

Chapter Seventy-Nine

SONJA DROVE THROUGH THE terminal twice before finally seeing Iris at the curb.

"Rico, sit down and stop touching your brother!" she yelled into the back seat, maneuvering the car across two lanes to the passenger pick-up.

Pulling up a few feet in front of where Iris was standing, she popped the release for the trunk and got out to help her sister-in-law with her bags.

"Damn, what happened to you?" Sonja asked, glancing quickly at Iris before taking a bag.

Iris ignored her sister-in-law and threw the suitcase in the trunk. She dodged Sonja's stare and moved to the passenger side of the minivan.

"Auntie Iris, Auntie Iris," the boys began chanting, as one jumped up from his car seat and attempted to crawl over the middle console to reach her. Sonja cursed under her breath in Spanish as she wrestled her younger son back into his seat and clicked the two security snaps shut.

Popping in a cassette tape and turning up the volume, she exhaled heavily and brushed a wisp of hair from her forehead while the boys began singing about someone named Thomas the Tank Engine. Iris couldn't help but smile as she looked back at the fat faces of her nephews, singing along with the English accent on the tape. Sonja put on her own seatbelt then slowly pulled into the traffic leaving Miami's airport.

They drove for a few minutes before Sonja said, "When are you going to tell me what happened?"

Iris shrugged and dropped her head back on the headrest, closing her eyes. "I really messed up this time."

Iris told her everything, stopping and starting to avoid crying, and only omitting the intimacies.

"Why you skimpin' on the sex?" Sonja asked, not missing the omission.

Iris smiled weakly. "A good girl never tells."

"Secretive ho'," Sonja accused.

Iris laughed for the first time that evening.

"Seriously, though. I don't know what to tell you, girl," Sonja said after a few moments.

"There's really nothing to say," Iris replied resignedly.

Chapter Eighty

Thursday, July 5

I T WAS 7:45 A.M., AND ZUMA SAT at her desk in the dark office, watching people and traffic on the street below. It was her first day back at work. She'd come early to gather her thoughts without interruption.

A soft rap at the door startled her, and she spun around in the chair to see Iris standing in the doorway.

"Good morning," Iris said.

"Morning," Zuma replied.

"I didn't think anyone would be here this early," Iris admitted.

"Neither did I."

Not knowing what else to say, Iris added, "Well, I just wanted to let you know that someone was here."

"Thanks," Zuma said with a genuine smile. She watched Iris walk away without the usual feeling of envy.

Iris moved to her cubicle and put her things away. Reaching to turn on the computer, she saw a single rose in a simple crystal vase with an envelope propped against it. Her name was scrawled on front.

She picked up the envelope and bent to sniff the flower's pink bud.

The fragrance was sweet, and she closed her eyes to inhale again. Sitting back, she opened the sealed envelope and pulled out two handwritten pages.

Iris,

I thought about some of the things you said at lunch the other day, and I felt it was imperative to write you this letter. First, because I owe you an apology and secondly, because there are some things that need to be clarified.

You were right when you said I should have told you about my daughter, Ginger. She's my heart and my world. I was waiting for the right time to bring you into that part of me, and I would still like for you to meet her before you go.

I didn't cheat on my wife. I'm not that kind of man. Right out of high school, I married my girlfriend and a year later, we had our daughter. My wife, Paula, stuck with me while I was working my way through college. She took care of Ginger and worked at night to bring in money to help me pay for school. She never complained, and I took it for granted that she was happy and content as I pledged a fraternity and partied my way through the last two years of college. When Shearing hired me after my graduation, I was grateful for my job. I worked long hours and was promoted for my dedication. But Paula was working full time and spending her evenings and weekends with Ginger. She wanted a taste of freedom, something she'd never had. She'd gone from living at home with strict parents to taking care of me and our child. When Ginger was 7, Paula left us to experience the freedom she'd never had.

After Paula left, my mother helped me with Ginger. For the first year, Paula never called or came to see her, and it was a difficult time for both of us. I wasn't angry at her. I understood her needs.

I met Zuma that year while we worked long hours on similar projects. It was natural for us to hook up. But, Bob O'Brien took over our department when our manager left on an extended maternity leave, and I think Zuma saw her ticket up and out. When Bob was promoted a couple of years ago, Zuma was suddenly slated to move up as well, and our relationship ended as quickly as it began.

I should have told you about me and Zuma, but there never seemed to be a right time or way to do it. I had no idea she'd say something to you, and it was never serious between me and her anyway.

I'm not asking you to give me another chance, I'm simply telling you that there are always two sides to a story, and I hope you'll forgive me for not telling my side first.

I know you're leaving in a few weeks and that there is probably no chance of our being together, but I want you to know that you mean a lot to me and always will.

With love,

Jonathan

Iris read and re-read the letter. Smelling the rose again, she placed the letter in her purse.

Across the floor, Zuma finally twisted away from the window and pulled up to her desk to begin the routine of checking voicemails. The first message was from Bob.

"Zuma, I've tried calling you at home, on your cell, and at the office. Call me as soon as you get this message."

The next one was from Margie Castor in HR. "Hello Zuma, this is Margie. Could you please schedule to meet with me sometime today or tomorrow? Thanks."

The final message was from Steven Searson. "Hi Zuma, this is Steven Searson. Please make sure to have the internship evaluation for Iris Pena to me by Friday, July 6th. Thank you."

Looking at email, it was much of the same. Do this, schedule that, meet with them. With a sigh, she picked up the phone to begin returning calls.

As Zuma started her first call, Betty walked on the floor and started getting settled at the reception desk. Iris saw her and made a beeline for the front.

"Hey, Betty."

"Iris! What are you doing here so early?" Betty asked in surprise, as she moved through the waiting area, straightening magazines and turning on lights.

"I had some work to do and thoughts to sort out."

Betty snuck a peek at Iris. "I know that feeling."

"Mr. Searson wants you to schedule a meeting for the two of us today or tomorrow, if possible," Iris said.

Betty stopped what she was doing and looked directly at Iris. "Really?"

"Yes. But I don't know what the meeting is about," Iris admitted.

Betty put her hands on her hips. "I guess it's time for me to tell you about that letter you signed."

Chapter Eighty-One

Friday, July 6

ZUMA SAT PATIENTLY IN THE human resources waiting area. Eventually, Margie appeared and said, "Sorry to keep you waiting, Zuma. Come on back."

Zuma followed Margie through the maze of cubicles to an office larger than her own. The sense of caution she felt escalated when she saw Steven Searson seated in the office with a folder and the Hispanic marketing proposal resting on his lap.

"Zuma," he said, nodding an unsmiling greeting to her before opening the folder and glancing down at a typed letter lying on top of the other papers.

"Hello, Steven." Zuma said, perching nervously on the chair next to him.

"Well, Zuma," Margie began, shuffling through a few papers on her desk. "There are a few reasons why you've been called in to talk with us today."

Zuma felt her pulse quicken.

"As you know, we're in serious negotiations with Ladd Tech to merge our two companies. As a part of our initial obligations, we are attempting to pare down our human resources."

Zuma felt her face growing hot and her breathing constrict. Margie continued.

"We began by offering our top tier of management early-out packages. Bob O'Brien has accepted that offer and will be leaving in two weeks."

Zuma inhaled sharply, but attempted to recover quickly. In her peripheral vision, she saw Steven Searson watching her.

"As Bob transitions out, the executives left in marketing will report directly to Steven," she said, flicking her eyes to him briefly and gesturing in his direction. She paused to allow Zuma to comment, but Zuma sat wordlessly waiting to hear what else she had to say.

"Do you have questions or concerns about what I've just explained?"

"No," Zuma answered simply.

"Great, then we can move on." Margie made a notation on one of the papers on her desk, then moved it to the side.

Zuma thought she saw the corner of one of Iris's Hispanic proposals under another stack of papers on the desk, but she didn't have to guess for long. Margie reached for the stack and pulled it directly in front of her.

She sent one to Margie! She always knew...

"I recently received a letter and samples of work completed from the intern assigned to you this summer—Iris Pena. It seems that she's somewhat uncomfortable working with you, to the point of writing me a letter addressing a few issues. Since Steven is now directly involved with you and the activities in your department, I gave him a copy of the letter as well."

Zuma's face turned to stone as she listened to Margie's voice drone on.

"The most important of Ms. Pena's concerns regards her

evaluation from you at the end of her internship." Margie stopped to sift through the papers. When she found the data she needed, she continued. "That date is Friday, August tenth. I know that Steven has asked you to complete a preliminary evaluation on her for our review, but he has yet to receive it. At this time, we would like for you to give us a brief summary of what you think her skills and areas of improvement may be."

Zuma was dumbstruck. *Right now?* She cleared her throat and searched for what to say and where to begin.

Then she thought about what she and Elijah had discussed during the last few days. It wasn't Iris who was at fault for the things that had happened recently. Zuma was doing it to herself. Her jealously and fear had triggered a series of foolish decisions and actions. Zuma knew what she had to say.

"Iris Pena is a very bright and thorough individual. Despite her youth, she has obviously worked in other capacities of management that make her an asset to our team in marketing segmentation. Specifically, her work on the current research of the Hispanic market and a segment of the youth market is admirable, and we will definitely benefit from her contributions."

Zuma saw Steven's eyes narrow as he watched her. She wondered why he hadn't spoken yet. She remained silent as Margie jotted down notes on the final sheet in front of her. Finishing, she looked up.

"Well, I would say that's in line with what we've received from the other managers in your department."

Other managers? They were setting me up.

Now Steven spoke. "I'm glad to hear that you have a high opinion of Ms. Pena, since we have decided to outsource a portion of our marketing and customer care to her father's company."

Unable to maintain a neutral expression, Zuma let her mouth gape open as her brows came together. "Father's company?"

"International Communications was founded by Oscar Pena, Iris Pena's father. It is one of the largest and most respected multilingual marketing consultancies in the country, with branch offices in New York, Miami, and Los Angeles. Iris Pena worked as an account executive with the company for three years before deciding to go back and get her M.B.A. at Columbia University. She is only with us as a requirement for graduation." He stopped speaking, but his message was crystal clear.

Chapter Eighty-Two

Saturday, July 7

I RIS SLOWED TO A JOG AND TROTTED to a stop as she neared the Inner Harbor. The heat was intense, but luckily it was a cloudy day. Tugging a small hand cloth from the front of her shorts, she mopped at the perspiration dripping from her chin. She walked through the crowd of Inner Harbor sight-seers and dropped down on an empty stone step at the water's edge. Shaking out her legs, she leaned into a slow stretch and closed her eyes, ignoring the passersby that looked her way. Breathing deeply and focusing on her stretch, she didn't hear the first time Jonathan called her name.

"Iris," he said a little louder.

Her eyes fluttered open, and she lifted her head to see him standing with a lanky girl in shorts and a halter top. "Jonathan?"

He didn't answer, instead he shifted awkwardly, draping his hand protectively around the girl's thin shoulders. Iris wiped her face again to make sure she was somewhat presentable, since the rest of her body was covered in perspiration.

"Hey. I didn't mean to interrupt your stretch, but I just happened to see you over here and thought you might like to meet my daughter,

Ginger." His eyes softened as he looked down at the girl with obvious love.

"Of course. I'd be offended if you didn't." Dropping her legs over the side of the stone wall, Iris sat up and looked at the girl. "Please excuse my condition, but I just finished running."

Ginger smiled shyly and said, "My father told me you were a runner."

He told her about me?

Iris extended her hand, "Well it's a pleasure to meet you."

Ginger took it and shook it lightly saying, "Nice to meet you, too."

"Um, did you get my letter?" Jonathan asked uncertainly.

Iris nodded. "Yes. Thank you."

"I wasn't sure if you'd gotten it. I wasn't even sure you were back since I haven't seen you on the floor."

"I've finished my part of the research for Tween Phone and have started work on a new project with Barbara."

"Yeah? What now?" Jonathan asked with genuine interest.

"A simple phone targeted to busy women and moms. No special features or buttons, just call and answer."

Jonathan smiled, and Iris remembered what she'd found so alluring about him. "I bet that was your idea, huh?" he said.

Iris nodded modestly, then said, "Yes, by way of my sister-in-law."

Jonathan nodded with her. Suddenly, an uncomfortable silence settled over the three of them.

Jonathan spoke first. "Well, we'll let you get back to your workout. It was good seeing you." He touched Ginger on the shoulder to guide her away.

Iris cleared her throat. "Um. Would you and Ginger like to have dinner with me this evening? My treat."

306

Jonathan looked down at Ginger's upturned face, and they exchanged a silent communication. This was a different Jonathan than the one she thought she knew.

He answered, "Sure. We'd like that."

"I'll pick you up around seven o'clock?"

Jonathan looked confused. "Pick us up? How?"

Smiling, Iris said, "There are some things about *me* that I haven't shared with *you*. I'll see you guys at seven."

Chapter Eighty-Three

ZUMA PULLED HER CAR INTO the garage and took her time gathering shopping bags from the back seat and trunk.

Ring. Ring. She heard the phone ringing in the kitchen and ran into the house, just in time to catch the last ring. "Hello," she answered, breathlessly.

"Zuma. It's me, Bob."

Zuma took a few seconds to catch her breath and check her anger. Curiosity was the stronger of her emotions. She actually wanted to hear what he had to say. Would he tell the truth about the package he'd been offered or act like nothing had changed since last week?

"Bob. How are you?" she asked in a cool voice.

Caught off guard by her chilly response, he stammered. "Good. Good. I wanted to know if you were busy. I'd like to stop by."

When Zuma didn't comment, he continued talking, hoping she'd let him come over for a little fun. "I know I've been busy and unable to talk or meet lately, but I thought we could discuss your opportunities for promotion with the new company."

Does he think I'm stupid? Was he playing me from the beginning of this thing? Zuma rolled her eyes and covered the mouthpiece to muffle the sound of her sucking her teeth. She couldn't contain her anger any longer.

"Anything we have to discuss, I'm sure we can do on the telephone," she said with an edge to her voice. But Bob wasn't so easily deterred.

"I know you're upset Zuma, but I have some information from my meeting with HR and Steven I thought you might want to hear." He waited to see if she would take the bait. When she didn't respond, he continued, hopefully. "I could be there in fifteen minutes." He held his breath, anticipating her response.

Zuma realized in that moment how ignorant and dumb Bob really thought she was. The heat of her anger bubbled up, and the old Zuma quickly took over the conversation. In a syrupy voice, she said, "Make it thirty minutes. And don't be late."

Bob pumped his fist in the air and congratulated himself on his sneaky maneuver to sleep with Zuma one last time before saying goodbye to everything Shearing.

As soon as she hung up, Zuma ran upstairs to her room and into the closet. She rummaged through several boxes on a shelf until she found what she was looking for and nodded, smiling wickedly.

* * *

Zuma slowly untied Bob's wrists from the corners of the headboard and allowed him to flip her over onto her hands and knees. As he rammed into her from behind, she turned and smiled into the lens of the camcorder resting obscurely under a silk wrap on her vanity.

Chapter Eighty-Four

"HEY SONJA," IRIS SAID into the telephone.

"What's up, chica?"

Iris heard the usual noise and mayhem in the background of her brother's house. "Should I call you at a better time?"

"Mi'ja, there's never a better time. You know how it goes."

"I went to dinner with Jonathan and his daughter last night."

"*What?* Wait a minute, let me find Dora to watch the kids so I can listen to this," Sonja said, shouting in the background for the housekeeper. A few seconds later, she was back on the line. "Okay, talk to me."

"Well, his daughter is cute and very smart and mannerable. She has his complexion and smile but obviously has her mother's eyes and build. I treated them to dinner and, afterwards, we had ice cream sundaes in Fells Point, a little hippie area outside Baltimore."

"Well?" Sonja asked.

"Well, what?"

"Don't play. Did he step to you or what?" Sonja asked impatiently.

Iris sucked her teeth. "Sonja, his daughter was with us. No! I'm beginning to realize you're just a big freak."

"Whatever. I keep it real, that's all."

They talked some more, and then Iris spoke to Carlos for a few minutes.

They discussed the company's upcoming annual meeting in Miami, and Iris promised to be there. As they were wrapping up, her phone beeped. They said their goodbyes and she clicked over.

"Hi, Iris."

Rey. Iris took a breath.

"Hello, Rey. When'd you get back?" she said formally.

"I flew in yesterday."

"I'm glad you made it home safely."

"Thanks."

Neither of them said anything, and Iris could hear the static on the line. Just then, her phone beeped again.

"Hold on, Rey, I have another call."

"Okay."

She clicked over.

"Hi, Iris. It's Jonathan."

Iris smiled widely and quickly said, "Hey Jonathan. Hold on a minute, let me hang up the other line."

Clicking back to Rey, Iris was happy to say, "Rey, I'm sorry. I've got another call I need to take."

"Oh, okay. I just wanted to check in," Rey said somewhat uncomfortably.

"No problem. Thanks for calling. Give your mother my love," Iris said.

"I will. Peace."

Iris clicked over and settled down for a long conversation.

Chapter Eighty-Five

"I RIS," BARBARA SAID, LEANING over the cubicle wall. "Zuma wants to see us in her office to discuss Simple Phone."

"Okay, hold on a minute." Iris finished sending a quick email to Jonathan before rising to follow Barbara across the room.

"Hi, ladies," Zuma said pleasantly as they entered and sat in front of her desk. Iris wasn't sure if it was fake or real, but something had drastically changed with Zuma. She seemed happier — almost cheery. And she was interacting with her staff in a more positive way. Everyone was commenting on it. To the dismay of the men on the floor, she was even dressing more conservatively. Her skirts reached her knees, and her jackets covered more of her cleavage. Something strange must have happened during the Fourth of July.

"I just wanted to let you know that we've gotten the green light to move forward with the Simple Phone idea that Iris proposed."

Barbara and Iris high-fived each other and turned back to Zuma as she detailed the specifics of the next steps.

"As usual, you two will need to work with Rick's group on the concept of the product, while continuing to test the market and gather statistical information on who would actually be interested in this type of product. As far as the service plans, we'd offer—," Zuma outlined the planned service options.

Iris nodded and jotted notes while Barbara asked a few more questions. When the brief meeting was over, Zuma asked Iris to stay.

When Barbara walked out, shutting the door behind her, Zuma folded her hands on the desk and took a deep breath before saying, "Iris, I owe you an apology."

Taken aback, Iris shifted uncomfortably while Zuma continued speaking. "When you first came here, I was going through something personal. I took out my frustration and pain on you, and it wasn't right. I know you only have three weeks left here, but I hope it's long enough for me to make up for being a total bitch the last two and a half months."

Iris didn't know how to respond. This was the last thing she'd expected from Zuma. "Uh, sure. I guess."

"I know you don't trust me, and I wouldn't either if I were you, but this was something I had to say regardless of whether you accept it or not. For me."

Iris saw the sincerity in her face and replied, "Thank you. I appreciate that."

"No, thank you for…" Zuma paused unsure of the right words to appropriately express her meaning. She kept it simple and said, "…helping me find me again."

Not knowing if Zuma was going to try to hug her or something, Iris quickly rose and moved to the door, waving goodbye.

Chapter Eighty-Six

"**S**URPRISE!**"** EVERYONE YELLED as iris walked into the twelfth-floor boardroom with Barbara. Confetti fell through the air onto her hair and the lapel of her jacket.

"Oh my gosh!" Iris said, shocked. She knew there was going to be a party at Kelly's tonight, but she didn't expect something at the office, too.

"Are you surprised?" Barbara asked enthusiastically.

"Yes!" Iris laughed, covering her mouth.

She looked around the room and was flabbergasted to see Zuma, Steven Searson, and Margie Castor in the room, along with Rick, Jonathan, Betty and her other co-workers from the two marketing departments.

"You guys are…" Iris was so stunned, she couldn't find the words to finish her statement. Everyone laughed at her surprise.

She walked through the room giving and receiving hugs. When she got to Margie and Steven, she shook hands professionally and thanked them for their support and help with the internship.

"No, Iris. Thank *you*. You've contributed more in three months than most of our employees do their entire career with the company," Steven said in a low voice. "We look forward to working with you through International Communications."

Iris smiled as a few people handed her cards. Eventually, Zuma moved forward and handed her a small wrapped box. Iris looked at her questioningly, holding the dainty box in her hands.

"A small gift for someone who's given me a big one," Zuma said, exchanging smiles with Iris. As Iris turned to thank another gift-giver, Zuma excused herself quietly from the room.

Eventually, people left to attend meetings, conference calls, and continue business as usual. Holding the door for a couple exiting, Will shyly entered the room. "Oh, Will! How nice of you to come up from the security desk. You didn't have to do that."

"Oh yes I did. I couldn't let my favorite girl in the building go without wishing her a proper goodbye." He hugged her before pressing a roll of bills in her hand.

"Will! I can't take this from you!"

He whispered in her ear, "Yes you can. I retire this year *and* I just hit the numbers. You made three months of my last year here a real joy, Sunshine." He squeezed her close, and Iris got the feeling that he was getting more than a goodbye hug.

Jonathan sidled up to her as Will slipped out the door. "You'll get my gift tonight," he whispered in her ear. For the sake of the others in the room, Iris pretended to give him a generic hug, but quickly whispered something back.

Back on the marketing floor, Betty pulled Iris behind the reception desk.

"Iris, you should really be proud of yourself. You've accomplished miracles at this company. Things I never thought I'd see."

Modestly, Iris looked down and mumbled, "Stop, Betty, you're embarrassing me."

"No, really. You should give yourself a big pat on the back. I know the company is under a big hiring freeze, but don't be surprised if you get a call from whatever big wigs are left when the dust settles on this merger. You're definitely something special."

Reaching under the desk, Betty pulled out a large box.

"This is for you."

"Betty. You didn't have to do that."

"You're right. I don't have to do anything I don't want to, but I *wanted* to do this," she said, handing the heavy box to Iris.

Iris placed the prettily wrapped box on the desk and took Betty's hand. "You know I couldn't have done half of what I accomplished here without you. I'll always be in your debt for that. Please don't hesitate to call on me if you need me for anything. Even if it's a job."

Betty looked surprised. "A job? What are you talking about?"

"Trust me. If you're ever in need of a job, just call or email this person, and you'll be taken care of." Iris handed her the business card she'd been holding.

Betty scrutinized the card. "This person, Carlos Pena, is a relative of yours?"

Iris nodded. Betty looked at the card again. Carlos Pena, CMO of International Communications. "Chief marketing officer of the whole company?"

Iris nodded again.

"I always knew I liked you for a reason. You know how to keep big secrets."

Chapter Eighty-Seven

Saturday, August 18

ZUMA PACKED HER MAKEUP and hair products in a red bag that matched the designer suitcases leaning against the wall. Placing the smaller bag next to the larger ones, she checked her image in the mirror. A loose-fitting cotton top hung tastefully over the waist of her shorts. The chimes of the doorbell rang, and she skipped down the steps to open the door for Elijah.

"Hi. Thanks for taking me to the airport. I'm all packed," she said giddily, running back up the stairs.

At a slower pace, Elijah followed her up the stairs. He took the largest suitcase from her and carried it down the steps.

"What time is your flight?" he asked.

She looked at her watch and said, "I have lots of time. It's not until two-thirty."

"Okay, but just in case, let's get going, and we can stop for something to eat along the way."

"Sounds good to me."

They packed her things into the back of his Volvo. She ran back to check the windows and locks and set the alarm.

Jogging down the front steps, she said, "Here," and handed him a single brown key.

"What's this?"

"I don't have anyone I trust more than you to watch out for my belongings. Just check the place out every now and then."

"Are you sure about this?"

"More sure than anything I've done in my whole life."

"How long will you be gone?"

"I'm going to stay two weeks this time. See how I like it down there. Give myself a chance to get to know my parents again."

"What about a job?"

"The package Shearing gave me pays my full salary and benefits for eighteen months. I think I have some time. Time to learn to like *me* again."

Elijah smiled with pride at the new woman standing in front of him. Unlocking the doors, he slid behind the driver's seat and started the engine to take Zuma to the next chapter in her life.

* * *

As Zuma left her house, another woman was just returning to hers. The woman was well-dressed in a colorful blouse, linen slacks, and cream loafers. She stopped her Mercedes at the edge of the driveway and stepped out to check the mail in the brick structure housing the mailbox at the edge of the street. Seeing her neighbor kneeling in a flower garden across the street, she waved, causing the large diamond of her wedding ring to blink in the sunlight. She pulled letters, a glossy magazine, and a small rectangular package from the box. She threw them all onto the passenger seat of her car and continued driving up the curving path into one of three garage bays.

Carrying her shopping bags and the mail into the mudroom off the garage, she tossed the letters and magazine onto a wooden roll-top desk in the corner. The package, however, piqued her curiosity.

Did I order something? she wondered, turning the box over to search for a company's logo or label. Not seeing one, she pulled the letter opener from the desk and cut the tape sealing the package shut.

Emptying the contents onto the kitchen counter, a single VHS tape fell out. "Bob's Office Party" was written on a white label stuck to the top. She carried the video to the den and pushed it into the VCR. Moving to sit on the edge of a stuffy leather armchair, she worked the remote in her hand.

As the image of her husband, Bob O'Brien, came onto the screen, his wife dropped the remote control with a clatter on the hardwood floor. Bob was naked with his head buried between the legs of a scantily clad black woman. Bob's wife clamped jeweled hands over her mouth to muffle a scream as the woman on the screen smiled directly at her.

Chapter Eighty-Eight

"I CAN'T BELIEVE TONIGHT IS really your last night in Baltimore," Jonathan said. He relaxed in the wide whirlpool tub with Iris between his legs, lying back on his chest. He leisurely ran one soapy hand over her nipples poking up through the bubbles. Iris moaned and reached under the water to place his other hand between her legs.

"What am I going to do when you leave me tomorrow?"

"Don't talk about it, Jonathan. Mm..." She trailed off, as his fingers moved in and out of the warm crevice between her thighs.

Finding his hardened dick under the sudsy water, she stroked him from base to tip and back again. They were both silent as they pleasured one another.

"Would you consider coming back to Baltimore?" he whispered in her ear.

"I can't consider anything when you're doing that," she murmured, guiding his hand faster between her thighs.

"Come here," he mumbled against her neck, rising from the suds and pulling her up with him.

Stepping out of the tub, he dragged a dripping Iris into the bedroom of the hotel suite. Shivering and giggling like children, they yanked the covers down from the pillows and jumped, wet and sudsy, into the bed, pulling the sheets, blanket, and duvet over them. Iris dove deep beneath the covers and took him fully into her mouth. Jonathan groaned as her head moved up and down, and she wrapped her tongue around the tip of his dick. Unable to stand another minute, he pushed Iris away, slipped on a condom, and positioned her on top of him.

Jonathan grabbed an ass cheek in each hand as she rode him hard and they began to climax together.

"Iris, Iris, Iris," he panted.

"Ohh," Iris moaned. "Oh, Rey…"

Acknowledgements

Sometimes, the words "thank you" don't seem adequate. That is definitely the case now.

Words cannot describe how much I appreciate my biggest support and cheerleader — my husband, Maurice. Our sons, Maurice and Malik, have grown up watching me write this book, and I appreciate their understanding, support, and love.

A huge "thank you" goes out to my friends who read it first and gave me the feedback to help make the story better: Lisa Thompson, Rosebelle Njoba, Julye Williams, Derry West, and Kevin Evans.

I may not have ever released it if it weren't for the eagle eye of my editor and friend, Raven Davis. She is a gem, and I truly appreciate her for helping me make my dream come true.

Thank you to Dr. Barbara King and Keith Hampton for helping me get the "perfect shot."

This page would not be complete without me thanking my mother, Dr. Thelma Lawton, for always supporting my many endeavors, watching my children, and sharing motherly advice along the way.

And my baby brother Carlos — I love him so much I made Iris's beloved brother Carlos, too. Thank you to every person who reads and enjoys my story. Peace and light… Althea

About the Author

A former corporate executive, Althea is a proud serial entrepreneur who loves the freedom of mountain hiking and the peace of daily morning meditations. Having lived in many different cities, she currently resides in an Atlanta suburb with her husband and their two teenage sons.

www.ingramcontent.com/pod-product-compliance
Lightning Source LLC
Chambersburg PA
CBHW030602180626
46816CB00005B/1641